A PLUM...

EAST OF ...

GREGORY HILL lives in Denver, w...
rock-and-roll power trio that include... ... on drums.

Praise for *East of Denver*

"This is writing on par with that of top-flight black-comic novelists like Sam Lipsyte and Jess Walter, and it deserves to be read."
    —Lev Grossman, bestselling author of *The Magicians*

"Gregory Hill . . . displays a keen, at times riveting, understanding of the absurdities and freedoms of small-town isolation and the dying way of life that was once the American standard."   —*Shelf Awareness*

"A breezily readable summer novel that not only entertains but also surprises. It explores the dynamics of family relationships without ever stooping to sentimentality, and it's one of this summer's most pleasant surprises."   —*Austin American-Statesman*

"All the characters are quirky if not downright bizarre and you never really know how things are going to play out. A witty, snarky, and thoroughly enjoyable read."   —*Portland Book Review*

"Hill gives up plenty of laughs to go with the pain . . . A fine first novel from a writer with a great sense of character."   —*Booklist*

"*East of Denver* is evocative, moody, funny, bleak, desperate, and, somehow, optimistic all at the same time. The story is chock-full of humanity and the images are chiseled with sharp, clean strokes."
    —Mark Stevens, author of *Buried by the Roan*

"[An] agreeable, offbeat debut novel . . . A story about a father and son who bond against the odds, with an ending as quirkily satisfying as the rest of the book."   —*Kirkus Reviews*

"An eye for detail, an ear for dialogue, and a knack for storytelling distinguish this unflinching novel of rural America."
    —*Publishers Weekly*

EAST of DENVER

Gregory Hill

A PLUME BOOK

PLUME
Published by the Penguin Group
Penguin Group (USA) Inc., 375 Hudson Street,
New York, New York 10014, USA

USA | Canada | UK | Ireland | Australia | New Zealand | India | South Africa | China
Penguin Books Ltd, Registered Offices: 80 Strand, London WC2R 0RL, England
For more information about the Penguin Group visit penguin.com

First published in the United States of America by Dutton, a member of Penguin Group (USA) Inc., 2012
First Plume Printing 2013

 REGISTERED TRADEMARK—MARCA REGISTRADA

THE LIBRARY OF CONGRESS HAS CATALOGED THE DUTTON EDITION AS FOLLOWS:

Hill, Gregory, 1972–
East of Denver / Gregory Hill.
p. cm.
ISBN 978-0-525-95279-4 (hc.)
ISBN 978-0-14-219688-5 (pbk.)
1. Fathers and sons—Fiction. 2 Farm life—Fiction. 3.Colorado—Fiction. I. Title.
PS3068.I4293E27   2012
813'.6—dc23   2011037050

Printed in the United States of America
10   9   8   7   6   5   4   3   2   1

Set in New Caledonia LTD Std
Original hardcover design by Francesca Belanger

To Mom, who works so hard,
and Dad, who keeps her busy.

PART ONE

CHAPTER 1

FUNERAL

I was driving from Denver to the farm with a dead cat in the back seat of my car. She was a stray I used to feed off my back step. She slept outside. She walked in the rain. Once, after a blizzard, she spent a month trapped in the sewers, where she survived by eating baby raccoons. When the snow melted, she crawled out of the storm drain, mangy and wet with a chunk of skin missing from her left side. She rubbed against my shin and got pus on my britches. She was tough. She got better. I don't mind cats but I hate cat-lovers. I loved this cat.

Nothing can survive poor kids. Poor kids in the city in the summer are apocalyptic. They wander the neighborhood with spray paint and sticks. Tag it, break it, steal it, kill it.

I don't know what they did to her or if they even did it. But when I found her wheezing on my back step, I could tell that something mean had happened. She was bent up all crooked and blood was coming out of her fur like sweat. I picked her up. She was a tiny thing. I held her until she died.

I put the cat in a cardboard box and waited for dark. I couldn't bury her in the backyard. I was a renter. I couldn't risk the next tenant digging her up and playing with her skull.

So I was driving to the farm with a dead cat in the back seat of my car with the intention of burying her in the pasture where my dad had been burying dogs for fifty years. Bing, Cindy, Jumper, Lady, Norman.

Denver to Dorsey. Two hours on a pale eastbound highway. Hawks sat on the telephone poles, watching. Juvenile sparrows dive-bombed the car.

A box turtle was basking on the highway, just begging to get run over. I hate to see a roadkill turtle. They look like bloody rocks. Not this time. I pulled over, backed up, got out, and carried it into a pasture. Got cheatgrass in my socks.

I stood in the pasture and looked west. Denver was gone. The mountains were gone, replaced by prairie, a shimmery horizon, and cumulus clouds building up for a prick tease of an afternoon shower. The dry world. It wasn't cracked or duned up like a real desert. Just dry. Grass, sage, tumbleweeds, wild sunflowers growing in the ditches. The color was bleached out of everything.

I pissed in a ditch. The puddle huddled to itself like mercury. The ground didn't want the moisture.

I have anosmia, which means I don't have a sense of smell. I was born that way. I was twelve years old before I became aware of the condition. I had always assumed I couldn't smell because I wasn't trying hard enough. But one day, I was driving the tractor and the cab filled up with dust. Then I noticed flames coming out of the steering column. The dust was smoke. I shut off the engine and emptied my water jug on the fire. Nothing serious was damaged. But it occurred to me that if I couldn't smell smoke, then maybe there was something wrong with me.

That night, I told my mom about my condition. She said I shouldn't worry. There wasn't anything wrong with me at all. I just couldn't smell. Then she whispered in my ear. "I can't smell either. Don't tell anyone. They don't understand." She was right.

There's lots of consequences to not being able to smell. You don't know when you stink. You don't know when something else stinks.

But you always suspect that something stinks because people are always reminding you. When someone asks, "Who stepped in dog shit?" I don't even bother looking at my shoes anymore. I just leave the room. It was me. Shit might as well be chocolate.

I climbed back into the car and cracked a soda pop. I didn't feel like driving yet. I just sat there. The windows were up, the air-conditioner was broke. Let it bake. I was an Indian in a sweat lodge.

A cop knocked on the window. I cranked it down.

He said, "Everything all right?"

"It's too damn hot."

The cop wrinkled his nose, peeked thru the open window. "You got yourself a dead cat."

"Yes, sir."

"Tell me what you're doing with a dead cat."

"I'm going to bury it on the farm."

He looked at my neck. "You're not a farmer."

"My dad is. Was. Emmett Williams. Maybe you know him."

"License."

I said, "What for?"

"You want me to, I can find something."

I gave him the license. He walked and sat on the hood of his cop car, smoking a cigarette. I watched him in the rearview. He sat there and smoked a cigarette.

He came back and handed me my license.

"Go bury your cat."

When I pulled into the driveway, Dad was next to the shed, poking a jack handle into a juniper bush he'd planted twenty-five years ago. In a land where things refuse to grow, he treated that juniper right. It was taller than he was.

He stopped poking the bush. "You come alone?"

"I brought a cat."

We drove to the pasture. Dad opened the gate. The barbed wire was stapled to cedar posts that had been hauled on the back of a wagon a hundred and twenty years ago by our homesteading patriarch Helfrich Williams. He was German, but he'd never been to Germany. In the early 1800s, Helfrich's ancestors moved from the middle of Germany to Russia. They were either escaping an oppressive regime or taking advantage of some sort of Russian government goodwill offering. Whatever it was, they settled someplace called the Volga River Plain. I don't know where that is. Another thing I don't know is why they were called the Williamses. Not very German. But if you look at the birth entries on the first two pages of our family Bible—a Bible written in German—there's Williamses all the way back to before Lincoln was president.

In the 1870s, the Russians decided to murder all the German immigrants living on the Volga River Plain. Shortly before the Russians burned his village, young Helfrich Williams and his wife, Margaretha, packed up, moved out, and jumped on board the first ship headed toward America. Three weeks on the ocean and a miserable train ride later, they marched across the prairie until Helfrich stamped his shoe in the dirt and said the German equivalent of "We're home." Then they huddled together underneath a washtub to avoid a sandstorm. The Homestead Act promised paradise and, unlike many of their neighbors in that rectangle of the Great Plains soon to be known as Strattford County, that's exactly what Helfrich and Margaretha found. To them, paradise was any place where they didn't kill you.

———————

The cedar posts were still solid. Good for another hundred and twenty years. Dad stepped out of the pickup, hugged a post, slipped the latch off, and dragged the gate out of the way.

I pulled the car into the pasture. Dad closed the gate and climbed back in.

He asked, "Where are we gonna do this?"

"Same place as Bing, I guess."

"Bing?"

I said, "Your first dog."

"We buried him?"

"I wasn't born yet."

"Bing. Here, Bing."

Dad's senile.

We bumped the car over the bunchgrass until we found a spot. A draw, a low place next to a high place. Here was sand like a real desert. Someone had dragged in a dead cottonwood tree to slow erosion.

We slid our shovels into the sand. Sweat dripped into our eyes. We slung the dirt over our shoulders, scoop after scoop. I wasn't going to quit until Dad got tired. Dad wanted to prove that at sixty-two, he could outshovel me. He won. The hole was big enough to hold a goat.

I dropped the cat into her grave. She was stiff now, like she'd been taxidermied. The sand was moist beneath her. We scraped the dirt back into the hole.

Dad patted the earth with the heel of his sneaker. "You got any last words?"

"The end."

"Here, Bing."

On the way home, we stopped in Dorsey. Dorsey is a wide part of the highway. There are no side streets. There are no traffic lights. Just beat-down houses and busted-up cars.

Briefly, in the early 1900s, Dorsey was on the way up. This was when they called 36 the Airline Highway. The Airline Highway brought cars. The cars brought travelers who stopped for gas and maps and hamburgers.

On Fridays, the citizens of Dorsey used to roll a portable bandstand into the middle of the road. They diverted traffic with burning bales of hay. There was live music and dancing. Then Eisenhower laid down Interstate 70 forty miles south and all the traffic disappeared.

The following businesses are gone: the Dorsey Grocery, Scamper's Fuel Stop, the Airline Motel, the Airline Café, Gabby's Mexican Restaurant, McPhail's Used Cars, the Corsair Roller Rink, the East Pacific Swimming Pool, the Lil' Dimple Golf Course, and Poeller's Automotive. The following businesses are open: Hi-Country Telephone, U.S. Post Office, Dee's Liquor.

The bandstand is firewood. The musicians are dead.

We went to the liquor store. Three kinds of beer, a shelf of dusty liquor bottles, faded bikini posters. Vaughn Atkins's mom was reading the *Strattford Messenger* behind the counter.

I'm not sure Dad had ever been inside Dee's Liquor. Getting drunk was never one of his priorities.

Vaughn's mom said, "Looks like you got yourself a farmhand, Emmett. Get any work out of him?"

"He can't take the heat."

She said, "Scorcher."

He said, "Hotter than a popcorn fart."

I set a twelve-pack of longneck bottles on the counter and asked, "What's Vaughn up to?"

"Worthless as ever. Sits in the basement all day."

"I should visit him."

Vaughn's mom shrugged.

I said, "Anyway, not this time. I'm headed back to town tomorrow."

I reached for my wallet. Dad pulled his out first. He said, "I got it."

He handed Vaughn's mom a hundred-dollar bill. She puzzled for a moment. I took the wallet from Dad's hands, found a twenty, and swapped it for the hundred. Vaughn's mom said thanks, but she looked at me like I was no good. Like I didn't need to be letting my poor, confused pa buy beer. Or maybe like we didn't buy enough. I'm not much for reading people.

On the way home, Dad leaned forward with his nose almost touching the windshield. "I sure like the way those big birds fly."

I followed his eyes until I spotted two hawks circling way up high. Below them, a tractor was dragging a rod weeder thru a field, all dust and exhaust. Farming turns up mice. The hawks get fat.

I parked my car in the shade of the locust tree next to the garden patch. "It's time for a beer."

"We have beer?" asked Dad.

"Yup. We earned it. We put a cat into her eternal resting place. Let's sit on buckets and drink a beer."

"Too hot to do anything else."

As we were walking toward the shed, Dad looked at the box of beers in my hand. He said, "We're only going to drink one, right?"

"Unless you want more."

"We should put the rest of them in the fridge before they get hot."

"We can do that after."

"We should put them in the fridge."

The distance from the house to the shed was thirty-three yards.

I ran that thirty-three yards a million times as a kid. At the moment, we were halfway there. Dad stopped walking.

"I don't wanna walk back to the house, Pa."

"I'll do it." He reached for the beers. I held them. He tugged the box. I let go. Dad was a pain in the ass. Always, ever since I was a kid. He made up his mind about some stupid thing, and if you don't like it, you'd best find a way to pretend that you do.

I followed him toward the house. He said, "You don't have to come with me."

"I gotta make sure you don't screw up and put 'em in the freezer."

He looked hurt. Sometimes I forget.

The house was a mess. Shit was broken. Water was sprung. Mold. Bugs. A hovel.

"Unabelle been around lately?"

He looked at me like I'd asked the dumbest question he'd ever heard.

Unabelle Townsend came by mornings and evenings to check on Dad. Tall, skinny lady with pretty grey hair. She gave him a D- in twelfth-grade English in 1963. She gave me a smiley face in elementary art in 1979. Retired in 1983. Nicest woman you ever met. For the past couple of years, she'd been helping out: laundry, food, oral hygiene. Her husband had died sometime in the nineties and I suppose she enjoyed having someone to care for. She talked to Dad about the weather and cleaned up his messes. She listened when he was willing to talk, calmed him down when he got mean.

I rephrased my question. "How long since Unabelle's been here?"

"Hard to say. Since yesterday, I think."

Nobody but Dad had been in this house for at least a week. Maybe a month. It made me mad. Mad at Unabelle for leaving him alone, mad at Dad for being helpless. I said, "Why didn't you call me?"

"I don't need to call you for every little thing."

He couldn't dial a telephone, that's why he didn't call. I should have brought him to live with me a long time ago. Except he couldn't live in Denver. He'd get lost and show up dead on my back step with blood in his hair. I didn't want to bury my dad in a pasture.

I sat him on his recliner and tuned the TV to a John Wayne movie. "Don't move."

I dug thru piles of trash until I found a phone book. I called Unabelle. No answer.

I went thru every room, just looking for something. Windows were open. Flies were thick. This house contained my childhood and it was covered with filth. The bathroom door was locked. He had locked himself out of the bathroom. Where'd he been shitting?

Goddamned pit. Twinkies. Cassette tapes. I didn't know where to start.

I went back to the kitchen. The beer was still sitting on the counter, getting warm. I opened the fridge. Ice cream, melted over a half-eaten microwave pizza. Dad appeared. "Everything okay?"

"I don't know how you do it, Pa."

He was sad. I was sad.

He said, "I'm not good at things anymore."

"You don't have to be good at things."

"I used to be able to fly."

"We'll take care of it. I'll find Unabelle and make things right and we'll take care of it."

I started by cleaning the fridge. It wasn't as bad as it looked. The ice cream had mushed on stuff but most of the food was safe in Tupperware dated in Unabelle's old-lady handwriting. The most recent date I could find was from two weeks ago. In the freezer I found a frozen pizza, which I set to baking. I wiped clean a couple of plates. We ate dinner. The sun was going down. I didn't have anything important waiting for me in Denver; I could stay another day.

After we finished the pizza, I started washing the dishes. I sent Dad around the house looking for dirty cups. If he was away too long, I'd holler for him. "What are you doing, Pa?"

"Not sure!" he'd yell back.

"Look for cups!"

He brought back a couple.

I started the dishwasher and then looked in the junk drawer for the bathroom key. I couldn't find it. Dad got curious. He said, "What're you after?"

"The bathroom's locked and I can't find the key."

"Come on," he said. He walked out the front door and headed toward the shed. I followed. Once there, he found a piece of welding rod and, using the table grinder, turned it into a key. Nothing fancy. Just a little flat-blade key. But he did it. When he finished, he looked at it. "What's this for?"

"Follow me."

Back to the house. I put the key into the knob, turned it. He was proud. I was proud. It was like old times. I opened the door. Unabelle was lying on the floor, dead, fat, bloated Elvis-style.

There are good things about being an anosmiac and there are bad things about being an anosmiac. Good: I didn't smell the rot. Bad: If I had been able to smell the rot, I would have known from the second I entered the house that there was a dead lady in the bathroom. Dad didn't wrinkle his nose. Evidently, senility also takes away your sense of smell.

"We found Unabelle," he said.

And so I quit my job and moved in with Dad.

CHAPTER 2

WHERE THE AIRPLANE WAS

The day after Unabelle's funeral, I removed my clothes from my suitcase and stuffed them into my old dresser. Thirty-six years old. I'd spent half my life away from the farm.

I sat on my bed and stared at the floor.

I decided to go thru Dad's finances, just to make sure he was doing okay. Pretty quick, I knew we had problems. I sat at the card table and tried to separate the bills from the bank statements. We were never rich but Pa was generally good with money. When everybody else was buying giant four-wheel-drive 8650s and brand-new combines, Dad got along with a 4020 and an antique John Deere 95 that didn't even have air-conditioning. He farmed his land and he farmed it well. He didn't try to own more than he could manage. And he never, ever paid anyone to fix anything. If something broke, he repaired it immediately, all by himself.

We got along okay, he and Mom and I, even in the years when hail flattened the entire wheat crop. Slowly, he expanded the farm to a little less than a thousand acres. He paid off all the land and managed to put some money in the bank. When Pa was ready, he'd be able to retire, which meant he'd rent out the land and let other people do the work while he invented things and Mom planted pretty flowers in the garden. They were going to be an old, happy couple.

Then Mom went in to the hospital and didn't come out until she was dead and all of the money was gone and half the land was sold. After that, Dad worked even harder, both to build back his savings and to fill the lonesome days. Not long after that, he started forgetting things.

At first the forgetfulness was cute, and then it was a hassle, and then it became a problem, and then it made it so he couldn't start a tractor. But he still owned some land and land was money. Before he became totally lost, he put most of that land into the Conservation Reserve Program. With CRP, the government pays farmers not to farm. It takes land out of production to reduce surplus, bring up prices, and increase habitat for critters of the Great Plains. It's goddamned amazing is what it is.

As he entered his years of decline, Dad fiddle-farted around the farm, cashed his CRP checks, and lived cheap. He'd drive his pickup around the countryside on afternoons. He mowed the weeds with the riding mower. He replaced burned-out lightbulbs. He didn't seem too upset about the situation.

Even as he got more and more senile, I thought all the money business was fine. Dad was smart. But as I was sitting there at the card table that morning, it became clear that things weren't fine. There should have been receipts for the CRP payments. But there weren't any CRP payments. The bank statements, the ones that I could find, went down, down, down. I needed to figure this out. I didn't want to figure this out.

Dad was watching TV. I brought him his shoes. Tennies with Velcro straps. He used to wear boots.

I shut off the tube. "Father, let's have a look at the estate."

"It's hot out there."

"It's hot in here."

We surveyed the farm on foot. Three hundred acres, half a square mile. A few acres were set aside for the house (built 1930), shed (built 1976), grain bins (1978, '81, '82), and two buildings from the old days: the granary (1899) and well house (1912).

We walked out to the runway. The overgrown runway. It had never been much more than a strip of mowed weeds. Now, you couldn't tell it from the rest of the prairie. All around was pasture that used to be wheat fields until the government started paying Dad not to farm. The wheat fields Dad had farmed for fifty years were full of rabbits, mice, and badgers all citied among the bunchgrass.

We walked past a stand of juniper trees that we'd watered by hand once a week until their roots got deep enough to survive on their own. It took years to teach those trees to live off the land. Most of them were still alive, but they had the twisted, dusty look that things get when they're not where they belong.

Every farm has a row of equipment, lined up and ready to mangle dirt. We inspected our holdings. The John Deere 4020 tractor, with three flat tires. A drill, which is a wheat planter. Dad had apparently failed to clean it out the last time he used it; little wheat plants were growing out of the hoppers. A disc, which is a weed killer, now obsolete in the low-till era. The ancient combine, which harvested wheat, with the windshield busted out. Everything had thistles growing up to the axles.

Farmers like their landscapes well kept. Dad had always made sure that the area around the house was mowed. The ditches and everything, acres of it. Mowing was my job. Hours and hours bouncing on the seat of a riding lawn mower. I hated mowing. It was all sneezing and flies and dust stuck to the sweat on your forehead.

The farm hadn't been mowed for at least two years. The place looked like shit, like one of those abandoned homesteads you see.

We stood in front of the grain bins, the giant, corrugated galvanized tubs that city folks mistake for silos.

Under our feet was a slab of crumbling concrete, the last remnant of the original sod house built by my great-grandparents a hundred and twenty years ago. I used to play inside that house. One day, Dad knocked it over with a bulldozer and shoved it into a hole in the ground. When I cried, he said, "It was ready to fall down. I didn't want it to fall on you. Anyway, it was ugly."

We stood on that foundation, scratched weeds with our heels.

"This is our dominion," I said.

"Hard to believe," said Pa.

"Hard not to."

We went to the shed, the laboratory where Dad's genius sprung forth. If he wanted it, he built it. If it broke, he fixed it. He was a machinist, a carpenter, a mechanic, an electrician, an inventor, and an artist. Since we didn't raise livestock (Pa once said, "I grew up with cattle. I feel no obligation to grow old with them"), there wasn't much to do during the winter on the farm. He spent that spare time tinkering.

When Pa was fifteen years old, he built an internal combustion engine out of scrap metal. When he was twenty, he made a calculator using a box of spare electronics parts he found at a farm sale. There was nothing he couldn't do. Even when he was working like crazy after Mom died, he still made time for his projects.

In one corner of the shed there was a stack of antique one-lung engines that he'd restored. When he got tired of fixing one-lungers, he built a miniature steam engine from scratch. He cast the flywheels, cut the gears, machined the governor. He built it. After that he turned an industrial fan into a jet engine. He was attaching it to an old John Deere R when his brain stopped working. It remained a half-finished tractor that looked like it was beamed in from the future. Dad looked at it carefully, like he wasn't sure where it had come from. I found a tarp and covered it up. It seemed more respectful.

His tools were spread all over the universe. Time didn't freeze for Dad; it slowed down real gradual. He didn't wake up one day and stop working. He kept trying until he couldn't do it anymore. And even then he still went out to the shed when he forgot he couldn't do anything. He moved things, organized them. All his gloves were piled on the workbench. A pile of bolts here, a pyramid of empty oil filters there. He'd stacked WD-40 bottles and spray paint on top of his oil-burning stove. The place was like a confused obsessive compulsion and it was eerie.

Dominating the shed, though, was the empty space that had once been occupied by the airplane. A four-seater, single-engine, high-wing Cessna 172.

Dad was raised in the forties and fifties when jets were amazing. When everybody wanted to be the first man on the moon. He got his pilot's license right out of high school. He flew anywhere, whenever he could. Landed on dirt roads when there was no runway.

Airplanes weren't unheard of in that part of the country. A handful of farmers had planes. They used them to survey the land or make quick trips to Denver. And of course there were the crop dusters zooming across the country all summer long. Still, planes were special. Like owning a fancy sports car. Dad took good care of his plane. Even if he got too senile to fly, I couldn't imagine that he'd get rid of the thing.

"Where's the plane, Pa?"

"Oh, it's gone."

"You sell it?"

"Yep, I suppose."

"You sold it?"

"Looks like it."

"Get some money for it?"

"It's gone, isn't it?"

"I wish I could have taken one last ride." Sort of. Riding in an airplane with a senile pilot has its downsides.

Dad stood on the empty concrete floor, right where the cockpit would have been.

I said, "I miss it."

He said, "Yep."

A shed is a big room. A cathedral. Up in the I beams, sparrows made clicking noises. Dad looked up. "I've been meaning to shoot those things."

"Remember when you used to take me up?"

"In the plane?"

"Yes."

"I suppose."

"You used to scare the crap out of me."

"You're easy to scare."

"That time we were flying back from La Junta and we got hit by the thunderstorm. Remember that?"

"I suppose."

I knew he didn't remember so I narrated. "I don't know what we were doing down in La Junta, but we were flying home and one of those afternoon thunderkickers popped up in the middle of a blue sky. Quick as a blink, rain was splattering all over the windscreen. The plane was bouncing up and down and left and right. You were flying by instruments only. You said not to worry. And then something went wrong. We stalled. I remember that stall alarm buzzing. We fell forever. If I hadn't had my seat belt on, I would have floated right up to the roof of the plane."

Dad said, "Floater."

"Somehow, you righted the ship. You tugged the wheel and twisted that airplane until it was pointing the right direction. We shouted like banshees when we busted out of that rain and into the clear sky."

"Clearly."

"You told me, after we landed, that you hadn't known which way was up. You said you'd never been so scared in your life. The next day, you went over the whole plane, looking for what went wrong. Finally, you found it: a twig stuck in the air-speed-indicator dealie. It was giving you bogus readings. We could of died."

"I think some of that may have happened."

He crawled into an imaginary cockpit. Held the steering wheel. Smiled into himself. Closed his eyes.

"Dad, did you really fly a loop-de-loop in that plane?"

"A loop-de-what?"

"Did you go upside down?"

"Like this?" He spread his arms and skipped a circle.

"You said so once. I was just a little kid. You said you did a loop. Would have been twenty, thirty years ago."

"You know better than me what I did."

Down nine stone steps into the basement of the house, all the way into the coal bin, a small square room lit with a bare lightbulb. Weak light, black walls, lots of shadows. We had upgraded to natural gas years ago. Instead of coal, the bin was filled with shelves stacked with ancient electronic equipment. A box of vacuum tubes. An oscilloscope. A twenty-pound voltmeter. Things that Dad understood, once. He caressed them all. Wiped dust. "I kept all this junk so I could show you how to use it. I don't suppose anyone would want it now."

Elsewhere in the coal bin, a computer purchased for $2000 in 1982. Wires, a soldering iron, cables, a Heathkit amplifier. An electric motor I made for 4-H. The trophy I won for that motor. Let me clarify: Dad made the motor. I won the trophy.

Farther in the basement, the cinder block walls were damp. I imagined it smelled like mold. I found a milk crate filled with quart jars. I pulled one out, held it under the light. I said, "Think these are still good?"

"What are they?"

"Pickles. Mom made 'em."

He said, "When did she make pickles?"

"She made them before she died."

Upstairs, in the kitchen, in the light. We pried the lid off the jar. I reached for a pickle. It turned to mush.

"Limp," said Dad. "That's one pickle that wishes it was still a cucumber."

I didn't feel like cooking dinner so we went to the softball games. In the summer, they had games every Friday night in Keaton, the sister city of Dorsey. Nine-mile drive. The Lions Club played host, ran the concession stand, paid for the lights. We sat in the bleachers and watched the Keaton State Bank take on the Dorton High School seniors. Dorsey and Keaton didn't have enough kids for separate schools so they built one exactly halfway between the two towns and, after much discussion, decided that "Dorton" rolled off the tongue more easily than "Kearsey." Kindergarten thru twelfth grade. Even with two towns, they were lucky to pull in ten students per grade.

The kids from Keaton said, "Guard your horsey when you ride thru Dorsey." The kids from Dorsey said, "The people in Keaton need a beatin'." Of course, since the majority of us were farmers, most of the kids didn't actually live in Dorsey or Keaton. But you picked a town for yourself and stuck to it.

Even though there was no scoreboard, it was obvious the bank was getting their ass handed to them.

Someone slapped me on the back of the head. "Shakespeare Williams!"

D.J. Beckman, a balding, red-faced, thick-necked jackass sat down next to me.

I'd known D.J. since we were both kindergarteners. That didn't mean I liked him. He came from Keaton. Okay basketball player. He could dunk but he couldn't pass.

He punched my shoulder. "What the fuck are you doing out here?"

"I'm hanging out with Pa."

"How long?"

"'Til I find an excuse to leave."

"So you're here for good."

"Here for something."

We watched the game. The pitcher for the Keaton State Bank was a fat girl I didn't recognize. She couldn't toss for anything. She was wearing a boob tube. Her face was goopy with makeup.

I asked D.J. who she was.

"Clarissa McPhail."

Another classmate. I said, "Wow. Last time I saw her, she was a skinny little thing."

He winked. "Believe it or not, she's still single."

"She's not much of a pitcher."

"Oh, she's a hell of a pitcher."

She threw another pitch. It flew over the catcher's head. The batter took a base on balls.

I said, "No, she's not."

"You're watching wrong. Keep your eye off the ball."

Next pitch, I watched Clarissa McPhail. Her boobs heaved.

D.J. gee-geed like Roscoe P. Coltrane. "If you wait long enough, a nipple will hop out."

I said, "She know you're leering at her?"

D.J. stood up, cupped his hands around his mouth. "Hey, McFailure! Shakespeare wants to know if you know we're leering at you!"

Clarissa stuck her tongue out and tossed another shitty pitch.

Pa and I got hamburgers at the concession stand and climbed back to our seats next to D.J. Dad ate his hamburger wrong. Took off the top half of the bun and ate it. Then he ate the burger. Then the bottom half. I wiped his face with a handkerchief. It shouldn't have been embarrassing. Everyone knows Dad is sick.

D.J. pulled a flask out of his back pocket, took a sip, handed it to me.

I drank, gagged, spit between my legs. Some of it splashed on the kids who were playing in the sand under the bleachers.

D.J. said, "It's a work in progress. I'm mixing corn, rye, and wheat. I'm gonna call it Nitro Whiskey. Whaddya think?"

I wiped my finger over my teeth. "Kitty Dukakis wouldn't drink that shit."

Dad said, "Watch your language."

"Who's Kitty Dukakis?" said D.J.

Who the fuck is Kitty Dukakis? Good question. I said, "I gotta take a leak." I wanted to be somewhere else. Being in public with Dad always made me want to be somewhere else. But, things being how they were, if I went somewhere else, I had to take him with me. We walked to the outhouse, which was in the shadows beyond the outfield lights.

It takes Dad forever to piss. I stood outside and waited. When Dad finally finished, we took the long way back to the bleachers. Past a row of parked cars. We were approached by the preacher from the church Mom used to go to.

"See you on Sunday?"

"Prolly not."

We continued toward the bleachers. Interrupted again.

"Beer?" Vaughn Atkins's mom was selling longneck bottles from a cooler in the back of her pickup. I said no, thanks.

She said, "Shame about Unabelle." She was wearing her judgmental face.

"Sure is."

"Something happen to Unabelle?" said Dad.

"How's Vaughn?" I said.

"He's in the basement."

We continued toward the bleachers.

D.J. Beckman saw us as we approached and held his hands out like a pair of giant tits. He yelled, "Hey, McFailure! Shakespeare said he wants to have your babies!"

My name isn't Shakespeare. My name is Stacey, but nobody ever calls me that. No one has ever called me Stacey. I am thankful for this. From the time I was a baby, Mom and Dad called me Shakes, which is almost as stupid as Stacey. Whenever I asked them why they called me Shakes, they'd say it's because I shook a lot. Then they'd smirk at each other. Growing up, I was Shakes, Shakesy, Milkshake, whatever. In seventh grade, D.J. Beckman made the connection between Shakes Williams and William Shakespeare. Yippee verily shit. A new nickname.

I veered us away from the bleachers and toward the pickup.

"You had enough softball, Pa?"

"Somewhat."

I said, "Let's go see Vaughn Atkins."

CHAPTER 3

PARAPLEGIC

We rolled down the driveway to Vaughn's mom's house. The place was dark, with cats creeping in the shadows. We stepped out of the car. I pounded on the front door. No answer.

"You trying to wake somebody up?" said Pa.

"Vaughn Atkins. We went to school together."

"Vaughn Atkins."

"He flipped a car when we were juniors. Busted his back. Rides a wheelchair now. You know him. Before the accident, he used to help us harvest wheat."

Dad snapped his fingers. "He spent more time backing over fences than hauling grain."

"Never was much of a driver."

I opened the front door and we walked in. The house was a museum of liquor propaganda. Buzzing neon signs, a team of plastic Clydesdales, clocks with beer bottle hands. Posters. A stuffed dog. It hadn't changed in twenty years. The same spider plant was hanging from the ceiling. The same rotary phone sat on the same table.

Dad whispered, "Are we supposed to be here?"

"We're fine."

A pounding shook the floor beneath our feet.

"Mom!" A voice from below. "The toilet's clogged!"

We climbed down the stairs into a paneled basement. The carpet was shiny brown, like the wings of a miller moth. The place looked like it was smelly. There were cups and cola cans scattered about. At the far end of the basement was a bed. On that bed was a fat, naked paraplegic pounding a broom against the ceiling.

When Vaughn saw us, he threw the broom. It bounced to the carpet at our feet. "You sons of bitches can start by finding the remote control."

While Vaughn flopped himself into a pair of pajama bottoms, Dad and I looked for the remote. It was hard to concentrate for all the crap. Shelves of books and record albums. Broncos' pennants from 1977, 1987, 1989. A liquor cabinet, chained and padlocked. A stereo with a phonograph, cassette, and eight-track. A console TV attached to an Atari 2600. Magazines: *Life, Sports Illustrated, High Plains Journal*. A twenty-inch-tall plastic Godzilla. Stacks of Lego boxes. A basement den from twenty years ago, preserved like a museum dedicated to failure.

I found myself squatting in the corner next to the stairs, flipping thru the 1989 *SI* Swimsuit Edition. All that sand stuck to all those thighs.

Dad tapped me on the shoulder and said, "What are we looking for?"

"The remote."

He was holding it in his hand.

I shouted to Vaughn, "We got it!"

Vaughn turned on the TV. Snow across all six channels. "She cut the coax, the shit-toothed devil." He clicked the TV off and threw the remote control at a beanbag.

I sat on the edge of the bed. Dad stood next to me. I said, "How're things?"

Vaughn wrinkled his nose. "I'm awesome, dude. I'm a jellyfish.

I eat whatever boiled horse meat my mom gives me, lube my cath-
eter, drag myself to the bathroom for a shit every two days, play
Atari, and watch TV. Not so much TV now that Mom's cut the wire.
You still in Denver?"

"I'm back." I gave Dad an easy shoulder punch. "Hanging out
with Pa here."

Dad growled at me. "Watch it, tiger."

Vaughn squinted. "That's right. I heard you're taking care of
him now that Unabelle's dead."

"Helping around the house for a month or two."

"'Cause he's senile."

What an ass. I gave him a silent glowering.

He said, "What? I can't state the obvious? You wanna go for a
jog with me? Oh, I forgot. I'm paralyzed."

"You're a peckerhead. How's that for obvious?"

He said, "So?"

"So have a nice night."

Between Vaughn, D.J., and Clarissa, I'd seen enough high school
chums for one evening. I put my hand on Dad's back. We walked
up the stairs and out the door, and then we drove home.

Back at the house, I helped Pa brush his teeth. I waited outside his
room while he got undressed and then I tucked him in. "Good
night, Pa."

"Good night, son."

While Dad snored in his bed, I sat at the card table and tried
again to read some of the financial stuff. It still didn't make any
sense. We had more land than the three hundred acres we lived
on. There was the pasture where we buried the dead animals. Pa
used to rent that out for cattle. There was another quarter section
to the south. It was in the CRP program. Maybe another parcel up

near Dorsey. I couldn't find any property tax statements. I didn't
have any idea what I was doing. I gave up.

I went upstairs to my room. Like Vaughn Atkins's basement,
my room was a time capsule. Except, unlike Vaughn Atkins's basement, this room had been unoccupied for the past eighteen years.
I went thru my bookshelf, found a novelization of *The Empire
Strikes Back*, and brought it to bed. The closest movie theater was
in Strattford, the county seat, which was forty miles north. In
Dorsey, we read our movies.

I woke up the next morning with Dad sprinkling water on my face.
When I sat up, *The Empire* slid off my chest.

I reached for the plastic cup in his hand, but he snatched it
away, spilling water on the floor. It was still dark. I looked at the
clock. It was in blink time. The power goes off at least once a month
on the farm. There was always wind or lightning or something
messing things up. Almost no point in even setting a clock.

He said, "Good morning, sunshine."

"Starshine."

"Moonglow."

I said, "Did you eat breakfast?"

"I dunno."

"Are you hungry?"

"I guess so."

After eggs and bacon, I went thru the drawers in the kitchen until
I found Mom's seed bag. Garden seeds. Corn and cucumbers and
so forth. Even though they were old, I figured they'd grow.

We went outside to the garden. It was overgrown with weeds.
Dad said, "You gonna do something with this mess?"

"I'm gonna plant a garden."

He said, "You can't plant a garden."

"Of course I can. It's only May."

I found a hoe and started attacking the weeds. The dirt was dust.

Dad sat under the shade of the locust tree and watched. He was smiling.

I said, "Do you know something I don't?"

"You're working like a Mexican."

I handed him the hoe. "Show me how a white man works."

He handed the hoe back. "Not this way. There's a dealiebobber."

"The rake?"

"No. It's like." He finished the sentence by moving his hands in circles.

"Is it something in the house or the shed?"

"In the shed."

"Is it powered by gas or electricity or humans?"

"Gas. It has handles."

I followed him to the shed. Inside, he asked, "What are we looking for again?"

"A gas-powered device with handles."

"State its purpose."

"Something that only white people know how to do."

He hurried to a dark corner, pushed a sheet of warped plywood off a mound of stuff, and there it was. An engine with handles attached to it. Where there should have been wheels, there was a set of blades. "That what you're looking for?"

Right. The rototiller. You stay away from home too long, you forget things.

I filled the tank with gas and pulled the starter cord. Putt putt zilch. I opened the choke and pulled again. And again and again until my arm hurt. Dad wandered off. He returned up with a can of starter fluid and a screwdriver. "You having trouble?"

"Do your thing."

He removed the air filter and squirted the starter fluid. He pulled the cord, and the machine came alive.

In the garden, behind the tiller, he knew what to do. Churn the dirt. I left him there. The man who used to steer gazillion-horsepower tractors was walking stiffly behind a rototiller.

While Pa tilled, I went in the house to give the money business another go. I dug thru the piles and files and couldn't figure out why we didn't have any money. I fetched Dad from the garden for lunch.

When he went down for his afternoon nap I headed to the bank for some advice.

CHAPTER 4

SOWING

The Keaton State Bank was a short, flat building made of beige bricks and covered with asphalt shingles. Inside, the paneled walls were covered with goofy signs of the sort you'd expect to see in a diner. "Flying lessons: $1 to fly, $50 to land!" "Lost Dog: Three legs, blind in one eye, missing right ear, tail broken, recently castrated, and answers to the name Lucky." And the timeless classic, "Complaint Department: Take a number," where the plastic number tab is attached to pin of a dummy hand grenade.

Mingled among the signs were several framed photos of a big-chinned skinny man in a brown suit smiling widely and shaking hands with various jolly farmer-types. I'd seen those photos a million times on a million trips to the bank with Mom and Dad. I didn't recognize any of the farmers or the man in the brown suit. But they conveyed the message that this was a good bank full of good people who liked shaking hands.

The bank had two teller windows. One of them had a "See Other Window" sign. The other window had Clarissa McPhail, starting pitcher for the Keaton State Bank softball team.

"Why dintcha stick around after the game last night?"

I said, "Is Neal in today?"

"You took off because D.J. was hollering those things."

"I'm hoping that Neal can help me figure out why my dad doesn't have any money."

Clarissa leaned forward until her boobs pressed on the counter. I saw veins, looked away.

"I hear you're back for the long haul."

"It's important."

She said, "We should get together."

"Bank manager, please."

"Maybe this week."

I said, "Give me fifty thousand dollars."

"I'll come by your place when I have a chance."

"I have a gun."

She said, "You're silly." Then she winked. She opened the gate and led me to the back, down the hall, past the safe and the computers, to Neal Koenig's office. She opened the door without knocking. More paneling. Another funny sign: "Will work for money."

Neal was sitting at his desk, eating an apple. Neal graduated in the same class as my dad. Never missed a free throw. Owned a mint condition '62 Oldsmobile Delta 88. He took it to car shows and won lots of trophies, which were displayed in a case behind him. There was a die-cast model of the car on his desk. He was going bald but, because he was a bank manager, business protocol prevented him from wearing a farm cap to hide it.

He set his apple on his desk and said, "Mr. Williams. Have a seat." He looked happy to see me.

Clarissa said, "Have fun," and shut the door.

I sat in a wooden chair in front of Neal's desk.

"How's your dad?"

"He's taking a nap."

"Some weather."

I said, "Boy, is it."

"Hotter than a two-dollar pistol."

"I hope I'm not interrupting."

"Just a snack." He took another bite of his apple.

"Can you help me make sense of this stuff?" I placed a stack of papers on his desk. "Dad's finances are murked up. I don't know if it's because he lost some things or if it's because I'm stupid."

"I'd have to question the intelligence of anyone who'd come to me for financial advice," said Neal. Big grin.

I slid the papers toward him. "Take this, for instance." I pointed to a recent bank statement. "He doesn't hardly have any money."

"That's never a good thing."

"Plus, I know for a fact that he put most of his land into CRP, but I can't find any proof that he's getting paid for it. I was hoping you could go thru some things. Dad always liked you."

"I'll go thru it. Can't promise anything. I do know that he was working with the bank owner a while back. Some kind of a deal or arrangement-type thing. I'll see what I can come up with."

I said, "I appreciate that."

Neal said, "He comes down every Saturday. He'll be here to-morrow."

"Who's that?"

"The owner. Mike Crutchfield. Flies down from Greeley every Saturday. He has a Cessna."

"Really? Dad used to have a Cessna. Maybe we can talk planes."

"You can definitely talk planes. That Cessna he flies used to belong to your daddy."

"No kidding."

"Yep. He got it as part of the deal they had."

"That so?"

"Yep. Give a call tomorrow. You can talk to him all about it."

Neal stood up and gave me a fatherly look, like all the kidding was aside. "Don't worry, Shakes. Everything's fine."

He shook my hand.

_____

When I got home, Dad was standing in the driveway looking at the sky.

I got out of the car. "Gonna rain?"

"Oh. I don't know."

"Let's plant the garden in case it does."

"Then for sure it won't." He made a pretend jab at my chin.

The ground was soft and it was churned up real good from the rototiller. I hoed rows. I tried to get Dad to sprinkle seeds. He couldn't figure out whether to eat them or plant them so I took over. He sat under the locust tree and watched me work. I was putting cucumber seeds in a mound when he said, "There's a frog!"

He stood and, following his index finger, took a few steps, bent down, and picked up a toad. A hibernating toad that must have been woken up by the tiller. It wasn't happy. First sunlight in months.

"Must have overslept," said Dad.

He played with the toad. I planted the garden.

Dad was looking to the southern sky. It was late afternoon. He said, "They're gonna kiss." A cloud shaped like a fist bumped a cloud shaped like a dog head. It didn't rain.

I cooked hamburgers on the grill. We sat on the dirt under the locust tree, dripping ketchup on our jeans. Dad ate his bun, burger, bun.

I said, "Pa, did you sell your airplane to the guy who owns the bank?"

"Well." He scratched his heel in the dirt. "I think I remember something about that."

"I need you to dig deep. Tell me anything you can recall about that transaction."

"About the airplane?"

"And the bank owner."

"The airplane and the bank owner." Dad poured a handful of sand on his knee. He closed his eyes. He opened his eyes. "The airplane. I sold it to the bank owner. Crutchfield."

I felt like a hypnotist. "What else? Take yourself back."

"Airplane. Bank owner. Airplane. Yep. He showed up one day in his cowboy hat. He made me an offer. It was a good offer."

"How much?"

"Twenty dollars."

"You mean twenty thousand."

"Twenty."

"Twenty thousand?"

"What's it matter?"

"It matters." I was pushing him. "Any idea where you'd put a receipt for something like that?"

"It was a long time ago."

"Yeah, but he was a *banker*. Surely he gave you a receipt."

"I'm sure he did."

"So tell me, where would you put a receipt?"

"I don't know. You're the one who's interested in everything. You tell me."

Don't let it get ugly. He's not trying to be a dick. He's just frustrated. "Maybe it's in your wallet. Let's see your wallet."

Dad reached for his back pocket. No wallet.

The receipt, if there was one, probably wasn't in the wallet. But a man needs a wallet so finding it became our new priority. We swallowed our burgers and started looking. And we continued looking. We poked around the house and all his pants pockets and the shed and everywhere else, and after the sun went down, I found it sitting on the dashboard of Dad's pickup.

There was no receipt.

CHAPTER 5

OGALLALA AQUIFER

The next day, Dad and I drove forty miles north to Strattford, which has stoplights, and bought a dozen tomato plants. Dad paid. We planted the tomatoes that afternoon. They were straight. We set wire cages around them. They were safe. These tomatoes would feed us in three months. We were farmers.

We laid out the soaker hoses. They hadn't been used since Mom died. When I turned on the water, the hoses leaked from dozens of tiny holes. Little fountains. The hoses still worked, even with the holes. I didn't think it was a bad thing. Dad couldn't stand it.

I said, "I'll buy new ones next time we're in Strattford."

Dad said, "We should fix them."

"There's gotta be a hundred holes. How you gonna fix a hundred holes?"

He shut off the faucet and unscrewed the hoses. He put them over his shoulder and dragged them to the shed. I told him he was an idiot. He ignored me. In the shed, he marked the holes with a felt-tip pen, drilled them out with a three-sixteenth bit, squirted a dab of silicone gasket sealer into each one, and then asked me what we were doing.

I dragged the hoses back to the garden, hooked them up, and turned on the water. No fountains.

"Those snake things."

I said, "Soaker hoses?"

"Yeah. Those soaker hoses. They work real good, don't they?"

"Sure do."

Water is important. The land in our corner of the Great Plains is irrigated by water from the Ogallala Aquifer. The Ogallala Aquifer is an underground reservoir larger than all five Great Lakes combined. At least that's what they told us in school. It's where all the wells that pump the sprinklers that water the corn get their water. Good water. It comes up unfiltered and tastes a hundred times better than the chlorine they feed you in the city.

The Ogallala Aquifer is dependable in a land where rain isn't. It's dependable, that is, except when the wells go dry, which was happening more and more often since the four-million-year-old water was being used up a thousand times faster than it could be replaced. When a well runs dry, you dig another, deeper well. Eventually, the water's going to be gone; they'll dig a hole a mile deep and find nothing but dirt.

Since everyone knows it's a limited resource, everyone does the sensible thing and uses as much Ogallala water as they can while the getting's good. I once heard a politician say you can't take water out of just your half of the bucket. The mentality in Strattford County is that you can't leave more than your share of water in the aquifer and expect it to be there for your grandchildren. Next thing you know, the damned government would start regulating the water. Probably give it to all those pricks in Kansas. Use it or lose it. But don't overwater the garden. And we weren't, on account of Dad fixing the soaker hose.

We watched as the water turned the dirt dark.

After the sun went down, we retired to the living room. Before I turned on the TV, Dad said, "Your mother used to play the piano."

"She sure did."

"You ever learn how to play piano?"

I tapped out "Twinkle, Twinkle, Little Star." Dad sat in his recliner, listening, eyes closed, face relaxed into a contented grin. I played it again and again. He began snoring. I closed the piano lid and snuck out of the house.

It was Friday, a softball night, which meant that Vaughn Atkins's mom was at the games selling beers.

I drove to Vaughn's house, walked downstairs, and found him moaning and looking at a magazine. He had his back to me. I quickly turned around and started back up the steps with the intention of waiting outside for a few minutes and then coming back in, this time with more of a racket.

Before I could sneak back upstairs, he said, "Hang on, Shakes, I'm almost done."

I stood with my back to him, one foot on the bottom step and waited.

With a final groan, he said, "Got it." The bedsprings creaked.

I turned around. He was under the blankets. I said, "Sorry to interrupt."

"I don't have a problem. You have a problem?"

"No. It's cool."

"Cool."

I said, "Yeah."

"So you came back."

"Sure did."

"And you didn't bring your dad."

"Sure didn't."

"Because you figured I'd be an asshole to him."

"Affirmative."

"And, although you resent the fact that I'm an insensitive prick, you still value my uncompromising friendship as you begin this bittersweet return to your loathed hometown."

"Exactly, except for the part about valuing your friendship. It's more pity. You're obviously lonely."

He tossed a piece of plastic at me. A skinny yellow tube about ten inches long. I tried to catch it but failed. It landed on my shoe, where it became stuck.

"Sorry," he said. "It appears that you have a catheter attached to your shoe." I shook my foot vigorously until the thing was dislodged.

"You weren't doing what I thought."

"Sure wasn't, pervert. I was, in fact, changing my catheter. I have to do that sometimes because they wear out. And I'm paralyzed. I can't even *do* what you thought I was doing."

"But the guys in that movie said that they can still do it."

"Which movie?"

"*Murderball.*"

He spit on the floor. "Fuck *Murderball*. That movie's as phony as the moon landing. Have you ever in your selfish, spoiled life bothered to wonder how a bunch of alleged quadriplegics could enjoy active sex lives and also beat the shit out of each other on a basketball court and also be *quadri-fucking-plegics*? They're fakes. Propaganda intended to make guys like me look bad. Christopher Reeve is an asshole."

"Was."

"Ditto *My Left Foot* and *Born on the Fourth of July*. The vast, *vast* majority of people in wheelchairs are pissed off and bitter just like me. Depressed? Yes. Alcoholic? Probably. Those fantasy films and celebrity role models are allegedly intended to inspire cripples like me. But the real purpose is to help walkers like you feel better about the fact that guys like me are rotting in their moms' basements. There's a black president. Big fuckin' deal. Call me when we elect a dude in a wheelchair."

"Ring, ring. FDR's on the line."

"You're missing the forest for the knees."

"You're being incoherent."

"I'm being clever. Remember the last time you were here and you stormed out because I was being mean? I was *deliberately* rude to your old man because I knew that, otherwise, you'd never come here without him. You're too much of a pussy to split a six-pack of beer with me with your dad watching."

"Well, I'm here. Your plan was brilliant."

He wrinkled his nose. It made his face look fake. "I know. Now go upstairs, open the fridge, and get us something to drink."

I fetched some beers and then came back down and put on a record. *Wings over America*. While Paul McCartney rumbled out of Vaughn's fat old speakers, we drank crappy beers and bullshitted like kids.

I sat on the beanbag and talked up to Vaughn, who was on his belly on his bed.

I said, "I'm a gardener. I'm getting back in touch with my agrarian soul. I'm going to can some vegetables this year."

Vaughn said, "Let's start a meth lab."

"Let's see how the vegetables work out first."

"I know how to do it. There's people could show us."

"Sounds fun, but I've got a farm to take care of. I'm a good son."

"You wanna be a good son, you start by breaking the knees of the bastard who fleeced your dad."

"Which bastard is that?"

"Everybody knows the bank ripped him off. After your mom died—remember that?—the banker got involved. Mike Crutchfield. He said he was helping. He was always out there on the farm, whispering in your old man's ear. He organized an auction, saw that they hauled off a bunch of tractors and all sorts of stuff."

"How do you know everything? You live in a basement."

"People know stuff."

"I didn't."

"That's 'cause you were in the city doing your city things."

"Nobody knew for a long time how senile he was."

"The banker knew."

"I went to the bank yesterday. Neal Koenig said things are fine."

"His boss—Crutchfield—bought your dad's airplane for twenty dollars."

"Where'd you hear that?"

"People know stuff."

"I'm gonna go talk to Crutchfield tomorrow. We'll get it sorted out."

"Good luck. The guy's a prick."

"I'm not your typical country bumpkin."

"You're a pussy."

"Coming from a guy who hasn't left his mom's basement in twenty years."

He waggled his empty can. "Get me another beer."

"The fridge is empty."

Vaughn said, "Go buy some."

"Where?"

"Softball games. Buy 'em from my mom."

"No."

Vaughn said, "I figured you'd say that. Too bad we can't open that thing."

He pointed his head toward the liquor cabinet on the other side of the room. It was draped with chains, padlocked.

"You and your mom have trust issues?"

"It's the special stuff for the store. If someone wants fancy booze, they let mom know and she puts the 'Back in Five Minutes' sign on the door, runs home, opens the cabinet, pulls out a bottle, drives back to the store, and sells it to 'em."

"Why not keep it at the store?"

"Meth heads."

"Nobody robs anyone out here."

"So you think."

We were slightly drunk. Not crazy. Not enough booze for that.

I said, "Good stuff in there?"

"Two-hundred-dollar bottle of scotch."

"I shouldn't drink. It makes me wonder about things."

"You are who you are."

I said, "I'm a guy."

"You're a whiner."

"Coming from you."

Vaughn said, "You might lose the farm, but you'll still have your legs."

I said, "You have a mom."

"She's a horse's twat."

"You have a basement."

"A prison."

"You have a record player."

He threw his beer can at the turntable. It missed. "McCartney's a pussy. And anyway, you have a purpose in life."

"To watch my dad get more confused every day."

Vaughn pulled a brownie sealed in plastic wrap out from under his pillow. "You want confused? Have a brownie. I been saving this."

He peeled off the plastic and handed me half the brownie.

"Take a whiff."

I pretended to smell it. "Smells like air."

"That's right," he said. "You're nasally handicapped."

"What would I smell if I could smell?"

"A brownie."

I chewed a bite. It was a brownie all right. I assumed it was doped with weed. I wasn't a fan of the stuff, but he was offering. I didn't want to be rude. And it was yummy. I ate it up. I said, "Permission to speak freely?"

"Yep."

"I don't know how Dad and I are going to keep the farm. We don't have any money. I don't have any money and Dad's is all gone. Without money, we can't pay taxes or eat. I've got to get a job and there aren't any jobs out here. If I *were* to get a job, I'd have to hire someone to watch Dad while I was at work. There's nobody out here who knows how to do that. At least not anyone who'd do it at a price I could afford."

Vaughn said, "Actually, there was somebody but she dropped dead in your bathroom."

"My family's been here for a hundred and twenty years. My contribution to the Williams family legacy will be to oversee the disintegration of everything my ancestors built with blood, sweat, and wind."

"Tragic. You know what would make you feel better? Try dating some high school girls. There's two that look like Heather Locklear in next year's junior class."

The Wings record ended. I flipped it over. I was starting to feel funny. Not relaxed and silly like pot should make you feel. I felt not-relaxed. My jaws hurt.

"Shakes, you're yellow." Vaughn said "yellow" like he'd learned it from watching *Bonanza*.

"Which one of us lives in a basement since . . . since before a long time ago?" Something was wrong with my planet. My arms felt huge. I wanted to mess some shit up.

Vaughn pushed himself into a sitting position and flipped me off with both fingers.

I slugged him in the mouth. He hit me in the ear. Paul McCartney sang about bluebirds.

Footsteps. Stairs. Vaughn Atkins's mom pounded halfway down the steps and screamed, "What the Christ?!?"

Busted. Mom's home. Act cool. Calm down. Calm down. Don't hit anyone. Relax.

Vaughn's mom stood menacingly on the stairway with an empty six-pack ring on her finger. "Who said you brats could drink my beer?"

I said, "Sorry."

Vaughn threw an Atari game cartridge at her. "You own a liquor store, remember?"

She ran down the stairs, elbowed me aside, and started slapping Vaughn upside the head. Vaughn bared his teeth, wrinkled his nose, and fought back.

I ran up the steps three at a time, out the front door, and jumped into my car.

Three beers isn't drunk. Even if it is, it doesn't matter. There aren't any cops in Strattford County. The roads are straight, flat, and empty. As long as you don't drive like a moron, the worst thing that'll happen is you'll get stuck in a ditch. So I drove.

I found an AM station beaming in from Oklahoma and screamed along to the Eagles. I was on the Long Run. I spun kitties on the highway. I made my car go faster than it had ever gone before.

I got home late. Dad was asleep in his recliner. The TV was still on. Some shiny-haired jackass was pitching a plan to make a million dollars. I shut the tube off, patted Dad on the head, went upstairs to my room, and lay in bed. I couldn't sleep. I tried to read *The Empire Strikes Back* but I couldn't even open the book. I stared at the ceiling and chewed my cheeks.

A couple hours later, the sun was shining. Dad stomped upstairs and splashed water on my face. I couldn't get up. I was tired. I stayed in bed. Claimed I was sick. I was bushed. Dad called me a wimp, but I must have looked bad enough for him to pity me a little. He brought me three cups of water.

At noon, I crawled downstairs and spent a half hour on the toilet. Then I made peanut butter sandwiches. Then I called the bank to ask for an appointment with Mike Crutchfield. I talked to Neal Koenig, who said that, unfortunately, Mr. Crutchfield was caught up with some business in Greeley and he wasn't going to be able to make it to Keaton today. I asked when would he be in. Neal said try next week.

After I hung up, I went back to bed. By sundown I felt better. Not right, but better. Never accept food from Vaughn Atkins.

CHAPTER 6

MOTORBIKE

Dad was poking the juniper bush with the jack handle again.

"Whatcha doin'?"

"Don't know."

"You sure do like that bush."

He tossed the jack handle into the dirt. "What's on the agenda today?"

"Fixing a window."

There was a broken window in the granary. It wouldn't be hard to repair. Find a piece of glass, cut it to size, pop it in the frame.

We walked to the granary. A granary is similar to a barn. A barn is a big wooden building where you store cows and hay. A granary is a slightly less-big wooden building where you store grain. Used to store. With the invention of grain bins, the granary lost its original purpose. Out with the grain and in with the miscellaneous farm junk.

The granary was the last original building still standing on the farm. It and the well house. The granary was older, though, and its contents held the greatest archeological significance. Harnesses from the pre-tractor era hung on nails, their leather stiff with age. There was a license plate collection from back when Colorado plates had a picture of a skier on them, and before. And lots of junk. Tires, scrap wood, boxes of glass insulators from old-time telephone poles. Lots and lots of dust.

A white barn owl used to nest in the ceiling of that granary. It was gone and dead by now, but for years that bird would scare the shit out of me. As a kid, I'd walk into the granary with the intention of finding a piece of whittling pine and that owl would glide out of its perch with wings wider than I was tall. Pass right over my head and circle out thru whatever secret hole in the ceiling it used for comings and goings.

I clapped my hands a couple of times to see if I could scare up an owl, just in case. Nothing.

As we made our way toward the cracked window, I had to step over an old bicycle frame lying in the middle of the dusty floor. Pa had modified it to hold a Briggs & Stratton washing machine engine. Homebuilt motorcycle. He did this when he was ten years old. He rode it seven miles to school each day until he got his driver's license.

At some point after he graduated, he'd dismantled the bike. Now it was in pieces with most of the parts stuffed into a wooden milk crate.

The hell with the window. "Hey, Pa, you think we could put that thing back together?"

"What thing?"

"That bike of yours. The one you turned into a motorcycle." I pointed. "It's right there."

He didn't recognize it. His eyes couldn't assemble shapes like they used to. I recognized it. I wanted to put it together and go for a ride.

We hauled the disassembled bike to the shed and spread the pieces on the cement floor. We had the original bike frame, a clutch assembly that Pa had built out of angle iron and wood, and a bunch of parts that could presumably be turned into an engine. The flywheel cover was decorated with hand-painted racing stripes. I laid the components of the bike out in more or less their original shape. It looked like a horse skeleton.

"That's my old bike," said Pa. "I put an engine on it."

"We're gonna put it back together."

He shook his head. "I don't know about that."

"It'll be a father-and-son project."

"I don't know."

"Everything's here. All we gotta do is put it all back together. Patch the tires. Nothing to it."

"That's a big job."

"It'll be more fun than fixing a window."

I sent him psychic messages: Stick with me. Trust me. I'm your son. I can do things. You and I.

He said, "I gotta take a leak." He walked away.

I squatted on the concrete floor and moved the bike parts around.

A red car pulled into the driveway. A woman wearing gigantic sunglasses stepped out. Clarissa McPhail with a movie-star scarf on her head. "You boys look like you're up to no good."

Dad appeared from behind the shed. His pants were unzipped. He said, "Why, hello!"

I said, "Dad. Barn door." He zipped up.

I said to Clarissa, "Shouldn't you be at the bank?"

"Hooky." She tilted her head.

Pa couldn't take his eyes off her.

Clarissa said, "You remember me, dontcha, Emmett?"

She lifted her sunglasses, winked.

"I wouldn't forget someone like you."

I said, "So you drove out here."

"Seeing how the bachelors are doing."

"You look like a movie star," said Dad.

Clarissa patted the back of her ear. "Oh, Emmett."

Dad continued, "You were in the TV, I think."

Clarissa looked to me for help. I shrugged.

She poked her toe toward the pile of bike parts. "Whatcha makin'?"

Dad strutted a little. "We could tell you, but then we'd have to kill you."

"A motorcycle," I said. "Actually, it's a bicycle that Pa turned into a motorcycle back in the fifties. He took it apart in the seventies and now I'm trying to get him to help me resurrect it."

"Neat. You coming to the softball games this week?"

"I don't think so."

"Don't worry about them things D.J. was yelling. He's a drunk."

"Maybe."

"You know what you oughta do? Haul Vaughn out of that cave he's living in. Bring him with you. I know you been hanging out with him. You drank all his mom's beer."

Dad's eyes popped comic-style. "You did what?!?"

"It's true, Pa. I drank some beers." I turned to Clarissa. "How the Christ does this stuff get out?"

"Vaughn's mom works in a liquor store. I work in the bank. We pretty much got it all covered right there."

Creepy. "Well. I ain't coming."

"I can tell you things."

"No, thanks."

She said, "I can tell you things about airplanes."

Dad said, "I used to have a plane."

I said, "Maybe I'll see you there."

CHAPTER 7

END OF THE
SOFTBALL GAME

After Clarissa left, I put Dad in front of the TV for his afternoon nap. Once he started snoring, I drove to Vaughn's mom's house. Vaughn was in the basement, clipping his fingernails.

I said, "Where's your wheelchair?"

"Up your ass."

I poked around until I found it, folded up beneath the bed. I dragged it out and set it up. The tires were flat.

I said, "Where's your bike pump?"

"Up your other ass."

I squatted and peered under the bed again. I reached as far as I could. I groped around teddy bears and Star Wars figures until I felt the cool metal of a foot pump. I pulled it out and filled up the tires. Vaughn continued clipping his nails. Snip. Snip.

When the tires were filled tight, I listened carefully. No hiss.

I said, "They don't sound leaky, but we'll bring the pump with us, just in case."

Vaughn looked at me curiously. "Bring the pump with us where?"

"Softball. Put on your outside shirt. Hurry up. Dad's taking a nap."

"I don't own an outside shirt."

"Yes, you do. Come on. We're gonna see some softball."

"No, we aren't."

"When was the last time you saw the sky?"

He tossed a chunk of thumbnail at me. "I know what the sky looks like."

"You owe me."

"What for?"

"That brownie you gave me the other night. What was in that thing?"

"Drugs."

I said, "It wasn't pot."

"Nope. Considerably stronger."

"It was speed, wasn't it?"

"So what if it was? There wasn't hardly any in there."

I said, "It's rude to give people speed when they don't expect it."

"Wrong. It's *polite* to give people speed."

"Methamphetamines rot your teeth out. Do you know how important it is to have strong teeth?" I smiled menacingly at him.

"Are you trying to smile menacingly at me?"

"You're coming with me."

"No." He looked scared.

I took a breath. "Look. You're a prisoner. You hate your mom. You hate yourself. And you're afraid to go outside."

"Go fuck a duck."

He was holding his pillow against his chest. This felt like an after-school special.

"Okay. Vaughn, you know how sometimes you know someone who's in a shitty relationship? Like Lacey and Calvin back in high school. Remember how they fought all the time? It was completely obvious to everyone that if they just stopped dating, they'd both be happier. But nobody was willing to point this out to them because we didn't want to piss them off. Remember? And remember how Lacey ended up missing the volleyball tournament because she and Calvin got in that huge hair-ripper and how that made everyone hate her because Dorton lost in the championship thingy?"

"I remember Lacey had huge tits."

"Listen, you gimpy fuck, if you don't get out of this basement, I'm going to burn your house to the ground. I'll do it while your mom is at work and I'll make it look like it was your fault. At the funeral, she'll lean over your grave and say, 'My son was worthless.'"

"She'll be right."

I sat down in Vaughn's wheelchair. "Okay. What if we don't go to the softball games? We can go to the farm and say hello to Dad. We won't run into anybody. There won't be any awkward conversations."

Vaughn said, "Every conversation with Emmett is awkward."

I said, "We used to have fun out there." I tried to pop a wheelie in the chair.

"Fun? We threw rotten vegetables at each other." He started digging at his cuticles.

"Yeah, and we pretended it was World War II. We made a fort out of tumbleweeds. We tried to catch lizards. And we rode the three-wheeler all over the place. Remember that? You loved the three-wheeler." It was true. The three-wheeler was a giant motorized tricycle with balloonish, knobby wheels. It could conquer any ditch, any mud hole. It had a top speed of thirty miles an hour. As kids, we spent hours on that thing. Vaughn would insist on driving while I bounced along on the seat behind him and tried not to burn my calf on the exhaust pipe. No hill was too steep for Vaughn. No corner too sharp. In short, he demonstrated the driving skills that would eventually send him flying thru the windshield of his first car.

Vaughn looked at me, serious. "You still have that thing? That three-wheeler?"

The fall after I graduated high school, Dad sold the three-wheeler to some pheasant hunters. It pissed me off at the time, but I got over it.

I said, "Oh, hell yes. It's still out there, in the shed. Just waiting for someone to ride it."

Vaughn folded up the fingernail clippers and placed them on his nightstand. "You think I could ride it? With my legs and all?"

"Sure. The throttle and brakes are on the handlebars. You don't need feet. Once I put it in gear, you can go nuts."

He held out his hands like he was driving. He squinted.

After a moment, he said, "Get out of my wheelchair and find me a pair of shoes."

I moved quickly. Dad could wake up from his nap at any time. If I wasn't home when that happened, he could get into trouble.

Vaughn dug a T-shirt out from under his pillow and pulled it on inside out. I found a pair of tennis shoes. Vaughn poked his feet into them and then heaved himself out of his bed and into his chair. He tested the wheels, leaned back and forth. His face started to look happy. It was odd. He flexed his arms.

I said, "You ready?"

He sat in his wheelchair, dressed in tennies, pajama pants, and an inside-out T-shirt. He leaned the chair back into a wheelie and spun a quick circle. He nodded.

This was great. This was the best thing that had happened since I'd moved back home. Of course, I'd have to do some apologizing when we got to the farm and he found out there was no three-wheeler. I didn't care. Anything to get him out of that basement.

He said, "Let's get out."

He wheeled himself to the bottom of the stairs.

I stood behind the chair and grabbed the handgrips, ready to help him up.

He said, "I can do this myself."

"Bullshit."

"Watch."

He reached across his body, grabbed the handrail, and tugged. With his free hand, he rolled the wheelchair and heaved himself up a step.

He quickly repositioned his rail hand and then climbed another step. It looked painful and awkward. By the third step, his face was red and he was breathing hard. He smiled.

"I haven't done this in a while."

I said, "You need some water?"

"Nope. Just gimme a minute."

Steps four and five went easy. Then he took a long rest. His breaths were shaky. He still seemed happy. The strain was new and it felt good. But it was taking forever.

I thought of Dad. He was surely awake by now. Wandering around the house.

"Vaughn, maybe you should save some strength for the three-wheeler. Lemme help you here."

I could tell he wanted to tell me to fuck off. But he cranked his head around and looked up the stairs. He was barely halfway up.

"You can help me."

I climbed up the stairs and writhed around him, conscious of how easy it was for me to move. I grabbed the handles of the chair. Vaughn counted to three and together we tugged him up another step. Then another. Then another. His breaths became focused. I was witnessing one of the great physical feats in the history of mankind. I was participating in this feat. My thighs began to hurt from squatting and lifting. The plastic grips were pulling my palms off. The back of Vaughn's T-shirt became dark with sweat.

I said, "Rest?"

"No. Up."

"Two more."

He counted to three. Tug. The chair climbed to the edge of the final step. It hovered a moment, shivering. I pulled as hard as I could. With a pop, the right handgrip slipped off the chair.

With the grip still in my hand, I flew backward and sideways and slammed into the wall. I continued holding on to the chair with my left hand. I tried to straighten myself out and grab the right-hand handle, but without the grip, the steel was slick and my hand slipped right off. Everything was out of balance. Vaughn's hands tightened on the wheels. For a moment, we held the chair, balanced on the edge of the step. It was only a moment.

I lost my grip. Vaughn tumbled down the stairs.

He landed on the basement floor. The chair landed on top of him. I ran down the stairs and pushed the chair aside. He was curled up into a ball, arms gripping his flimsy knees. His eyes were closed.

I said, "Sorry."

With his eyes still closed, he shook his head.

I said, "You all right?"

He shook his head again and raised a middle finger.

"Let me help you up." I reached down to grab his shoulder.

His eyes opened. They were bloodshot and wet with tears. He said, "Get out."

"You don't want me to leave you here."

"Get out. Get out. Get out."

I got out.

When I got home, Dad was watering the house. Thumb over the end of the garden hose, spraying the roof. He'd been at it for a while. The ground around the gutter spouts was deep with wet.

I got out of my car and hollered, "Working on a new addition?"

He nodded. I wasn't sure he'd gotten my joke so I elaborated. "You're watering the house. Gonna make it grow?"

He said, "Gonna make it wet."

"Why's that?"

"It's hot." He looked toward the sun. It was hot.

I said, "Yep."

Then he pointed the hose at me. I ran and hid behind my car.

I yelled, "You wanna go to the softball games?"

He said, "Softball's okay."

In the car, on the way to Keaton, he said three times, "How'd you get so damned wet?"

Clarissa's team was at bat. She was sitting on the bench. I waved at her thru the chain-link fence. She came outside the dugout.

She said, "Why didn't you bring Vaughn?"

"Too many stairs." I tried not to think of Vaughn dragging himself across the basement and back into his bed.

"At least you brought Emmett." She made eyes. Dad made eyes back.

The batter flied out. End of the inning. Someone called Clarissa's name. She jogged back to the field.

I shouted, "When are we gonna talk about airplanes?"

She ran backward and waved.

I got a hamburger. Dad got nachos. We sat on the bleachers. D.J. Beckman climbed the bleachers, sat between us, and said, "How's it hanging, buddy?"

I said, "Not bad."

He said, "Ask me how's it hanging."

"How is it?"

"Loose as a goose, full of juice, and ready for use."

"Thrilling."

D.J. said, "How's your girlfriend?"

Dad enjoyed that one. "You've got a girlfriend?"

I shook my head. "D.J. lives vicariously thru his fantasies of other people."

"Shakespeare and Boob Ruth have got something brewing."

I said, "We don't. How's your whiskey concoction coming?"

"I gave up."

"That's a shame."

"I found another hobby."

"Neato."

"Brownies." He winked at me. Then he winked again. "You ever want some brownies, lemme know."

An aluminum bat pinged. A batter knocked one of Clarissa's pitches right back at her. The ball smacked her on the knee. The batter ran around the bases while Clarissa curled up on the ground and hugged her leg. Players in their blue jeans and three-quarter-sleeve softball shirts jumped around and slapped each other five. Clarissa waved off any help and stood up slowly. She had dirt on the skin of her back where the tube top didn't cover up.

D.J. shouted, "Hey, McFailure! If that ball was a little higher, it woulda got stuck in Cleveland!"

I gave him my disapproving look.

He rolled his eyes. "Relax, Shakes. She don't have feelings." He whispered in my ear, "You ever want any brownies, I got some real good ones." Then he was gone.

Clarissa looked like she didn't want to be there anymore. I wanted to pat her on the arm, tell her things were okay. And encourage her to quit playing softball. But I just sat there, spectating away.

Dad—who was apparently missing all this excitement—pointed at the sky and said, "I believe it's going to rain."

He was right. In an instant, the weather went from summer pleasant to the opening scene of a horror movie. Lightning bounced from cloud to cloud. Thunder shook our eyes in their sockets. Wind blew clothes tight against bodies. The first few drops of cold, pebbly rain fell square on my back and made me wince.

The ballplayers sprinted off the field. Spectators leaped out of the stands, off tailgates, grabbed coolers, ushered children, held farm caps, and dove into pickups. I tried to hurry Dad, but he walked slowly. "It's just some damn water."

God almighty, there's nothing like a thunderstorm on the Great Plains. I'm serious when I say this. It's like looking at the Grand Canyon—that's how amazing the sky is. You ever notice how county fair artists are always trying to paint huge clouds into their landscapes? It's because those clouds are mighty, mighty things. You ever notice how all those paintings look like shit? That's because it's impossible to capture the essence of those clouds in paint. It's the quickness. You can't paint that. It took millions of years for the Grand Canyon to form. It takes half an hour for a fifty-thousand-foot thunderhead to appear out of nowhere. It bubbles and rotates. Little pigtails twirl out, trying to make themselves into tornadoes. Hell, you can't describe how amazing it is.

By the time we got to the car, I was soaked. Dad didn't seem hardly wet at all.

He said, "I believe it's raining."

"I believe you are correct, Father."

It wasn't night yet. Just sunsetty. The clouds took away the setting sun. The softball field lights came on. The wind whipped up and shook the car.

A hand slammed against the windshield. I yelped. Dad laughed. Before I could slap the locks down, Clarissa McPhail climbed in. Back seat. The car sagged.

"I got a six-pack." She passed bottles to Dad and me.

Dad took a sip from his beer and said, "This here's the good stuff."

I said, "How long you think this'll last?"

"Half hour, maybe," said Clarissa.

"That sounds about right," said Dad.

"Too bad about the game," I said.

"Yeah. Too fucking bad," said Clarissa. She covered her mouth with her hand. "Sorry, Emmett."

Dad took another sip. "Cuss all you want. I don't give a damn." He said "damn" like it was the dirtiest word that ever came out of a human mouth.

"Softball's stupid," said Clarissa. "Whyncha turn on some music?" She wedged herself between the front seats until she could reach the radio. She pushed buttons and twisted knobs. Only one station. Talk radio, and you couldn't hear a word due to all the lightning static.

"Middle of damn nowhere," said Dad.

Clarissa twisted the switch off.

Lightning sent glowing capillaries across the sky. Before the sparks had faded, thunder snapped. The softball field lights blinked and turned black. It was dark now.

"You better hope there's no tornadoes," said Clarissa. "We wouldn't be able to see one until it picked up this little car of yours." She added, "I don't know why you drive this puss-mobile when your dad has a perfectly good pickup."

"Tornadoes," said Dad. "You can hear 'em from a mile away."

"Better hope so," said Clarissa.

We listened to the rain.

I heard something. I said, "Did you guys hear that?"

"Alls I hear is rain," said Clarissa.

A whistling sound. Growing louder. Dad and Clarissa tipped their ears. We peered thru the windows, looking for a funnel cloud. All we saw was dark, distorted by the rain running down the glass.

Nobody spoke. The whistle grew louder, like a siren.

"It's a siren," said Dad. He pointed out the back window toward the road. A red light grew, the siren shrieked. It passed, the pitch dropped.

"Fire truck," said Clarissa.

All around us, headlights came on. Engines revved and pickups pulled out of their parking spaces to zip down the road behind the fire truck.

Clarissa slapped the back of my seat. "What are you waiting on, Poindexter?"

"I don't follow fire trucks."

"Someone's house is on fire."

"Don't you have a softball game to finish?"

"Not when lives are at stake. Let's go!"

I turned the key. We went. I thought I was driving fast, but it wasn't long before the last taillights had disappeared before us. I drove on, following Dad's finger, which took us off the highway and onto squishy dirt roads. He thought he knew where we were going and I didn't care where we went. Clarissa sat in the back seat and shivered in her tube top. I turned on the heat and said, "If you feel around, you'll find a blanket back there. Prolly wedged under the passenger seat."

With much shifting about, Clarissa bent over and found the

wool blanket I kept in my car because Mom always told me it could save my life.

She said, "It's kind of ratty."

"It'll warm you up."

I looked in the mirror. She put it over her shoulders. She seemed more decent that way. We drove on.

The rain moved east, taking the lightning with it. Except for some tatters of wind, the night became pleasant again.

"Tell me about airplanes," I said.

"Not when we're looking for a fire." She and Dad had their noses close to the windows, breathing steam, watching for the fire truck or a fire or a tornado. Anything.

"We're wasting gas," I said.

"There it is," said Dad.

CHAPTER 8

VOLUNTEER FIRE DEPARTMENT

Lightning had struck the lonesomest cottonwood tree in the world and split off a branch, which landed crossways on the power lines. The wind was bouncing the branch on the wires. Every little gust made a quick electrical short and sent up puffs of sparks. The branch, with its wiggling leaves, was dark against the sparks.

I stopped the car and rolled down the window. We watched for a while. Wind hummed thru the power lines. Heat lightning flitted in the east.

The situation didn't seem terribly dangerous. But we reckoned we should do something; one of those sparks could fall into the pasture grass and set off a real burner.

We drove toward the nearest yard light, about a mile away. Ezra Rogers's house. Ezra was ninety-nine years old, the oldest person in Keaton. He was older than Keaton itself. When he walked, he leaned on a homemade cane. The flesh over his left eye sagged down low, with an ugly yellow eyeball peeking out underneath. He went to my mom's church. I'd seen that eye plenty. Ezra's first wife had died decades ago. His second wife, Mirabelle, had come to him via mail order. They'd been married for sixty years. He taught her to drive when she was eighty-six. Her first lesson ended with a car-shaped indentation in the Keaton State Bank. The bricks got replaced, but the outline was still there.

Peering thru the window, we could see that he and Mirabelle

were watching TV. The volume was loud enough for us to understand the dialogue from outside.

Clarissa hit the door with her fist.

Ezra and Mirabelle continued watching their TV show.

"Why don't we just walk in?" I asked.

"Ezra keeps a shotgun," said Clarissa. She hit the door again.

"Shotgun, my ass," said Dad. He opened the door, cupped his hands around his mouth, and yelled, "Ezra!"

The old man spun around in his chair, stood up, and hovered toward us. He was dressed in a T-shirt and a baggy pair of underwear. He leaned on his cane all squinty-like and said, "You hungry?"

"That depends," said Dad. "What's on the menu?"

Clarissa stepped forward and stamped on the floor. "Ezra, there's a fire!"

"A far?"

"A fire. Across the road and up a piece. Lightning hit a tree. There's a branch in the telephone lines and it's gonna start a grass fire and we need your phone."

Ezra was skeptical. "Wasn't no lightning tonight. I felt the thunder. Wasn't a peep of no lightning."

Dad took our side of the argument. "Say, Ezra, I'm pretty sure there was lightning. I mean." He paused, trying to put together a sentence. We waited. "What they're saying. It's the truth."

Ezra nodded. "If you say so, Emmett."

Phone call made, we shouted good night to Ezra and Mirabelle and returned to the scene. The branch was smoldering now. Bits of glowing ash floated to the ground and made the moist grass smoke.

Ten minutes later, the fire truck arrived, followed by the caravan of pickups. The volunteer firemen stood under the tree and discussed the night's events. The original fire alarm, the one that had killed the softball game, had been a falsie.

After some mild debate, the volunteer firefighters concluded that they didn't want to mess with an electrical fire so they radioed Jimmy Young, the local representative of the Rural Electric Association.

As they waited for Jimmy to arrive, folks drank beers and discussed the time Troy Earhardt tipped up a section of sprinkler pipe to scare out a rabbit that had hidden inside. The rabbit wouldn't leave so Troy stood the pipe straight up and shook it. The pipe touched a power line and Troy died. He was a good kid. The whole thing was tragic.

His school record for the triple jump still stands.

Half an hour later, Jimmy Young arrived in his company truck. He looked like he'd just woke up. Thirty drunken softball enthusiasts watched as he extended a fiberglass pole, jiggled the wires, and let the branch fall to the earth. Without a word, he got back into his truck and drove away.

CHAPTER 9

BREAKING AND ENTERING

We were driving back to Keaton.

"Worth every penny," said Dad.

"What's that?" said Clarissa.

"The fire department," said Dad.

I said, "I'm not following you."

Clarissa said, "They're volunteers, dummy. He made a joke."

I turned to Clarissa. "Tell me about airplanes."

"I wish we had some more beer." She said, "Six beers between three people only makes you thirsty."

"If I get more beer will you tell me about airplanes?"

I looked at her in the rearview mirror. She nodded.

Keaton doesn't have a liquor store so I made a detour to Dorsey.

Dee's Liquor was closed. We sat in the parking lot and watched fluorescent lights blink in the refrigerators.

"Why would a liquor store close on a Friday night?"

"In the summertime, it's always closed on Fridays," said Clarissa. "It's her mobile day. Bring the booze to the people. Usually she's at the softball games. But since the games are rained out, she'll be down at the gravel pits. That's where the high school kids hang out nowadays. Later she'll make a run to the poker night at the Catholic Church."

"Since when is there a Catholic Church out here?"

"There isn't. That's just what they call the Quonset hut on the old Bennett place." Clarissa shrugged. "Whatever. The store's closed and we need something to drink."

"Shit yes, we do," said Dad. He looked at me and Clarissa to see if we heard him.

"Language, Pa."

Clarissa sighed. Dad sighed.

I said, "You know what she oughta do? She ought to leave a key out so responsible people can go in and buy booze even when the store's closed. We're responsible people. I'd even tip her some."

Clarissa said, "Leave a key out. Wouldn't that just be hilarious?" She got out of the car and tried the door of the liquor store. Locked. Then she lifted up the doormat. There was a key.

I rolled down the window and said, "Okay. Time to go home."

She put the key in the door and turned it.

"Pa, tell her to knock it off."

"Looks like she's got things under control."

Clarissa looked left and right. No witnesses. She tiptoed inside, opened a fridge, and exited with a case of beer.

"You leave enough money?" I asked.

"I don't have anything on me."

"Then you just committed larceny."

She put the key in my hand. "You pay. Go on. It's fun. Kinda creepy in there with all those half-naked women looking at you from the walls."

She was right. It was creepy. It didn't feel like I was committing a crime. I felt like I was snooping in someone else's bedroom. I was ready for Vaughn's mom to pop up from behind the counter with a shotgun and fill my belly full of rock salt. I walked very carefully. I opened my wallet. I didn't have to look—I knew I had eighteen dollars. I left it all on the counter and was about to walk out when a car pulled into the parking lot. The engine thumped loud, as if the muffler had rusted off. I hid quick behind a cardboard swimsuit model.

Talking. Laughter. Footsteps. The door to the liquor store opened. I saw high-tops and blue jeans. I heard a cooler open and close. A voice said, "That looks about right." A hand slapped the counter. Footsteps out. Door closed. I squatted behind the swimsuit model until my knees went numb. The absolute worst thing in the whole world would be for someone to find me hiding like a chicken.

A hundred years later, the mystery car revved up and backed out of the parking lot with a friendly toot of the horn. I stayed put. Another hundred years later, there was a knock on the door. Laughter. The door opened. Clarissa said my name. I crawled out from behind the swimsuit model.

"There's my boy!"

She hugged me close. She seemed drunker than before.

I said, "What's the deal?"

"What's the deal?" she repeated.

"Who was that?"

"D.J. Beckman. You didn't recognize him?"

"I didn't look."

"Surely you recognized his car. You don't need to see that thing to know it's him."

"That was the Nova?"

"Yep, but uglier. Just like him."

When D.J. Beckman was a sophomore, he bought a beat-up, shitty 1972 Nova for two hundred dollars that he'd most likely pinched from his parents. The car was fast and loud and cool. It was a muscle car, built right before anyone started giving a fuck about mileage or safety or anything. It was also one good-sized badger mound from busting into a hundred pieces.

He always said he was going to restore it to mint condition. He never did. Instead, it remained perpetually on its last legs. Apparently, for twenty years and counting.

I said, "Was he on to us?"

"I told him that me and your dad were on a date."

She was still holding me. I shook out of her arms. "That's disgusting."

She was hurt. "What'd you want me to tell him? That you were robbing Dee's Liquor?"

"You coulda come up with something better than that. Anyway I was *paying* Dee's Liquor. *You* robbed the place. If D.J. starts telling people you're dating my pa . . ." I didn't know what to say. There was nothing nice to say, that's for sure. "That was dumb."

Clarissa stopped being happy. "He ain't gonna tell people me and your dad was on a date. In fact, I didn't tell him that me and your dad were on a date. I was messing with you. What I really told him was that we came up here—the three of us—to buy some beers but the store was closed. We were about to leave when you decided you had to take a shit. And I told him you were behind the building squatting. He wanted to go scare the you-know-what out of you, but I talked him out of it.

"Then he said, 'If you want something to drink, you just need to use the key under the doormat. Everyone knows that.' Then he looked under the mat and didn't see the key. I thought he might suspect us of something but he didn't 'cause he's an idiot. He just tried the door, pulled it open, walked in, and got some beers and schnapps. I even saw him put money on the counter."

She pointed to the counter, which had no money on it.

She frowned. "Maybe he didn't put any money on the counter. I couldn't really tell from outside."

"Maybe he took the money *I* left on the counter."

She said, "That seems likely."

"We need to leave something."

"Even though Vaughn's mom's a creep."

I said, "Even though."

"I ain't got anything, Shakes. You know that."

"Everything I had is now in D.J. Beckman's pocket."

"Let's just go," said Clarissa.

"It ain't right."

"You wanna see if the credit card machine's working?"

"You think?"

She grabbed my wrist and dragged me out the door. "You got no sense of sarcasm."

Dad was in the car with an empty beer bottle in his hand. "Where's the party?"

I said, "Night's over."

Clarissa said, "The night ain't nothin', Shakespeare."

"It's not even night," said Dad. I didn't correct him.

"Let's go see Vaughn Atkins," said Clarissa. "He's all alone."

I said, "No."

"You said I was dumb," said Clarissa.

"No."

She dragged her finger under my chin. "We'll talk about airplanes."

We went to Vaughn Atkins's house.

When we got there, Vaughn was lying on his bed watching a Kirk-era *Star Trek* episode on the TV. No sign of the wheelchair. He was still wearing his inside-out shirt and pajama pants. No tennis shoes. His legs looked straight.

He waved at us like nothing was wrong, like he hadn't fallen down a flight of steps a few hours ago.

I said, "You doing okay?"

He said, "Fine. Why?"

If he didn't bring it up, I wouldn't bring it up.

He said, "How was the game?"

Dad said, "Everybody lost."

Laughter. We settled in.

Dad fell asleep on the beanbag almost instantly.

We watched TV, talked, and drank the beers we'd stolen from Vaughn's mom's store. During a commercial break, Clarissa asked Vaughn, "You sure your mom isn't gonna come home and start yelling at you?"

Vaughn shut off the TV. "Who cares? Anyway, nights like this, she never gets back before midnight."

I said, "What's she doing, do you think?"

"Selling beer to minors, whoring around, skinning coyotes. What do I care? She's a grown-up. You figure out how that banker ripped your dad off yet?"

"Yeah, you figure that out yet?" asked Clarissa. "You figure out how Crutchfield ripped you off?"

I said, "I'm not really interested in the *how* of it. What I really want to know is why he thinks he's gonna get away with it. I'll get answers. He's going to meet with me. We were supposed to get together last Saturday, but he couldn't make it. Neal Koenig said he'll be back this next week. When I go in there, we'll get it all cleared up."

Clarissa burped incredulously. "You're a sucker. Crutchfield was at the bank on Saturday. I don't work on Saturdays, but I know that airplane. He lands it on the road and taxis out back behind the bank. I drove by. I saw it parked there. If the airplane was there, then Crutchfield was there. If Crutchfield was there, then Neal was lying to you when he said he couldn't make it. You got lied to." She made a face. "You need to figure out how to tell when people are fucking with you."

"I need someone to empty my colostomy bag," said Vaughn.

"We're trying to converse," said Clarissa.

"One of you's gotta do it."

"It ain't gonna be me," said Clarissa, waving her finger and head back and forth in a sassy maneuver that could have only been picked up from daytime TV. "Let Shakespeare do it. He can't smell."

I said, "Don't use my handicap as an excuse to make me do your third-world bullshit chores."

Vaughn said, "If this bag of shit doesn't get off me, I'm gonna catch hepatitis. And which one of us is handicapped, again?" He glared at me.

I had dragged him up the stairs and watched him fall on his face. I should probably do anything he wanted for a very long time. "Fine," I said. "Gimme."

Vaughn reached under his shirt. He pulled out his fist and raised his middle finger. "You, my bard, are one gullible little bastard. Colostomy bag! I shit natural."

He and Clarissa giggled. Dad snored.

Clarissa opened two more beers, handing one to Vaughn and tipping the other into her mouth. When her gulp was finished, she wiped her mouth with her forearm and said, "I feel like we're really connecting."

"You've got that right," said Vaughn.

Clarissa said, "I feel like we're on the same level. Like we're part of a kinship." She gritted her teeth. "Like that."

"Like a waterfall," said Vaughn.

"You wanna know something about me?" said Clarissa. "A secret?" She had reached the confessional stage of drunkenness. I was not at that stage.

I said, "Only if it's intended to humiliate me."

"Why you gotta say that? This is totally, totally, totally true. I want to tell you guys, both of you, 'cause you're my friends."

"We're your friends, too, Clarissa," said Vaughn. "Say anything you want. We're right with you."

She took a breath. Then, solemnly, she said, "I have emetophobia."

Vaughn and I were silent. Without opening his eyes, Dad said, "I never met a phobia I didn't like." He resumed snoring.

"It means I'm afraid of vomit."

"How *do* you survive?" asked Vaughn. He was not connecting with Clarissa quite as much now as he had been a moment ago.

Clarissa plowed on, oblivious to Vaughn's sarcasm. "That's not the point. Survival doesn't apply to this situation. The point is that the situation applies to why I'm an anorexic. That's my confession. I am Clarissa McPhail and I suffer from anorexia nervosa."

Vaughn was fully not connecting with Clarissa now. "With all due respect—"

"Don't you even say it. I know what you want to say and it's crap. Just because I'm fat, you think I can't possibly have an eating disorder. You're wrong. I haven't had a bite in over a week. If I keep this up, I'll die. You're the only people who know. Listen to me. I wanted to be bulimic, but I couldn't because I'm afraid of vomiting. So I'm anorexic. I've stopped eating."

"You aren't anorexic," said Vaughn.

"Yes," said Clarissa, "I am."

"Why?" asked Vaughn.

"Because." She spoke in a tiny voice. "Because sometimes I feel ugly."

She was sitting on the edge of Vaughn's bed with her spandex bra and tight britches, hunched over, belly fat folded, hair messed up, a frown mushing up her face. Vaughn and I exchanged glances.

Vaughn looked her over. "You aren't ugly."

"No, I am," said Clarissa.

"I don't think you're ugly," I said.

"I think you're purty," said Vaughn.

I said, "You're downright attractive."

"A real looker."

"Cute."

"Hot."

"Sexy."

"Beautiful."

Clarissa was glowing. We were all connecting again. We were all on the same side.

"Hey, Vaughn," she asked, "you got any of those famous brownies I keep hearing about?"

Vaughn reached into his pillowcase and pulled out two plastic bags full of brown goop.

I said, "You sure that's not your colostomy bag?"

Vaughn ignored me. "One bag contains hash brownies. One bag contains meth brownies." He looked carefully at the bags. His eyes were crooked from the booze. "I can't remember which is which. Anybody wanna play guinea pig?" He pulled a brownie out and handed it toward me.

I said, "Thanks, but kiss my ass."

"Pussy," said Vaughn.

Clarissa said, "Vaughn, you take one from one bag and I'll take one from another bag. That way we'll know which is in which."

"Brilliant!" said Vaughn.

"You know," I said, "you'd be just as successful if just one of you ate one brownie."

The way they looked at me, I knew I had missed the point.

Vaughn tossed a brownie to Clarissa. It stuck in her cleavage. They both thought that was hilarious.

While they goofed around, I went upstairs to get another beer from Vaughn's mom's fridge. All the lights were off. I walked thru the living room, absorbing memories. The bathroom. That was the first place I ever took a shower. My family didn't have a shower until I was twelve. Just a tub. It was a sleepover night and Vaughn and I had been playing in the mud all day. Vaughn's mom told us to clean up for dinner. I went to the bathroom and stood in the shower stall. I didn't know what to do, how long to stay in there, how to clean my toes. I remember I turned the hot water on full blast and stayed until it went cold. Luxury.

I heard Clarissa and Vaughn laughing downstairs. I contemplated leaving. I didn't really want to go back down there and watch those two get messed up and stay awake all night confessing their insecurities and talking about old times and letting them make fun of me and us all just being losers in a basement. But Pa was down there.

I decided to slam a beer. That would improve my mood. I opened a bottle and started pouring it down my throat.

A car pulled into the driveway. I dropped the beer on the floor and sprinted downstairs.

"She's home!"

"Shit!" said Vaughn.

"Who gives a fuck?" said Clarissa.

"Gimme another brownie," said Pa.

Clarissa, Pa, and I hid in the downstairs bathroom with the lights off. We were all breathing heavy. On the other side of the door, I could hear Vaughn grinding his teeth in his bed. Footsteps on the ceiling above us.

The basement door opened. Vaughn's mom yelled, "Whose car is that?"

Vaughn shouted, "What car?"

"That car in the driveway."

"I didn't know there was a car."

"It looks like that faggot-mobile the Williams kid drives."

"You're drunk, Mom. Go to bed."

A hand groped my crotch. I slapped it away.

"Sorry," whispered Clarissa. "It's so dark."

"I'm over here," whispered Pa.

I hissed at them both to shut up.

The basement door clunked shut. Safe. Footsteps upstairs. A toe struck a half-empty bottle of beer. A muffled what-the-fuck-is-this? The door to the basement opened again. "How'd this bottle get on the floor?"

I could hear Vaughn squint his eyes. He yelled up, "You probably dropped it on your way out the door."

Vaughn's mom was silent. Then she said, "I guess."

Vaughn muttered, loud enough for me to hear thru the bathroom door, "Bitchosaurus."

Vaughn's mom said, "What did you say?"

"Nothing." Muttering again, he added, "Hitler with tits."

Something was flung. "Don't you ever!" Stomping down the stairs. Tripping, tumbling. Vaughn's mom moaning in pain. Vaughn laughing.

I cracked the bathroom door. Vaughn's mom was on her face on the carpet right where Vaughn had fallen earlier that day. Her legs were akimbo.

Vaughn cackled with glee. "The drunken toad fell down the stairs! Come on, run! Git! Before she gets up."

Seemed reasonable. "Pa, we're moving out!" No response. I turned on the bathroom light. He and Clarissa were in the deep embrace of— Oh, Christ. I nearly retched.

"Move it!" shouted Vaughn in evil delight. "She's gonna get you!"

I grabbed Pa by the hand and dragged him away from Clarissa's lips, out of the bathroom, past Vaughn's whimpering mother, up the stairs, and out of the house. Clarissa followed, stopping to get more beers out of the fridge before she joined us in the car.

I drove us thru the country wild and fast.

CHAPTER 10

PANCAKES

I woke up in my clothes, in my bed. I looked at the clock. It was after noon. Downstairs, in the living room, someone was playing piano. "Old Rugged Cross." It sounded just like Mom. I stayed in bed. This was what happened on Saturdays. Mom woke us up by rehearsing the songs she was gonna play at church on Sunday. "Trust and Obey." "Ten Thousand Angels."

I stayed in bed until the music stopped. Then I stayed in bed some more.

There was noise in the kitchen. Pots and pans. Someone was cooking breakfast, or trying to. I snuck down to the bathroom. I took a leak, splashed water on my face, and then walked thru the hallway toward the cooking noises. I felt hopeful.

Clarissa McPhail was making pancakes. She was wearing Mom's robe and her hair was wet. Dad was sitting at the table, watching her like she was a movie star.

She saw me and said, "His mom's not dead. She doesn't remember anything."

I thought about this for a moment. I said, "I don't know what you're talking about."

"I just got off the phone with Vaughn. His mom. She's okay. She got a rug burn on her face but that's all. She was so drunk she doesn't remember."

I didn't remember.

Clarissa said, "*You* don't remember, do you?"

"What's there to remember? We went out, got drunk, and came home."

"Softball, lightning, Dee's Liquor, Vaughn's basement. Your dad."

I looked at Dad, who shrugged. He said, "Whatever."

"Sit down," said Clarissa. I sat down. She set a plate of pancakes in front of me. Strawberries and whipped cream.

"I don't much care for whipped cream," I said.

She took the plate back.

I remembered parts of the night before. Things came back.

Clarissa said, "You like strawberries, don't you?"

I put my hands on the table. Took deep breaths. Gradually, I began to recollect. The softball game and the quest for fire and going to Vaughn's and then there was a panic and we were hiding in the bathroom and Vaughn's mom fell down and we escaped and then nothing.

Clarissa put another plate of pancakes in front of me, this time without the whipped cream. She said, "I think he's remembering."

"Lucky him," said Pa.

"Fun night, huh?" said Clarissa.

I squirted syrup on the pancakes. "I'd rather not talk right now."

Clarissa shrugged.

Clarissa had kissed my pa in Vaughn's bathroom.

I put my fork down. "Where did you sleep last night?"

"That's none of his business, is it, Emmett?"

"None of your damn business," said Pa.

"It's my house," I said.

Pa corrected me. "Not yet, it ain't."

I put my fork down. "I'm going to take a shower. This will take me approximately fifteen minutes. When I get out of the bathroom, I'd like you to be gone, Clarissa."

"You gonna drive me home?" She looked out the window. "Or do I need to call a cab?"

"You're clever. Figure something out."

I showered until the hot water was gone. And then I stayed in the cold water until I started shivering. Shameful. I was responsible for Pa.

After I got dressed, I went back to the kitchen. Clarissa was gone and so was Pa. So was Pa's pickup.

Clarissa had left a stack of pancakes on the table. There was also a note:

> Emmett is driving me back to my car. I'll make
> sure he gets home. It's true. Crutchfield bought the
> airplane for $20.

I sat at the table, listening to the clock tick.

Eventually, I ate the pancakes. They weren't bad for an emeto-phobic anorexic.

As I was washing my plate, Dad pulled into the driveway. Clarissa's little car followed. She honked and drove away. I watched from the kitchen window. Dad idled the pickup in front of the garage for a few minutes. He bent down in the cab, looking for the garage-door opener. He finally gave up and shut off the truck.

He stepped out of the pickup in a very good mood. My own father sleeping with a girl I went to school with. With an eating disorder.

I stepped outside to greet him. He asked, "You just get up?"

"I been up."

"I've already gotten a whole lot of things done today."

"Such as?"

"This and that." He was smiling real big.

"Terrific." I didn't want to babysit him. I needed a babysitter for my own self. I led Pa into the house, made him brush his teeth, and then sat him in his recliner. "Watch TV. I'll be back."

I took the pickup to the Keaton State Bank. Dad's airplane was parked in the grass behind the building.

I went in. Clarissa wasn't working. The teller was Charlotte Sackett. A fifty-year-old woman with long fingernails and frosted hair. I liked her all right. She used to go to all the high school basketball games. She cheered loud and cackled insults at the referees.

"Hey, Charlotte."

She smiled at me. "I heard you were back in town."

I said, "Here I am." I didn't feel much like talking. "Is Mr. Crutchfield in today?"

Charlotte half-rolled her eyes. "He sure is. But he's pretty darned busy." She shrugged apologetically.

"I was hoping I could talk to him."

She squinted at me. "You look so much like your dad. How is he doing, anyway?"

I do not understand why some people feel compelled to screw up a perfectly normal conversation by bringing up the most depressing subject they can think of.

"He's on a long, slow decline." I said it with a smile.

"Well, tell him hi for me."

"Will do. Can I see Mike?"

"He's awful busy. You understand."

"Charlotte, I need to talk to him about that airplane he's been flying. It'll take five minutes. I just want to talk to him." My voice was getting loud. I tried to sound calm. "Tell him I'm here, willya? It's important."

She stopped smiling. She pointed to the one of the goofy signs on the wall behind me. *There will be a $5 charge for whining.* I said, "I'm sorry. I didn't mean to. Please."

Without speaking, she turned and walked toward the back of the bank. A moment later, she returned. "He said he can spare you a few minutes."

Mike Crutchfield, master of the Keaton State Bank, was staring at a laptop. He was just a skinny guy with thick ears and a big chin. In his fifties, probably. Brown suit and bolo tie. He moved the computer aside. He grinned at me and his whole face stretched.

"Mr. Williams," he said. He didn't stand up. He leaned back in his chair. "Thanks for taking the time to come by."

The people of Strattford County have an accent. It's not Southern, it's not cowboy, and it definitely isn't Texas. A linguist might say that the Strattford County accent can be identified by the fact that "pen" and "pin" sound the same, or that, depending on the usage, "do" sometimes has one syllable and sometimes has two. In reality, the Strattford County accent is defined by the layer of bullshit that coats every word, like the speaker is always messing with your head. I've seen funerals where I wasn't sure if the preacher wasn't maybe *glad* that the so-and-so had died. I don't know what it is, but it's there and, even though I grew up with it, I can never tell what people are saying.

Mike Crutchfield didn't have that tinge. He sounded completely sincere. And he pronounced every vowel in every word he spoke.

He said, "I understand you're living with your father now. It is noble of you to take on this responsibility. Emmett is a great man. He has always been an upstanding member of this community. He lives a respectable life, he is known throughout the region for his wits, and, together with your mother, he contributed a great deal of time and money to those who needed both.

"Unfortunately, things have changed and now your father has neither a great deal of time nor money. I cannot speak on the subject of the thing that has shortened his time other than to say that his most precious years are being robbed of him, plain and simple, by a universe whose ultimate plans for us all are as mysterious as they are unfair.

"I can say more about the subject of money and perhaps what I say will be of help to you. Before his capacity to manage his affairs became overly restricted, your father enrolled much of his land in the Conservation Reserve Program, of which I am sure you are aware. Income from this program was instrumental in maintaining his quality of life. CRP contracts last for ten years. Unfortunately, your father's contracts expired two years ago and he was not able to renew them in time for the payments to continue. What's more, a quirk of the latest farm bill makes it impossible to bring land back into the program once its contract has expired.

"Without being farmed and without the government handouts, the land has no value to your father. I suppose you could attempt to rent it for pasture or even sell it, but I am not currently aware of anyone who would be willing to pay anything, much less a fair market price, for that land at this moment. I work with most of the farmers in this community and I can tell you that the economy is not strong. Plus, the land has been in your family for generations and, in spite of the fact that you currently do not have plans to farm it, I suspect you are very reluctant to sell it outright."

He was correct and he knew it. He smiled so that his eyes deepened in their sockets.

"Naturally, you're also curious about the subject of your father's airplane." He reached into his desk and pulled out a piece of paper. "This should answer any questions you have. What you're holding is a copy of a good faith contract signed by your father and me."

I looked at it. There were lots of words.

"The contract clearly states that your father is selling me his airplane for a discounted rate in exchange for my extraordinary helpfulness in helping him organize an auction of most of his farm equipment last year. I'm sure you've noticed that several tractors and implements are no longer on his property."

I hadn't, and it made me feel bad.

"'Extraordinary helpfulness.' Those were your father's words, not mine. I presume that his copy of the contract has been misplaced. I'll be happy to have a duplicate mailed to you if you'd like."

Before I could answer, he rotated his laptop so I could see the computer screen.

"Here's a photo taken the day your father sold me the airplane."

It looked like Elvis and Nixon shaking hands. Except, instead of shaking hands, Dad was accepting a twenty-dollar bill from Mike Crutchfield. Dad was wearing jeans and a clean shirt. The banker was wearing a leather jacket and a goofy fighter helmet. They both looked delighted.

"As you can clearly see, your father is not under duress. He was, in fact, very happy that day. He told me it would be a relief not to have to worry about how his airplane would be taken care of. His exact words were, 'You'll be a good daddy to my girl.'"

Crutchfield pressed a button on his computer and the printer started working. "Mr. Williams, I worked very hard to help your father get along after his wife passed on and as his illness has progressed. With my assistance, he was able to sell much of his unused equipment for more profit than he otherwise could have. He was simultaneously grieving and suffering from a degenerative brain disease. He was all alone."

The banker looked right into my eyes.

"What I did for your father was nothing that I wouldn't do for any other long time customer of any of the banks I own. What your father did for me, however, was a kind and generous act, the likes of which I'll not soon forget. He insisted that I accept the airplane on the very terms on that contract. Consequently, every time I climb into that cockpit, I feel nothing but pride and humility."

Crutchfield handed me the piece of paper from the printer. It was the photo of him and Pa. He walked me to the door, shook my hand, and said, "Thank you so much for coming in."

I didn't notice Charlotte as I walked out of the bank. All I could see were the photos on the wall, mingled among the goofy diner signs. All those photos of Mike Crutchfield shaking hands with jolly farmers.

On my drive home, I tossed the picture out the pickup window and watched in the rearview mirror as it fluttered in the wind.

When I got back, Dad was burning the trash. In the country, there is no Wednesday garbage truck that rolls down the alley at six in the morning. Instead, you cut the top off a fifty-five-gallon drum, set it down several yards from any flammable buildings, and burn your trash. As a kid, I learned to set trash afire in any weather. Windy, winter, whatever. It was like Boy Scout training but without the dopey outfits. Bring three strike-anywhere matches, tear some junk mail envelopes into strips, light them, baby them, feed them with cereal boxes until the fire can take care of itself. Everything has its own way of burning. Cardboard burns hot and smoky with a skinny yellow flame shooting out of each corrugated hole. A stack of magazines won't burn completely unless you crumble them up. Aerosol cans aren't as dangerous as everyone says.

We kept an iron rod next to the burning barrel so we could stir the trash, open it up for air. At the moment, Dad was poking the rod into the barrel, playing with a piece of plastic that looked like the remains of a busted-up laundry basket I'd put in the throw-away pile a couple of days ago. He didn't know I was watching him. He got a glob of the melting plastic on the end of the rod and held it in the flame until it started burning. The plastic dripped burning drops of itself into the barrel. Like tiny bits of napalm. Even though I was standing behind him, I could tell Dad was fascinated. I'd done the same thing a hundred times. You could watch that stuff drip for hours and it would never stop being amazing. It was lava and water and a really pretty window into hell.

By now, the end of the rod was all aflame with that glob of plastic. With two hands, Dad held it upright, straight above his head. The flames sent up black smoke. The glob started to ooze toward his hands. Then he said, "Hyaaa!" and swung the iron around like a samurai.

An arc of flaming spit flew off the end of the rod. Halfway thru his spin, Dad saw me standing there several paces away. His eyes widened. His mouth said, "Oh shit!" He let go of the iron, but it was too late. Napalm flung toward me. I turned sideways and got splattered with whizzing pelts of liquid fire.

I know you're supposed to stop, drop, and roll. But, really, it was a few drops of burning plastic. They stuck to my shirt and jeans. I patted them out. By the time Dad had run up to me, there was nothing but some smoking holes in my clothes. Little things, no bigger than a raisin.

"Gee whiz," said Dad. He took deep breaths.

I showed him my palms. There were little bits of charred plastic stuck to them. "Not even a blister."

"I dang near burned you up." He touched my shirt, making sure all the fires were out.

"Aw, hell."

"I thought I was all alone."

"You were. I mean, I just got back from Keaton. I was talking to the banker."

"Crotchfield?"

"Crutchfield, yep."

Pa nodded. "I believe he's flying my airplane these days."

Something popped in the burning barrel.

"Yep, he's flying it."

Pa's eyes squinted. He got a look. It was real quick and then it was gone. "Let him fly her. I don't have any business in that thing."

I wanted to say, "What are you talking about?!? He stole your plane!" But I didn't say anything. In that little chunk of brain that still held his soul, Pa knew what that banker bastard had done. Pa also knew that he couldn't fly a plane anymore. And he knew that between the two of us, we didn't have the money, wit, or mean-headedness to get back what Crutchfield had took.

We played with the fire until it went out and then we ate dinner and watched TV and went to bed.

I didn't sleep very good. First, I contemplated doing cruel things to the banker. Then I thought about Clarissa McPhail and whether I'd ever want to look at her again. Then I wondered what kind of dreams Pa was having downstairs in his bed.

CHAPTER 11

LIVERS, TONGUES, AND KIDNEYS

When I got up the next morning, things were clear. Sometimes that happens when you go to sleep with a lot of things on your mind.

First off, we'd been screwing around too much. *I'd* been screwing around too much. Drinking and going to softball games and putting us in dangerous situations. In a world full of temptation, the only way to keep out of trouble is to keep out of the world. We had to hole up.

I resolved to never let anyone take advantage of Pa ever again. Not a banker, not a drunken anorexic, not a paraplegic fuck-up, and definitely not me. Henceforth, Pa and I were going to hunker down. Avoid the townsfolk.

Food and gas, that's all we needed. We had both of those in abundance. We had a three-hundred-gallon fuel tank, a deep freeze, and a pantry full of canned food, and in a couple of months, we'd have a garden. On top of that, we had a shed full of tools and piles and piles of scrap metal. There was nothing we couldn't do.

In the country, your home is the universe. If you do it right, you don't ever have to see anyone, ever. That's how my ancestors did it. They dug a well with shovels. Made a house out of dirt. Grew crops, milked cows, shot jack rabbits.

We could do it just as good as them.

———

Just like turning a switch, the outside world disappeared. Me and
Pa on the farm. Like Huck and Jim floating on the river, without
the river. Every morning, while Pa was figuring out how to put
on his britches, I took a walk around the property. The birds would
gather in our little stand of trees and make their morning racket.
The cottontails liked to sit on bare patches of dirt and bask in the
morning sunlight. Dad had quite a few guns. I figured that someday I'd use one of those guns to shoot one of those rabbits. I'd
skin it, spit it, and cook it on a fire. For now, they were pleasant
to look at.

After my walk, I'd go inside and help Dad reassemble his razor.
It was an electric, which he dismantled every single morning. He'd
unplug the power cord, remove the head, take out the blades, and
shake the grey beard dust into the sink. He could never put it back
together. The parts would migrate to the kitchen or his nightstand,
but I always found them. Put it together, then turn it on and put it
in his hand. He shaved pretty good except for his throat. Every few
days, I'd make him tilt his head back so I could run the razor over
his Adam's apple. He enjoyed it with a look of a dog when you're
scratching its ears.

With enough time, he usually dressed himself good. He'd put
on two or three shirts. He took them off, one by one, if he got hot.
If it was hot enough, he'd take off all his shirts and walk around
sweating thru his grey chest hairs. You get used to it.

He didn't always put on socks on his own. But I was strict about
socks. I made him put them on even if he didn't want to. When you
don't wear socks, your feet sweat and you can catch a fungus.

Breakfast was whatever. We didn't differentiate between meals.
Kidney beans and frozen peas. A TV dinner. Graham crackers. It
was all food. Find something in the pantry or the deep freeze, heat
it up, eat it. Pa, especially, didn't care what we ate. He had strong

teeth. Once, when I wasn't paying attention, he ate half of a frozen sausage before I could thaw it out.

After breakfast, we pulled weeds in the garden. The tomato plants were growing. Most of the rest of the seeds—the onions, carrots, cabbages, and corn—had poked themselves up from the dirt. The garden was doing all right.

After weeding, we'd take a walk around the farm or go inside for a nap. Then lunch, then more weeds or walking or wandering or a nap. After dinner, it was TV time, then brushing of teeth, then bed.

We didn't talk much.

In the third week of June, it rained for five days straight. It was the monsoon season. The landscape shifted from bleached brown to sage. Buffalo grass turned green. Dew hung on everything. The bare wood of the granary was soaked dark.

One afternoon, it rained too hard for us to go outside. Not a downpour, but the kind of rain that made you want to stay in and listen to the pat-pat on the roof.

I pulled out the old photo album. All photo albums are the same. Just like all dreams are the same. They mean the world to the person who owns them and they're boring as dirt to everybody else.

Funny-looking '70s pants. Dad with an Amish beard. The family in front of the Christmas tree. Always the family in front of the Christmas tree. Trying to imagine that the baby in that picture is you. Trying to imagine that the pretty gal in the tintype is your grandma, or that the woman sitting at the piano is your mom.

That woman was my mom. I held the photo for Pa to see. "There she is," I said.

Most senile people lose their short-term memory but hang on to the old stuff, the foundations, the bygone days, which they recite over and over until you want to kill them. You know, Great Aunt

Beatrice can't remember what happened five minutes ago, but she knows exactly what she was doing the day Kennedy was shot. Pa's senility was weird. First, it had hit him early. He was only sixty-two and his brain was already three-quarters gone. Second, he didn't have his foundations anymore. He was losing everything.

Pa looked at the picture. Mom at the piano in the church. She was wearing a crafty Christmas sweater. Her mouth was open. I imagined she was singing "Glo-o-o-o-o-o-ria." The preacher's wife probably took the photo. I'm sure Dad and I were standing at a pew just out of the frame. There would have been maybe thirty people in the church. Dad and I would have been singing like clowns and elbowing each other. Mom would hear us but say nothing. She was just glad to have us there for our annual Christmas Eve appearance. They let everyone hold candles on Christmas Eve.

I think both of us would have gone to church more often if Mom hadn't played piano. Since she was always at the piano, we never got to sit next to her. What would be the point of going to church if we couldn't sit with the person who invited us?

Dad said, "Merry." He was trying to read Mom's sweater. "Merry Christmas."

"You know who that is?"

"Seems like I should know that gal," said Pa.

Sometimes it's necessary to leave the room. Come back a few minutes later with a handkerchief and a runny nose. He didn't notice that kind of thing.

It was raining real gentle.

When it stopped raining, we cleaned out the deep freeze. The deep freeze was in the well house. Before the Rural Electric Association rolled thru the country, farms got their water by way of a windmill. The windmill pumped water up from the Ogallala Aquifer and into a huge tank, which was planted on top of the well house. Like everyone else in Strattford, we had converted our well to electric fifty years ago. This made the windmill unnecessary. Over the years, Dad had dismantled it and reused the metal for various projects.

The well house remained, though. Mom used it mostly as a garden shed. In addition to the hoes and fertilizer, there was just enough room for the deep freeze.

When I had first moved back from Denver, the freezer was filled up full. On top was nothing but frozen dinners. Beneath those were Tupperware dishes filled with Mom's homemade cookies and banana bread. Since I'd been back, we had eaten everything on those first layers. Now all that remained were blocks of meat wrapped in butcher paper and stamped in red block letters that read "liver," "tongue," and "kidney."

Mom used to buy sides of beef from the Keaton Locker. We would gobble down the ground beef, chuck, rump, steaks—all the good stuff—but none of us wanted anything to do with the low-class meats. Mom grew up poor. Leaving that low-class meat in exile at the bottom of the freezer probably made her feel a little rich. As for me, I just didn't like livers, tongues, and kidneys.

Still, Mom couldn't bring herself to throw the meat out. Probably because she grew up poor. We must have gone thru a half dozen sides of beef over the years. Now the deep freeze was three-quarters full of nothing but those livers, tongues, and kidneys.

Dad and I were poor now and it looked like we might have to eat some of those cow parts. I took a liver from the top of the freezer and thawed it out. When I peeled back the butcher paper, it was freezer-burned, leathery, no good. That meat wasn't just low-class; it was inedible. If the stuff on top was bad, then everything below it would be bad, too. Enough food to feed a football team for a month and all of it was dried-up white.

We loaded hundreds of pounds of no-good meat into the back of Pa's pickup and drove out to a pasture.

This was a different pasture from the one where we buried my stray cat. You don't put rotten food in a pet graveyard. It's disrespectful. This pasture was further south. It had been in the family for decades, maybe even a century. It used to be a wheat field until Dad put it in the CRP program and sent it back to its native state. To get there you had to drive on a two-rut road. That field was the first place I ever saw a rattlesnake.

In the corner of the pasture was an ancient cottonwood tree next to an old, dead windmill next to the foundation of an old, dead house. The existence of that tree only reinforced the notion that trees don't belong in Strattford County. It lived, somehow, but it was bent. Branches thicker than my waist tried to grow up tall but then gave up and curved to the earth and then tried again and failed. All the bark was gone. Nothing but white wood. The tree looked like it could have been a thousand years old.

We wandered around the foundation of the house.

"You know," said Pa, "this here is an important piece of land."

"Why so?"

"This was the old." He snapped his fingers. "You know who I'm talking about."

"Relatives?"

"No! They were."

Walking along the outline of the foundation, we deciphered where the bathroom had been, the kitchen. Some barbed wire, the door from an old car, all rusted.

"Look here!" said Dad. He pointed to a sod brick. "That's old."

We found a few more bricks, something that could have been a corner post. We traced the outline of a sod house.

"You think this is an original homestead?"

"That's right," said Pa. "Your grandma lives here."

"My great-grandma?"

"The Schleichers."

I said, "That sounds about right."

The Schleichers were from Dad's mom's side. Those sod bricks were made by my ancestors. I wondered if any of them had anosmia. I picked up a brick. It looked like a big square dirt clod. I squeezed it and it fell apart.

"I don't think you should do that," said Dad.

"I agree."

While the cow livers thawed in the back of the pickup, we wandered the pasture. We followed a meandering trail, looking down every few steps to avoid prickly pears. Buffalo grass. Sagebrush. Grama. Yucca. Watch for rattlers.

We walked until the pickup was small. We found the skeleton of a cow. It was cleaned up, bleached. I dragged a rib across the top of the spine, hoping it would sound like a xylophone. It went clunka, clunka.

"This here's the skull," said Pa.

"That looks like a pelvis to me."

Pa dragged his heel thru the dirt. "I don't know about that."

When you find a cow skeleton, you look for the skull. You bring the skull home and hang it on something. The person who finds the skull gets to feel proud. Saying that thing was a pelvis, that took away Pa's pride. I looked around for the real skull. Couldn't find it. Someone else must have got there before us.

The ground was etched with tiny animal tracks. I said, "Pa, does that look like a lizard to you?"

He peered into the dust. "Looks like dirt."

"You can see where it was dragging its tail."

We bent our heads to the ground. We found more lizard tracks, bird tracks, ground squirrel tracks, and lots of dog-looking footprints. I said, "Those look like they were made by wolves."

"They were made by coyotes."

"They're so big."

"Coyotes have big feet," said Pa.

As we walked further, the coyote tracks were everywhere, as if the footprints had rained from the sky. I studied one, pretending to be a boy pretending to be an Indian. They looked brand-new, like they'd been put down five minutes ago.

Pa said, "Look here!"

He'd found the den. It was a hole, big enough for a baby to crawl into. I crept toward it.

"They know you're looking. They won't come out of that hole for nothing."

"You think they killed that cow?"

"Coulda been a steer," said Dad.

We retrieved the pickup and drove it to the coyote den. We peeled the butcher paper off the livers and left them piled up as a gift to the coyotes. When we were done, our hands were numb with cold and covered with cow blood.

With the deep freeze empty, we went on a canned food diet. We had a huge pantry, which Mom always kept stocked in case of a blizzard. No need to go grocery shopping yet. Mom was still feeding us.

At lunchtime, while the beans or mixed vegetables or whatever were warming up on the stove, I'd plunk the piano and Dad would sing. His favorites were "Twinkle, Twinkle, Little Star" and "Old MacDonald." When he sang, his eyes closed halfway. When I was growing up, Dad never, ever sang. But he liked to do it now. He was transported. I'd never seen him like that. He was a terrible singer. Didn't know the words. Didn't matter. He was focused.

After lunch, he'd lay on his back on the carpet and nap for an hour.

One afternoon, I went out to the shed and decided to get the riding mower running. I put some gas in the tank and, amazingly, it revved right up. When I showed it to Dad, he jumped in the seat and started putt-putting it around. It became a hobby for him. He enjoyed mowing, it made the place look nicer, and it kept him out of my hair for half-hour chunks. He had a hard time keeping track of where he went. He left random scribbles of mowed swath. Over the course of a week, he'd cover the whole place. It was good to look out and see the weeds trimmed.

Once, he drove a whole day without the belt on the mower deck. It must have snapped and dropped off into the weeds. He didn't mow a damned thing that day. I found a replacement and installed it. I got him going again. Didn't even bloody my knuckles.

I fixed squeaky door hinges. Replaced the rubber washer in the dripping faucet. Painted the front door. Little stuff like that. The place started to look okay.

Breakfast, piano, garden, housework, yard work, lunch, nap, watch the clouds, eat dinner, TV, sleep. Sometimes the phone would ring. If Dad felt like answering, he did. It was always somebody selling something. He'd talk to them until they hung up. Nobody we knew ever called us. The people of Dorsey were always willing to leave you be. I appreciated that.

Every day was beautiful. Sometimes it was windy and we'd stay in the house all day. Huge winds would fill the world with corn shucks blown from miles away. Most afternoons, we'd get some nice weather. A few clouds. Maybe a drop of rain.

The garden came up. The tomato plants got big. The rest of the plants were runty. But it was all growing. Dad wasn't allowed to hoe. He killed things when he hoed. While I worked, he sat in the shade and watched the jets drag their contrails across the sky.

I found a kite in a closet. It was a nice canvas kite. Mom gave it to me for my birthday a long time ago. It came from a store in Boulder. Pa loved that thing. The string was a couple hundred feet long. Pa was always nervous to let it out all the way.

He'd point at the contrails of the jets that crisscrossed the sky. "I suppose they can see it, but I'd hate for it to get in their way."

"I think they're farther up than that kite can reach, Pa."

"I dunno. It's gotta be a quarter mile."

I'd let the string all the way out and he'd slowly reel it in. I could weed the whole garden in the time it took him to bring the kite down.

One day, a giant gust ripped the kite off the string just as Dad was reeling it back in. The string slid back to earth. The kite flew higher and higher and got smaller and smaller. When it disappeared, Dad looked at the spool in his hands and said, "What the heck is this deal for?"

I'd occasionally find Pa wandering around the shed, poking in the pile of parts that was his old motorized bicycle. We hadn't touched it since we'd dragged it out of the granary. I still wanted to get that thing going again.

I took my time. I wasn't gonna push him. If we were going to put that motorbike back together, I wanted him to initiate the process. Let him feel like he's running the show.

One day, he said, "What's this?"

"Your bike."

"Why's it all apart like that?"

"Hard to say."

He said, "It'd sure be neat to put it together again."

I said, "Maybe we could go for a ride."

"Real fun."

"Too bad I don't know the first thing about engines and stuff."

"You're ignorant."

Another day I found him out there, holding the piston in his hands, like it was a newborn baby.

"Whatcha doin'?"

"I was thinking how it'd be neat to put this thing back together."

"There's thinking and there's doing."

He said, "Well?"

I said, "Well."

"Then get off your duff and get to work."

"Where should we start?"

He squinted his eyes at me for being stupid. "The engine. You can't propel yourself without an engine."

I squatted and stared hard.

He squatted next to me, looked at the parts for a moment, and said, "You're missing a carburetor."

"That all?"

"Looks like it."

I ran to the granary, poked around. Found something that looked like a carburetor and brought it back to Pa, who was still staring at the pile of parts.

"Will this do?"

"Depends. You trying to carburete something?"

"Yes, sir."

"Well, that's what a carburetor does."

Something good happened. Pa's switch flipped to the "on" position. There's this look that he used to get when he was working. His eyes would dart around and his mouth would flatten out with a tiny hook of a smile on one corner. As a little kid, I'd ask him what was so funny and he used to say, "Nothing." He loved to work.

I watched him. He watched his hands. The half-smile arrived. We began assembling the engine, I anticipated when I could. I knew he would want to clean grime, so I filled a coffee can with gasoline from the tank out back and dipped greasy things into it. I gave him wrenches. I became ten, he became forty. The morning turned to afternoon. We took a break. Drank water from the hydrant outside. Spat on the dirt.

Everything had a place. The piston and the crank and the flywheel. We did not move quickly. We spent several afternoons working on it. I started to get an understanding. I don't know how, but I eventually turned into the point man on the project. Actually I do know how. Dad was slow. His bursts of genius were followed by hours of searching for tools he'd set down in random places. I stared at that engine and it metamorphed from a block of bolted-together bits of metal into a tangible collection of parts. Like when you understand that an Elvis song is not just noise coming from your stereo; it's a collection of sounds made by guitars and a giant bass and a singer. When constituent parts become visible, you can begin to understand how they cooperate to make music or move a bicycle or, if you go far enough, why the last two surviving members of a family are squatting on a concrete floor trying to locate a lock washer.

I dreamt of valve lifters and ignition points. There was a linear path from fuel to fire to kinetic motion. I didn't understand the guts of the thing like Dad did, but I understood that it had guts. It got to the point where I'd send him on an errand and work by myself. He'd spend an hour trying to locate the 9/16″ combo wrench while I put the rings on the piston.

And then we were ready to start the engine. Everything was in

place. The engine was sitting on two four-by-fours on the floor. I
checked the spark plug. I made sure there was gas.

I said, "We're ready."

Pa was impressed. "We did some real good work."

I said, "Let's wait and see."

"Step on it."

I stomped the kick start. Nothing. I stomped again. Nothing. I
opened the choke. Closed the choke. Nothing, nothing, nothing.
Sweating. Piece of shit. It should be working. Pa watched patiently.
To him, each of my attempts was the first one. But he saw me getting riled up and he enjoyed that.

I said, "I gotta take a break." I walked around back of the shed
and took a piss. As I was walking back, I heard the engine come to
life.

Dad was standing with his hands in his pockets, watching the
washing machine engine putt-putt.

Delighted and mystified, I said, "What'd you do?"

"I fixed it."

Things like that made me wonder if he wasn't faking it all.

With the engine restored, we started working on the bike frame.
My dad was ten years old when he did this the first time. That
young version of my pa acquired a bike frame, removed the pedals,
built a pulley mechanism that would operate as a variable-speed
centrifugal clutch, welded a contraption that would hold the whole
thing together, and then rode it all over the place.

The frame was in pretty good shape yet. Unlike the engine,
there wasn't much to it. All we had to fix was bearings and rubber.
The bearings were easy. We unpacked them, soaked them in gasoline until the grit floated off, slathered them with grease, and put
them back together. Cleaned and packed, everything spun smooth.

Using some vulcanizing fluid and the rubber from an old inner tube, we patched a dozen holes in each tube. Before we put them on the wheels, we filled them fat with air and ran them thru a bucket of water. No leaks. Not now, at least. But that wouldn't last long.

There's a plant called the goathead. It grows flat the ground. The seeds are hard as rocks and pointy as the devil. Goatheads kill bike tires. We had goatheads everywhere. It didn't use to be like that. Back when, we fought them hard. I fought them hard. For my seventh birthday, Dad built me a special tool. It was a hoe handle with a little V-shaped blade on the end. It slid under the plant and allowed you to snip it off right above the taproot. Pa would give me two dollars for every five-gallon bucket I could fill with those weeds.

I spent many summer days walking thru ditches, looking for yellow flowers. Any time I wasn't working with him on farm stuff, I was expected to fill a bucket with those damned plants. Homework? You can do your homework after dinner, when it's dark out. I killed so many of those plants I used to hallucinate them.

Pure, boring misery, and all so we wouldn't have flat tires. The thing is, the goddamned things were too short to puncture a car tire. The only danger was to bare feet—which wasn't a problem since we always wore shoes outside—and bike tires. I stopped riding my bike when I was twelve years old, which made the entire endeavor a waste of time. I argued that we were engaging in a pointless war. I drew analogies to Vietnam.

It didn't matter. Pa was stronger than me. He didn't have to raise a fist; when I told him he was an idiot, he said, "That's fine. Now go fill that bucket up." I'd fill it up, burn the weeds. Cuss under my breath. Sing Billy Joel songs angrily. It didn't matter. It's daylight, so work. I wore that V-blade down to a sliver on those damned weeds. Eventually, I got them under control. Or they got me under control. Whatever it was, I took pride in it. When I'd go to another farm and see a mat of green vines, I'd feel contempt for the lazy bastards who couldn't bother to kill the goddamned goat.

I pointed to the sole of my shoe. It was covered with burrs. "Pa, unless we take some preventative measures, our maiden journey won't last long."

I got an idea. I went to the paint shelves. I said, "Maybe we can put some rotten paint in the tubes and it'll act like that hole sealant stuff they advertise on TV." Dad ignored my brilliant idea. Instead he pulled out a sheet of copper from behind the workbench. Using tin snips, he sliced it into two strips.

"Try these."

I lined the tires with the copper. Put the tubes in the tires. Put them on the rims. Filled them with air until they were tight and hard. Bolted the wheels on. We had a frame. We had thorn-proof tubes.

We bolted the engine to the frame, found a V-belt, linked the chain, filled the fuel tank. The bike was ready.

"It needs paint," said Pa.

"Sure," I said. "We'll give it a coat after we test-drive it."

"I think we should do it now."

"It'll run fine without paint."

"It doesn't look good."

"It's beautiful."

"It needs paint."

It's about aesthetics. We painted the thing. Not a five-minute spray-paint job. No, we had to look thru the entire shed until we found the compressed-air spray gun, then stir and mix some red and yellow paint into a perfect shade of orange, then tape off everything, and then deal with Dad taking the spray can out of my hands because I was getting drips.

The bike was orange, the engine black, the racing stripes freshened up and tidy.

As we watched it dry, Dad said, "It needs a . . ."

"A horn?" I said.

"No! A word. A thing to call it by."

"A name?"

"Close."

"A logo? A company? A means of identifying it by manufacturer?"

He snapped his fingers. "Like Ford."

"Williams Bicycle Company?"

"Just the letters."

"WBC?"

"And another word."

I looked around the shed for ideas. My eyes stopped on the half-finished jet-tractor resting under the tarp.

"WBC Rocket?"

"That's it."

Dad let me pencil the letters on the frame. He painted the letters in black using a tiny paintbrush. The words looked shaky. We agreed to let it dry overnight.

The sun went down as we walked from the shed to the house. Pa was in charge. I was the best helper in the world.

Pa said, "You wanna race?"

Before I could say, "Yes," he started running.

I didn't let him win. I ran as hard as I could and he won anyway.

I made chili with canned beef and canned beans. We sopped it up with busted-up crackers. We watched TV for a couple of hours and then I helped Pa brush his teeth. When I put him to bed, he said, "What's the big plan for tomorrow?"

"We're going to take the WBC Rocket for a spin."

"What's that?"

"The WBC Rocket? It's your old bicycle. The one with the washing machine engine."

"That thing? It's just a pile of bones."

"You'll see." I turned off the light and started out of the room.

"Say," said Pa.

"Yes?"

"It's real good having you out here."

I said, "You, too."

He said, "Sounds like a personal problem."

I sat in bed and read the novelization of the second Star Trek movie, *The Wrath of Khan*. It's pretty good for a novelization. There's a lot of blood and torture. Khan hangs people by their ankles and slits their throats. In the book, the brain-eating worms are a million times nastier than the puppets in the movie.

I finished the last chapter just after one A.M. When I got to the part where Spock dies, I swear to God, I cried. It didn't matter that he comes back in the third movie. He was dead. I rubbed the tears away, turned off the light, and went to sleep.

I woke up at 3:23. I remember because I looked at the clock. There was a noise downstairs. It sounded like it came from the kitchen.

I thought of Clarissa McPhail. Was she sneaking into our house to take advantage of my pa? I heard Dad laugh. Was he watching TV? Probably watching TV. He was talking. Having a conversation. An argument. Maybe he was on the phone.

I went downstairs. Pa was standing in the living room, in his underwear, talking to Mom.

"You shouldn't be gone like that," he said.

His eyes followed a figure that I couldn't see.

"You're my damn wife! I'm lonesome. I can't eat."

I spoke his name, real softly. He looked at me, unsurprised, and said, "*You* try talking to her."

"You want me to talk to Mom?"

He spoke to a space a couple of feet in front of his face. "The boy knows."

"Dad, I think you're dreaming."

He turned to the ghost. "Tell him."

It was dark. It was quiet. I was watching my dad discuss me with my dead mom, who wasn't there.

I clapped my hands. "Dad! Wake up!"

"Quiet!" he said. "She's talking."

There's no such thing as ghosts. Dad was straddling waking life and slumberland. I was quiet. I wanted to see what my dead mother had to say.

I waited a minute. Dad was listening with his ear cocked. He nodded.

I said, "What's she telling you?"

"Let her finish." He listened. He nodded. Smiled. It was the smile of someone who'd just been blessed. "You see?" He was talking to me.

"Nope. What's she saying?"

"She's not saying anything. She went away." He flapped his arms like a bird. Skipped around his recliner. Started chanting, "She went away. She went away. She went away. She went away."

"What did she say?"

He ignored me. I watched. He skipped, flapped his wings, chanted. The clock chimed for four o'clock.

He ran circles faster and faster. He said, "Wheeeeeeeeeeee!"

He kept running circles until he crumpled to the floor.

CHAPTER 12

HOSPITAL AND HOME

It was a seizure, or maybe a miniature stroke. Maybe a seizure brought on by a miniature stroke. Or just light-headedness. Hard to tell. The doctor said Pa would probably be fine but they wanted to keep him in the hospital for a few days to make sure there wasn't anything serious going on. I asked if not remembering how to tie his shoelaces would qualify as something serious. The doctor laughed pretty good at that one. Dr. Shepard. He had checked my nuts for ruptures once a year from seventh grade thru twelfth grade. Nice guy, but I always felt uncomfortable when I was alone in a room with him.

I went in to see Pa before I left. He was real groggy. He'd gotten panicky when he first woke up in the hospital bed. I was there right when his eyes opened. He kicked his blanket off and dumped orange juice all over the floor. "Don't put me in this place. I'm not going here. I'm not an old folks' home."

I explained to him that he was in a hospital and that things were okay and that he'd be out of here and back home lickety-split. He told me to go to hell.

He got out of bed and fell down on his ass. A couple of nurses heard the racket and hurried into the room. When they tried to help him up, he told them they were no-good bitches.

I calmed him down by singing "Twinkle, Twinkle, Little Star." He was sitting on the floor, all splayed out next to his hospital bed. The two nurses were watching him like he was a carton of bad milk.

I said, "Twinkle, twinkle, little star, how I wonder . . ." and Dad started singing along. Right there on the floor, he bobbed his head back and forth, closed his eyes, and tapped his knee. The nurses started singing as well. We were able to pick up Dad by his armpits and guide him back to bed. With everyone still singing, one of the nurses hustled out of the room and then hustled right back in carrying a couple of little blue pills and a paper cup full of water. She handed me the pills and I said, "Time for dessert."

Dad stopped singing and opened his mouth. I dropped the pills on his tongue and gave him the paper cup. He drank the water down, swallowed his pills, and lay back with his head on the pillow. A few moments later he was snoring.

Now it was mid-morning and he was just coming out of his dopey slumber.

"How you doin', Pa?" He looked pathetic, all stuck in that hospital gown. His skin was red from the sun. Hard, cracked. Skin like that didn't belong in a hospital. Trolls like Vaughn Atkins belonged in the hospital.

"Somewhat." He knew he was in a hospital. You could tell that. But he was in a hospital someplace a long way from here. His eyes were shrunken and gooey.

I set my hand on his shoulder. It felt too intimate so I took it off and hitched my thumb into my belt loop. "They'll take care of you real good."

He said, "I'm sure they will. They've got a real normal. Normal way here."

"I'm going to go now."

He said, "Say, do you know what's the procedure?"

"You have to stick around for a few days so they know there's nothing wrong with you."

He chuckled. "I know the answer to that question."

"I'll call you every day."

It's thirty-nine miles from the Strattford Hospital to our house. I drove home as slow as I could. I was tired. There was nobody else on the road.

The farm was quiet. There wasn't any wind. And there wasn't any Pa. It was remarkable.

I could breathe. Watch whatever I wanted on TV. Read a book without him staring at me. Take a shower without him knocking on the door. I could think without thinking about him or where he was or what he needed.

I took a nap on the couch. I woke up in the afternoon and ate a bowl of canned ravioli. I stared out the kitchen window as I ate. The world was calm.

After I washed my plate, I went outside and weeded the garden. The tomato plants looked good. Little green tomatoes on their way. The peppers and onions were alive. I ate a baby onion in one bite and chewed my way up the green stem. I pulled up a carrot. A tiny thing. Yummy. Right there in the garden with sparrows and black-birds and robins jumping around. I can't tell you how free it feels to be out of sight of the whole universe, right under the sun, especially when you don't have a two-hundred-pound three-year-old to keep an eye on.

It was hot. I dragged an old horse tank out from behind the shed and filled it with water. I had to patch some holes with chewing gum and duct tape. Dad wasn't the only guy around these parts who could fix stuff. I filled the tank with water, stripped down to my drawers, and climbed in. I sat there and watched the clouds just like some cowpoke from a cartoon. I stuck it out as long as possible. Sitting in cold water isn't as comfortable as you'd imagine.

After my dip, I went to the shed and tried to start the Rocket. Of course it didn't work. I used starter fluid, choked it, checked for spark, fuel, and compression. Nothing. Dad was the only guy around these parts who could fix stuff. He was a magician. I was just a dumb son in a big shed staring at a motorized bicycle my dad built when he was in elementary school. I stood in the spot where the airplane used to be.

The next day, I called him at the hospital.

"Morning, Pa."

"Morning."

"Tell me what you see out the window."

"The moon's just getting tired. Been up all night."

"Are there clouds in the sky? What's the sky look like?"

"The sky? It looks hot."

"Are there clouds?"

"Yep. Well, a jet. A jet cloud."

"You getting enough food?"

"I think so."

"Okay. I gotta go now."

"What's the hurry? Big plans?"

"Weeding the garden. I might mow the lawn. There's a doorknob that needs fixing. That window in the granary. Various stuff."

"How much longer am I going to be in here?"

"Not much longer."

I called him every morning for four days. On the fifth day, the hospital called me. They said I could come get him. When I walked into his room, he was eating pudding. He saw me and gave a big smile. His eyes were normal again. I felt like a parent. While the nurses were helping Pa into his clothes, Dr. Shepard brought me into his exam room so we could talk privately. I sat on the table, paper crinkling under my ass, legs dangling. He sat in his swivel chair and twiddled his stethoscope.

"Your dad's a real character."

"Yep."

"Strong, too. He's going to be okay. I mean, as okay as he can be."

I said, "No more of those spells?"

"He's been here almost a week and we haven't seen anything to suggest it'll happen again. Whatever it was—stroke or seizure—it was very mild. We did tests. Scans, evaluations, everything. I spent some quality time on the phone with some very good physicians in Denver. While nothing was definitive, everything suggested that he made it thru this in good shape."

I nodded.

"He's been absolutely stable. Probably no significant brain damage. Hard to say, though. Obviously."

"Obviously."

Dr. Shepard took a breath. "It's a shame. Emmett was so brilliant. And a good man. He helped me save a patient's life once. Did he ever tell you about that?"

I shook my head.

"It's been twenty-five years. There was a car wreck a few miles south of Strattford. A man driving a pickup fell asleep and went into the ditch. Rolled the truck, flew out the windshield. No seat belt, of course. This happened pretty close to where the Griffith ranch used to be."

I nodded, as if I knew where that was.

"It was a bad one. Head injury, punctured lung, spinal. The whole damn caboodle. There was no way we could treat him here in Strattford and there was no way he was going to survive a two-hour ambulance ride to Denver.

"Your dad—this was when everyone had a CB—your dad over-heard us talking on the scanner, jumped in his airplane, and scam-pered himself right to the scene. He landed on the road. There wasn't enough room to put the fellow in the plane lying down so, just as quick as you can imagine, your dad unbolted the two rear seats and dumped them in the ditch. We stuck that fellow into the plane with his feet poking into the tail and flew straight to Denver. I rode in the copilot seat. Your dad was as cool as the bottom of a rock. It was amazing."

"He never told me about that one."

"It was gruesome. The kind of thing you don't want to think about."

"What happened to him?"

"The guy in the pickup? He hung on for a couple of weeks and then he died. Those couple of weeks mattered, though. Long enough for his family to say good-bye." Dr. Shepard looked at me real closely. Probably looking for a piece of Pa in my eyes. Good luck.

I nodded my head solemnly, figuring that would be appropriate.

"Yes, sir," said Dr. Shepard. "Your dad's a great man and a good man." He rubbed his knee, returned to the present. "Even in his situation here, he's still curious about everything."

"Yep."

"He climbed out of bed every chance he got. We'd find him walking the halls. Once, he even wandered into the OR in the middle of a surgery. We eventually had to find someone to keep an eye on him all the time."

"That's probably what he wanted. Someone to watch over him."

"Likely as anything."

We looked at each other.

The doctor said, "Any problems with depression?"

I said, "I'm getting used to it."

Dr. Shepard said, "With Emmett, I mean."

"Oh. He seems fine. Gets a little sad sometimes. But I try to distract him."

"If that works, then good. Sometimes people in his situation will get depressed. It's difficult to cheer them up because you can't explain to them why they shouldn't be sad. They feel sad and that's that. If Emmett should get that—the melancholy—let me know. I'll prescribe something."

"Will do." Won't do. People don't use antidepressants in Strattford County.

"How's his diet?"

"We eat regular stuff. Meat and vegetables."

"Since the dementia hit him so young, he's very healthy, physically."

"He's a tank."

"He could live a very long time."

"Yep."

"The end will be difficult."

"I know." I wanted to leave.

"Does he enjoy fatty foods?"

"Like hotdogs?"

"Oh, anything. Steak, cheese, fast food. Pizza."

"He'll eat whatever I put in front of him."

Dr. Shepard said, "At this stage, I encourage you to feed him anything he wants. And, even though fatty foods can contribute to so-called bad cholesterol, that's not always a bad thing, especially in the case of someone as healthy as Emmett. As his condition worsens, your father could spend years in a bed, with no idea who you are or who he is. Fed thru a tube. Diapers. It can be difficult."

"I expect that will be the case." I hadn't thought of that part yet.

"There's always the chance that he could die of natural causes before it comes to that. A heart attack is a natural death. Fatty foods increase the risk of a heart attack."

"And?"

"A heart attack isn't a bad way to die."

In the pickup, driving back from Strattford, Pa said, "Wish I had a comb."

I patted my shirt pocket. "No comb here. You're gonna have to lick your hand and wipe it on your head."

"Wipe it on your ass."

I said, "Good one."

A few minutes later, Pa said, "Wish I had a comb."

I patted my shirt pocket. "No comb here. You're gonna have to lick your hand and wipe it on your head."

"Wipe it on your ass."

I said, "Good one."

When we got home, he wanted to walk around, so we did. We walked around the property and got cheatgrass in our socks. I pointed out the work I'd done. The granary window was fixed. The front doorknob was fixed. The garden was weeded. He approved. It wasn't so bad, having him back.

I took him to the shed and showed him the Rocket. "Say!" he said. "That's a good-lookin' little dude you have there."

"You and me. We put it together."

"That so?"

I said, "I can't get the damn thing to start."

"I bet I can."

He squatted down. Pa's ass never touched the ground. At sixty-two, straight out of the hospital, he could still squat like a Hindu holy man. He ran his hands over the engine. I watched with squinted eyes. I knew he couldn't explain what he was doing but I figured if I paid close enough attention, I'd see the precise moment when he worked his sleight of hand.

He wiggled the spark plug cable and then made a yip sound. Must have pinched his finger. Blood started flowing. The cut wasn't any bigger than a mouse bite. But that dark red blood went drip, drip on the floor.

He was unconcerned. "You got something that could mop this mess up?"

I turned to fetch a rag. I wasn't two steps away before the Rocket revved up.

He was holding his hand above his head, finger wrapped in his hankie, a little river of blood creeping down his forearm. He didn't care. He waved me over. The Rocket chattered, leaning hard on its kickstand. He's home half an hour and just like that.

He said, "Give it a go."

"You sure? It's your bike."

"Get on."

I straddled the Rocket. Old-fashioned fatso seat. The throttle was a knob bolted to the frame. I revved the engine. It putted like a Briggs & Stratton washing machine engine should.

"Ride it!"

I didn't know what to expect. You get your expectations up and then they fall. This here was a bicycle with an engine on it. It wasn't a magic carpet. I put some weight on the clutch pedal.

The Rocket flew. My ass slid halfway off the seat before I pulled myself back into position. Headed right toward the house, I took my foot off the pedal and the bike came to a stop. I eased back the throttle. I walked the bike around. Dad was watching me from the shed, hands on his hips. He shouted something at me. I gave him a thumbs-up and engaged the clutch real gentle. The bike drove much better now. I took it around the shed, between the grain bins. The seat springs were the only suspension. An anthill felt like a molehill. Mounds of bunchgrass jerked the handlebars. The whole frame felt like it was flexing. But I held on and that old, heavy iron held together.

I cruised the farm with gentle wind cooling the sweat in my armpits. When I'd had enough, I rode back to the shed and stopped easy, right in front of Pa. The hankie was tied around his finger. The blood had dried.

I said, "Your turn."

I climbed off the bike and he climbed on. He revved the engine, stomped the clutch. The rear wheel showered me with gravel. The bike reared up with a roar. A lesser man would have panicked and dumped it right then. Pa leaned forward, put the front wheel back on the ground, and took off like a rabbit. He sped past the house and onto the road. He headed north, face crouched into the handlebars, elbows wide like wings.

A quarter mile down the road, I saw him turn right at the intersection. He was circumnavigating the section. A four-mile trip, it was a required test run for any homebuilt motorized device. The bike got smaller and smaller and then disappeared behind a rise. Blackout time. I would not hear from him until he reappeared rounding the corner three-quarters of a mile south of the house.

The dirt roads of Strattford County were on the grid system. Instead of city blocks, they used sections. A section is a square mile. Every mile, another intersection. In spite of the uniform design, every road had its own personality. Some held their shape in the rain, some sank your car up to its axles. Some roads were solid, some were washboarded, some were soft and sandy. The road that Dad was roaring down was terribly soft. Even in dry weather, the sand could wrench the front wheels of a pickup and squirrel it into the ditch.

I scratched some calculations in the dirt. The blackout zone was a little less than three miles. If he was traveling twenty miles an hour, those three miles should take him around nine minutes.

Twenty minutes later, he still hadn't showed up at the south corner. I wasn't worried exactly. Still, I got in the pickup and followed his route. The tire tracks weaved back and forth across the road. On that sand, the Rocket must have been meaner than a snake. I wondered if all that bouncing didn't dislodge a blood clot, give him another stroke. Pass out, veer into a barbed-wire fence. Death by Rocket would have been faster than feeding him fatty foods by a long shot. I became a little worried.

I found him on the homestretch. Walking the bike. When I pulled up, he stuck out his thumb. I rolled down the window. "Need a ride?"

He nodded. "Got any gas?"

After a trip to the fuel tank, we spent the rest of the day riding the Rocket. Up and down the road, scaring up pheasants. Down the old runway, where the badger mounds would bounce you right up off the seat. It was glorious. Just before sunset, we went in to the house, ate canned food, watched TV, and slept wonderfully.

CHAPTER 13

THE POSTMAN
DELIVERS BAD NEWS

Dad wasn't much good for chores, but there was one job he did and he did it well. He could get the mail. Several times a day, he'd go to the mailbox, which was up the driveway, next to the road. Once a day, excepting Sundays, he'd actually bring something back. He'd put the mail on the counter, where I'd go thru it and sort out the good from the bad.

Since the mail usually arrived around noon, I'd cook lunch while he read random snippets from catalogs, brochures, anything. From one flyer advertising a Hawaiian vacation he read, "Kobe Japanese Steakhouse," "Easy Rider," "Meteor Shower Night Trip." Very serious. I don't think he knew what he was reading. He was just impressed with himself for being able to translate letters into sounds. Words that were composed by an ad agency in New York were being recited with zero context in a farmhouse in Strattford County, Colorado. It was the opposite of poetry.

The day after we rode the Rocket, Pa went to the mailbox and brought back the hospital bill. Of course we didn't have any insurance. At sixty-two, he was too young for Medicare. We were too ignorant to apply for Medicaid or take advantage of any other program that could have possibly helped us. Five days in the hospital plus a bunch of tests came out to $87,332.23.

I stuffed the bill in my back pocket and we spent the rest of the day working in the garden. Weeds. They grow so damned quick.

The sun was cooking pretty good. We wore long-sleeved shirts.
Most people think you should wear a T-shirt in the hot sun. Or go
shirtless. Bullshit. You want a worn-out, long-sleeved button-down
shirt. Keeps the burn off your arms. A good shirt and a mesh farm
cap and you're safe from everything but the flies.

I dug a hole and dropped the hospital bill into it. I buried it. I
had failed to pay bills before. I wasn't worried. You always get plenty
of warning before they send someone after you. Letters, sneaky
phone calls. In the end, it wasn't going to matter. There was no way
we'd be paying that bill.

All Pa and I had was the farm. We could have sold it, maybe,
but I doubt it'd bring in eighty-seven thousand dollars. And even
if it did, we'd have no farm and no money.

A process had started, and there wasn't any stopping it. Eventually we were going to lose the farm on account of my dad having a
conversation with his dead wife in the middle of the night. I dug
up the letter and put it back in my pocket.

That evening, after Dad was in bed, I called Clarissa.

"Mind if I come over?"

She said, "It's been a while."

"I know."

"I thought you were all done with me, Stacey Williams."

"Please don't call me that."

"It's your name."

"I got a question."

She said, "It's late."

"It's not even ten o'clock."

"I have to be at the bank tomorrow morning."

"It won't take long."

She sighed right into the receiver. "Come over."

I made sure Pa was asleep and then drove my car the eight miles to her place.

Clarissa lived in a trailer. It was solid in the ground. The windows and the front door were open, hoping to catch a breeze. I walked in. Clarissa had the TV tuned to a program where sexy cops sliced open sexy cadavers. She turned down the volume and offered me a drink.

I said, "You got any root beer?"

"Did you give up on the real kind?"

I nodded.

"I'll see what I can find."

She went to the kitchen and poured me a cup of iced tea. We sat on her couch while an oscillating fan ruffled the edges of her nightgown. She'd lost some weight.

"What's the emergency?"

I handed her the envelope. "You know anything about things like this?"

She looked at the bill. Raised her eyebrows. "If I'd of known Emmett was sick, I would have sent a card."

"I thought you knew everything."

"I usually do." She tapped the letter. "Take this, for instance. It's called a bill. It's a request for money in exchange for services rendered."

"It's not right to charge that much just to keep a guy in a bed."

"It's a hospital. What do you expect?"

"What if I don't have any money?"

"They'll let you do it in payments."

"We aren't going to get any money any time soon. Dad can't work. I don't know how to farm. There's no jobs here, at least none that I can do."

"Then move back to Denver."

"I'd have to hire someone to take care of Dad. That's expensive. And anyway, I can't take him off the farm. He'd be lost."

She shrugged. "Then you're screwed. They'll take the farm and sell it and you and your Pa will end up in a shack like this."

"They're not going to take the farm."

"Unless you've got some plan for earning eighty thousand dollars real quick, they damn sure will."

"Okay. And say I did have a plan for earning eighty thousand dollars real quick?"

"Yeah. What are you gonna do? Rob a bank?"

"Yep."

She pointed to the door. "Out."

I stayed on the couch. "That bastard stole my dad's airplane."

Clarissa said, "I'm not helping you rob the bank."

"I bet ol' Mike Crutchfield is a prick to work for."

"It's a job. And anyway, he's only in one day a week. I hardly ever see him."

"You live in a shitty trailer house in a rotten town. You're thirty-six years old, you're afraid of vomit, you're anorexic, and nobody loves you." I picked up a book off her end table. "And you're reading something called *Furious Desire*?"

She pulled the book out of my hands. "I read it because it's funny." She was defensive. "You know, telling me I'm pathetic isn't news. I know all that shit. I know I'm a nobody doing nothing in nowhere. I know people laugh at me. Fuck. I know Crutchfield is a dripping asshole of a man. He's everybody's best buddy until he repossesses their house. He's the world's best boss until he slaps your ass. But you know what? You better get over it because if you whine, you can say good-bye to your job. Next stop, you'll be commuting forty miles to Strattford to wait tables at Billy's for three bucks an hour and zero tips. So, yes. I'd love to rob that place. Who the hell wouldn't? But it's impossible. Never happen."

"Why not?"

"For one thing, there's a gun behind the counter and instructions for the employees to shoot first and then shoot again."

I said, "Nobody's gonna shoot us. Except for Saturdays when Mr. Crutchfield comes in, there's only three people who work in that bank. Not you, nor Neal Koenig, nor Charlotte Sackett would shoot anybody. But that doesn't matter since we're going to do it at night when there's nobody around."

Clarissa said, "Which brings me to point number two. If you try to break in at night, you've got to deal with a fancy alarm system whose code I am not privy to."

"We'll figure that out."

"If you think I'm gonna sleep with Crutchfield in order to get that code, you're a shit-tongued moron."

"You won't have to sleep with anyone. I promise. We can cut the power or something. Alarms can be tricked. Look at your TV show. They do it all the time."

Clarissa shut off the television. She said, "Thirdly—and, may I point out, most significantly—it's a vault. With a lock and a combination and everything."

"That'll be the easy part."

"Oh yeah?"

"We have a secret weapon."

"And that would be?"

"Emmett Williams. He's a genius. Well, he was. He still is. You just gotta get him started. We'll put him in front of the vault with a stethoscope and wait. He's automatic."

"We're going to base our entire plan on your senile father's ability to crack a safe?"

"Yep."

"Emmett's got morals. He'll never agree."

"He doesn't have to know we're breaking the law. I'll lie to him. He's gullible."

"That's taking advantage of him."

"Coming from a woman who slept with him while he was drunk."

"I was drunk, too." She winked at me.

"And it's not taking advantage. It's just using him to retake what the banker stole."

"It won't work."

"I don't care."

She said, "Lucky for you, I do care."

"You're looking skinny."

"Don't flatter me."

"Will you do it?"

"Yes."

She threw *Furious Desire* at the TV. The pages spread out in a way that made the book appear to fly for a moment just before it bounced off the screen.

On the way back from Clarissa's, I drove thru Dorsey to make sure Vaughn Atkins's mom was working at the liquor store. She was; thru the window, I could see her leaning on the counter with a cigarette on her lips.

I went to Vaughn's house. He was in the basement, eating fudge, watching TV. The same show Clarissa had been watching.

He said, "The prodigal son of a bitch returns."

"After that night."

"My mom."

"What happened? Did she ground you?"

"Nah. She forgot the whole thing. Drunk. She even got my TV rigged up again."

"I see that," I said.

He shut off the television. "You could have called."

"I wanted to spend some time with my pa."

"I heard he almost died."

"I thought nobody knew."

"Everybody knows everything."

"It was just a little stroke."

"Is that why you're here?"

"No."

He said, "You want something."

"I don't want anything."

"You want some fudge?"

"What's in it?"

"Opium. But it must have cooked out in the oven because I've had half a pan of this shit and I can't feel a thing."

He offered me a cube. I waved it away.

He said, "Have some fudge."

"I don't want any fudge."

"Then what do you want?"

"Can you keep a secret?"

"Of course I can."

I said, "Are you telling me you can keep a secret because you really can keep a secret or because you're a liar?"

"What's it matter? You're going to tell me anyway."

"No, I'm not."

"Let me guess what you're going to tell me. If I get it right, then all you have to do is nod."

"Okay."

"You want to rob the bank."

"Good guess."

"It wasn't really a guess. Clarissa just called."

"Goddamn. That bull—"

"Hold on. She said she thought you were going to drive over here and ask me to help you rob the bank and that I should say yes because she totally has faith in you."

"That's nice." It actually was nice.

Vaughn said, "You should have asked Clarissa if *she* could keep a secret."

"So you'll help?"

"Of course. And you can trust me."

I said, "What about . . . ?" I looked at the stairs.

"They remain an obstacle."

PART TWO

CHAPTER 14

FIRST STEPS

Obviously, I didn't go right out and tell Pa about the bank robbery, but I did tell him that we were going to go to Vaughn's place for a meeting next week. At first, he didn't seem interested. I told him it was important. I explained that we were writing a play and we wanted him to be our creative consultant. I told him this several times over the next few days. Slowly, it started to work into his brain. He began saying things like "When's the conference?" or "We have something coming up, don't we?"

The night of the meeting, he put on his suit. His pants were tight. His belly was getting bigger. I couldn't tie his tie. Didn't know how. Never learned. He did it just fine. He shaved twice. He even brushed his teeth without my help.

When I brought him to Vaughn Atkins's basement, Clarissa was already there, sitting on the bed next to Vaughn. They didn't look at us. They were playing *Adventure* on Vaughn's Atari.

I remembered when Vaughn got that game for Christmas. The game cartridge came in an orange box decorated with a golden dragon weaving its way thru a green labyrinth. We were all thrilled at the time, me and him and D.J. Beckman. It was going to be the most amazing game ever. We'd fight dragons and a flying bat and enter three different castles.

The game was less amazing than the box implied. Instead of dragons, you—a small square—fought squarish chickens. Instead of a labyrinth, you wandered thru a maze that looked like it had been cut out of construction paper.

Still, once you got over the fact that the box had lied to you, *Adventure* was a brilliant excuse to sit on your ass for hours.

Vaughn put his hand in the air. "Hang on." His square was carrying the bridge thru the blind labyrinth in the black castle.

I said, "Gettin' the dot?" You had to find the dot to get into the secret room.

"Just about." The red dragon glided onto the screen. It made its blippy roar. Vaughn wiggled the joystick desperately.

It was no use. The dragon was too fast. It gobbled up Vaughn's square with a cheerful bleep.

Vaughn tossed the joystick onto the floor. "I had the sword, but the fucking bat."

Dad, who had been standing silently, said, "Are we going to talk about bats all day or are we going to get something done?"

Vaughn and Clarissa looked at me dumbly. Dad wasn't supposed to assert himself like that.

I shrugged. "He's right. We're here for a meeting. Let's meet." I turned off the TV.

Dad was comfortable. In control. He said, "What's the? What's the first thing on the?"

"Agenda," I said.

"What are we doing?"

"We're trying to figure out how to rob a bank," said Vaughn.

I said, "And we need to know if it would be possible to crack a safe."

Dad looked worried. "Why are you robbing a bank?"

"We aren't really robbing a bank, Emmett," said Clarissa. "We're writing a play about it and we'd like you to help us."

"Whatever," said Pa. "You want my help or not?"

I led Pa to Vaughn's mom's liquor cabinet. It was a big old thing, about chest high. Dark wood. Wrapped with a thick chain, secured by a padlock. "Can you open this?"

"What for?" He was getting riled up. Bratty. He could tell we were excited and he knew we needed him. I had to calm him down or we wouldn't get anything done. It was a balance. Let him be important without feeling indispensable.

Vaughn started to say something, but I gave him a look.

I said, "Pa, it's okay. We're trying to get in that cabinet so we can see how hard it is to open a safe so we can write a play. We can probably do it without you but it'd be easier with your help."

"Why don't *you* do it then?"

Clarissa said, "Because none of us is any good at stuff like that."

"Well, then." He crossed his arms.

I said, "Can't you just try?"

He looked at the cabinet. Touched the padlock. "That thing is closed up for a reason."

I said, "We're not going to take anything out of it. We're just going to open it up and close it again."

Vaughn pulled a stethoscope from under his pillow. In the friend-liest voice he could muster, he said, "I got one of these if you need it."

He handed it to Pa, who looked at it as if it were a snake. He said, "It doesn't seem right."

Clarissa got off the bed and put her hand on Dad's arm. "Emmett, you don't have to worry about it. It's not that important. It's just a play."

"It's just a play, huh?"

"Sure. Research. For the theater." She smiled.

"Well." He shook his head. "I'm not that good at stuff anymore." His confidence was gone. The suit looked silly on his fat belly. He said, "Nope. You do your thing. I'll only make you slow."

Clarissa nodded. "That's all right, Emmett. It's just a play. You don't have to open that lock if you don't want to." She turned to Vaughn and me. "Right, boys?"

With teeth clenched, Vaughn and I nodded. I said, "Yeah. Don't worry about it, Pa."

The three of us played *Adventure* while Dad wandered around the basement.

Eventually, Clarissa said, "I'd sure like something to drink. Anyone else thirsty?"

You'd think, by now, that I'd be on to him, but I was still surprised when Dad said, "How about you drink some of that stuff in that big box of yours?"

He had, of course, opened the liquor cabinet.

"Bring me over there," said Vaughn.

Clarissa said, "Where's your wheelchair?"

He hesitated and then said, "Under the bed."

Clarissa dragged out the wheelchair and opened it up. The tires were half-flat. One of the wheels was bent, but not badly. The grip was still missing from the right handle.

She said, "Your wheelchair is a piece of shit."

I thought it looked pretty good, considering the tumble it took.

Vaughn said, "I don't use it very often."

Clarissa said, "How do you get to the bathroom?"

He pointed at a footstool sitting next to his bed. "I use that thing. It's got wheels. I scoot."

Clarissa said, "But the wheelchair . . ."

"It annoys me."

Clarissa looked at me for help. I shrugged. Given my track record with that wheelchair, I didn't feel qualified to weigh in on the subject.

She said, "You shouldn't scoot on a footstool."

"It works fine," said Vaughn. "I haven't shit my pants yet."

Dad raised his voice. "Use the damned wheelchair and get over here."

We stuffed Vaughn into the chair and rolled him to the liquor cabinet. Inside, there were dusty bottles of scotch and whiskey, a bottle of wine with a peeling yellow label. "That one's old," said Pa.

In the very back was a small gunnysack. Vaughn pulled it out of the cabinet and poured the contents onto his lap. Coins, all sorts. Buffalo nickels and silver dollars and things I'd never seen before. One of them fell onto the floor. Pa picked it up, looked closely.

"This one's gold. 'United States of—'"

Vaughn took the coin from Dad. "Eighteen fifty-five. Three dollars. A three-dollar coin."

Dad said, "Queerer than a three-dollar bill."

I said, "Did you know your mom had these?"

"She got 'em when Grandpa died."

"I wonder what they're worth," said Clarissa.

"A lot," said Pa.

"We wouldn't need to rob the bank, maybe," said Clarissa.

Vaughn started scooping the coins back into the sack. "We're not taking them. They're my grandpa's."

Pa said, "You kids are robbing a bank?"

"Can't we just tell him?" said Clarissa.

"Tell who what?" asked Dad.

"Tell you that we're gonna rob the Keaton State Bank," said Vaughn.

Dad said, "What would we do that for?"

I said, "Dammit."

Vaughn said, "Because you spent a week in the hospital and you can't afford the bill. And because the son-of-a-bitch banker stole your airplane. And because Clarissa's fat and because I ain't got no legs and because Shakespeare here is half a hippocampus from being an orphan."

Pa said, "Somebody stole my airplane?"

I said to Vaughn, "Don't get him revved up."

"And so what? The guy needs to be revved up. We all do. We're zombies. We gotta eat some fucking brains or we'll die. Right, Emmett?"

"Damn right!" said Pa.

"I'm not fat," said Clarissa.

"Hell no, you aren't!" said Pa.

"But I am going to rob a bank," said Clarissa.

"Rob it!" said Dad.

"See?" said Vaughn. "Clarissa and Emmett are ready to eat brains. Are you?"

Dad was twitching, he was so happy. Vaughn was grinding his teeth. Clarissa's stomach growled.

Suddenly, I wondered if this was all a terrible idea. I said, "Eating brains is a big commitment."

"I fell down the stairs," said Vaughn. "Did Shakes tell you that, Clarissa? He came over the other day and talked me into getting out of the basement. We made it all the way to the top step and then the chair"—he punched the arm rest—"the chair fell apart and I fell down. You ever fall down a flight of stairs?"

Clarissa said, "Shit. Are you okay?"

"I don't think I broke anything. I felt sorry for myself. I still do. But I don't care about that because I'm going to rob a bank. I'm okay. We're all okay. We're going to eat brains. Right, Shakes?"

Clarissa, Vaughn, and Pa all looked at me like I was supposed to raise my fist in the air and shout something inspirational.

Instead, I said, "This is stupid. We should go home." I took Dad by the elbow and tried to lead him out. His arm stiffened. When he flexed his muscles like that, he turned to stone.

He said, "I don't want to go home."

That's it. That's how you plan a bank robbery. You sit in a muggy basement with a paralyzed asshole, an anorexic fatso, and your prematurely senile father. Let everyone talk at once and eventually, if you allow yourself to become too annoyed to fight, they'll form an idea. Nobody took notes. No need. It was simple. We'd do the job in the middle of the day. Dad and I would go to the bank with the bag of coins from Vaughn's mom's liquor cabinet and say we wanted to put them in a safe-deposit box. Clarissa would lead us down the hall and toward the vault. Neal Koenig, the bank manager, would open it up. At that moment, Vaughn, who would be in an undisclosed location, would call in a false fire alarm for an imaginary spot at the edge of the Keaton Volunteer Fire Department's jurisdiction. As news of the fire spread, the bank would be emptied of its patrons, who, as we knew from the experience at the softball game, would chase the fire truck like hounds after a rabbit. Clarissa would volunteer to watch the bank until everyone got back. Of course, Neal Koenig would lock the vault before he ran out to follow the fire engine. But that didn't matter because we had Pa.

With the bank empty, Dad would crack the safe. We'd fill up a suitcase with cash, hop in the car, pick up Vaughn, and then skedaddle the hell out of the county. No need to sneak in at night. No alarm. Simple. Easy.

It wasn't the best bank robbery plan in the world. In fact, I suspected that there might be some serious flaws. When I mentioned that it seemed like the collectible coins had more of a symbolic purpose than anything, Vaughn agreed. "If I'm not going to be there helping you guys out, I want to be represented by my grandpa's coins." Reasonable enough.

Still, we decided to wait a week, just to make sure we had our ducks in a row. Knock out a few details. Such as what we were going to do immediately after the robbery. Go into hiding? Leave the county? Leave the country? But those things would sort themselves out.

It seemed possible.

CHAPTER 15

BATH TIME

After the meeting adjourned, Pa and I drove home. Pa brushed his teeth on his own. Twice in one day. This bank-robbery business was good therapy.

I went upstairs and read an Indiana Jones movie and then went to sleep. It wasn't long before Pa woke me up. It was still nighttime.

"There's a noise out there."

We pulled on some clothes and went outside. The yard light was burned out. No moon. Cloudy. Couldn't see anything. The birds were asleep. It can be terrifying out there at night. Nothing but wind.

In the daytime, we both knew that land with our eyes shut. But in the dark, there were things. Coyotes, badgers, deer, raccoons, all kinds of shit. It was scary and I wanted to go back to bed, but Dad had heard something so we had to investigate. We walked around the house. Fat, clumsy beetles flew around our heads. Wind and bugs and ghosts. Then something.

I heard a noise near the base of the house. I crawled thru the grass. Scratching sound. Panting. A critter was stuck in the window well. It was too dark to see.

"Stay here."

I ran into the house, turned on the basement light. When I came back out, Dad was gone. With the basement light on, I could clearly see the critter. Little, cute baby skunk. It was terrified. Scrambling up and down in the window well, ripping apart the screen. It couldn't climb out.

I backed up quick. When you can't smell, you don't risk skunks. Being scared like that, the thing might have already sprayed. I could be walking in a mist of stink. Since Pa couldn't smell either, we had no way of knowing. Stay away.

I shouted for Pa. No response. I put my hands on either side of my mouth and shouted again. Nothing.

Sneaky footsteps behind me. Pa liked to surprise you. He used to put his cold hands on Mom's back every time she was at the sink. It made her yell and it made him laugh.

I said, "Don't try any funny stuff, Pa. We got a skunk situation."

He sidled up to me. "Not for long." He was holding his .22. My grandpa shot a lot of rabbits with that rifle. Some of those rabbits made it into Pa's belly. In my generation, the gun was fired primarily at empty soup cans and horny tomcats. I shot the cans. Pa shot the cats.

I stood back. "Don't bust the window."

My eyes had adjusted to the dark. I watched Pa's silhouette. Feet at shoulder width, he entered a standard upright firing position. He pointed the gun into the window well. The skunk's nails made scratching noises against the glass. Pa waited. The scratching stopped. I could hear the skunk breathing in short, wheezy bursts. Then a *pop!* and Dad said, "Got the bastard!"

He got it, all right, but it wasn't dead. The skunk was thrashing. Pa fired again. This time, he hit the sweet spot. The skunk exploded. Red blood, green goop. A bright yellow fountain of viscera, shit, and piss splattered against the window.

Dad leaned in close. A droplet of the yellow landed on his glasses. He was laughing like a kid. "It's the Fourth of July!"

I dragged him away. "I think we just got sprayed, Pa."

He sniffed the air. "I don't smell nothing."

"I know."

This was a crisis. I had to call for help, but the phone was in the house and I didn't want to go inside for fear of stinking the place up. We couldn't drive for help because I didn't want to stink up my car. We couldn't stay outside forever. It was warm enough, but it was night and night is scary.

I made Dad sit down on the front step and tried to think. Maybe there was an old telephone in the shed. If I could find it and then plug it into the spot where the phone line ran into the house, I could make some calls from outside.

Pa stood up and said, "What the hell are we doing out here?"

He started for the front door. I said, "Stop!"

"I'm going inside."

"You can't. There was a skunk."

"*You're* a damn skunk."

I pretended to hear something. "What was that?" I tried to sound worried.

He got interested. "Something out there?"

I pointed toward the well house. "I heard something."

Pa said, "Well, go see what it is."

"Absolutely not. What if it's a badger?"

Pa raised up the .22. "Then we'll shoot it."

"I ain't going over there."

Pa looked at me, disgusted. "You're a wimp." He swaggered toward the well house.

I made an executive decision. I couldn't bother with trying to find a phone and plug it in. I had to get in the house and call for help. While Pa wandered behind the well house, I quickly stepped out of my britches and took off my shirt. If figured I'd stand less of a chance of skunking up the house if I was down to my skivvies. I ran inside, locking the door behind me, and picked up the telephone.

First, I dialed Clarissa. It rang a thousand times but she didn't answer. I hung up. Every second I remained in the house, more particles of stink were floating off my body and sticking to the walls.

It was no good calling Vaughn. His mom would answer and then she'd yell at me and then yell at him. I had to call someone. We couldn't sleep in our beds until we knew we were clean.

As I contemplated who to call next, Pa tried the front door. It may have been the first time that door had ever been locked. It was certainly the first time Pa had been locked out of his own house. He pounded on the door. He shouted, "What the hell's going on in there?"

I ignored him.

I tried D.J. Beckman. Jackass that he was, I figured he'd be up for an adventure. He answered halfway thru the first ring. "Yepper."

I explained the situation. He laughed at me. I hung up on him.

Dad kept knocking on the door.

The phone rang. I answered. It was D.J. "Shakespeare, why you gotta be so dramatic? I'm on my way." He hung up. I put the phone back in its cradle and hustled out the door.

When he saw me, Pa stepped back. He was still holding the .22. "What in the world are you doing out here in your undershorts?"

I said, "What are you doing with that gun?"

He looked at the rifle in his hands. "I suppose I'm going to shoot someone."

I slipped past him, found my clothes, and got dressed.

In order to keep Pa distracted while we waited on D.J., I walked with him up to the road. I pointed out the North Star. He pointed out the blinking light of a jet zooming overhead.

Having accomplished our stargazing, we turned and headed back down the driveway toward the house. As we approached, I saw a little peak of a thumbnail moon rising just above the top of the shed. I paused and said, "Look, Pa, the moon's rising."

We stood together and watched as that grey sliver climbed over the silhouette of the building. Once it cleared the top, Pa said, "That was neat." Then he sighted the gun at the moon and pulled the trigger. *Pop!* The bullet zoomed over the shed and into the night.

I said, "Think you got it?"

He said, "Shoot the moon."

We took a couple more steps toward the house. With the gentle descent down the driveway, the angle between us, the shed, and the moon changed so that the moon was once again hidden behind the shed.

Once again, I said, "Look, Pa, the moon's rising." Once again, we watched the grey sliver climb over the top of the shed. Once again, Pa said, "That was neat," and then shot at it.

We watched the moon rise five times.

Target practice was interrupted by the distant sound of D.J.'s car. When we looked north, we saw the headlights from a mile away. He drove fast. Soon, he was skidding to a stop in the driveway, twenty feet from where we stood. The famous two-hundred-dollar 1972 Chevy Nova. Beat up and ugly. But still cool.

He shut off the engine, leaving the headlights on, and leaned out the window. "I hear you boys are having skunk trouble."

"Is that so?" said Pa.

"According to Shakes." D.J. pointed toward the rifle Pa was holding. "Is that a .22? That's a nice-looking gun."

Pa said, "I'd shoot you but I'd have to kill you."

D.J. made har-har noises. "You're a funny man, Emmett."

Pa said, "You wanna have a look at it? It's a pretty neat old gun."

Pa started walking toward the car. D.J. raised the palm of his hand. "Hang on, there. I got a job to do."

I said, "Yeah. Smell us, willya?"

"Smell for what?" said Pa.

"Shakes thinks you've been sprayed by a skunk," said D.J. He pointed at me. "Walk toward me, real slow, Skunkspeare."

Here's the thing with anosmia. You gotta humiliate yourself in order to make sure you don't stink. And the only reason you care if you stink is so you don't offend the smellers. Go to all this trouble and they still make fun of you. At least when people make fun of the blind, the poor bastards can't see it.

I took a step. D.J. sniffed and said, "Keep coming."

I walked closer and closer as he waved me in. When I was standing right next to his car, he gave me a thumbs-up. "You smell like a farm rat. But there ain't no skunk on you."

"Now do Dad."

Before Pa was within five steps, D.J. held up his hand. "You been sprayed, Emmett."

"Sprayed by what?"

"A damned skunk," said D.J.

"I don't smell nothing."

"Is it bad?" I asked.

D.J. gave me a pitiful look. "It's a skunk."

I leaned in the Nova's window and whispered, "You wouldn't be messing with me? Taking advantage of the situation?"

He shook his head. "I don't joke about skunk stink. And if I did, I wouldn't put it on Emmett."

I looked him in the eye. All I could see was that his pupils were dilated.

I said, "So it's tomato juice, then."

"Don't bother with that shit," said D.J. "Use baking soda and peroxide. My dog got sprayed once. It works good. Cheaper, too." He opened the glove box and pulled out a bag of brownies. "Speaking of cheap."

"No, thanks."

"It's nothing but the green, green grass of home. It's real fresh. Might help you trust people."

"No."

He turned the headlights off. "After all I've done for you."

"You haven't done that much."

"I drove here in the middle of the night just so I could smell you two bobbleheads. I'd call that doing very much. In fact, I'd call it a charitable act."

Dad said, "Give to charity."

D.J. reached in the back seat and retrieved a six-pack. "Have a beer. Visit. Relax."

I said, "I don't have time for a beer. Dad needs a bath."

D.J. said, "Come on. He can sit outside for a minute. He's not gonna get any stinkier." To Pa, he said, "You want a frosty beverage, Mr. Williams?"

Pa said, "I love frosties."

D.J. pulled a can off the plastic ring and handed it to me. "Give that to your father, please."

Pa said, "I can get it myself." He started walking toward the car.

D.J. said, "Hold it! Not a step closer."

Pa said, "Why the hell not?"

D.J. winked at me. "Because my car just got sprayed by a skunk. If you come too close, you'll get the stink on you."

Pa took a few steps backward. "Hell. I wouldn't get within a hundred miles."

I tossed the beer to Pa. He caught it in his left hand—the hand that wasn't holding the rifle—and threw it right back to me.

I said, "If you don't want it, you don't get it." I pointed the can away from me and popped the top. It fizzed a little over my hands, but not too bad. I took a sip.

"That's better," said D.J. He opened a beer of his own and took a theatrical drink.

I said, "All right. We're visiting."

A quick breeze stirred thru the yard. D.J. said, "It's nice, isn't it? Being out on a beautiful night. Look at the stars."

I didn't bother looking up. I'd seen them.

D.J. said, "You ever wonder why I'd be up at all hours, answering the phone?"

"Is Channel Twenty showing a *Dukes of Hazzard* marathon?"

My cleverness had no effect on D.J. He said, "It's because life is difficult, Shakespeare. My life. The lives of others. I know you sit at home with your old man and mope all the time, but other people's lives are equally complicated. My own included."

Dad said, "Hope is a thing with fathers."

D.J. raised his beer in a toast. "Emmett, you are a genius. Always have been. Always will be. You've inspired me to explore vast landscapes of invention that I otherwise would never have dared to traverse."

Pa nodded his head in humility. "Thank you, sir."

I said, "How's that? How's he inspired you?"

"By being himself. But mostly thru 4-H. Remember that, Emmett? You taught me how to troubleshoot a lawn mower engine. We spent all those afternoons in your shed." D.J. grew wistful. "You showed us carburetors and taught us about timing. And you were always in the middle of your mad-scientist projects. Remember that hot-air balloon you made out of a pair of polyester britches? Always something. Ever since those days, I've wanted to be an inventor. And now I've found my place. I create new and unheard-of recipes with various pharmaceutical and herbal ingredients. One day, one of these recipes will catch on and the world will remember me. Thanks to you."

Dad was proud.

I wanted to bring the conversation back home. "Your life is complicated, D.J. How so?"

"So many people in the world need our help, Shakespeare. Poverty. Pain. I'm not a rich man. I do what I can. Sometimes, it keeps me up nights."

I didn't know where he was headed but I was sure wherever it was involved lots of meandering. Maybe a confession. Whatever it was, I didn't particularly care. I raised my beer and said, "To altruism."

D.J. took a drink, wiped his lip, and looked at the can in his hand. "A malt-truism for altruism."

Nobody spoke for a while. We listened to the sounds of the night.

Then D.J. said, "So you wanna buy a brownie or not?"

Sensing that this would be the only way to bring an end to our visit, I said, "How much?"

"Fifteen dollars."

"No, thanks."

"Ten?"

Pa got curious. "What's that you're buying?"

D.J. said, "Brownies."

Pa said, "I like brownies. Buy a brownie."

I said, "I'm almost broke, Mr. Altruist."

D.J. sighed. "Five."

We exchanged goods for cash. D.J. drove away, his taillights barely visible for all the dust his car kicked up.

_____

Pa didn't want to take a bath.

"I'm not a baby."

"You been sprayed by a skunk. You gotta take a bath."

"If I'd of been sprayed by a skunk, I would smell it."

"You don't have a sense of smell."

"How would you know?"

"Get in." It was after four A.M. Way too late for us to be up. We were standing in the bathroom. I had failed to get Pa to take off his clothes before he pushed his way into the house. I could almost see the stink particles floating in the air.

The tub was filled with steaming water. I had poured in a bottle of peroxide and half a box of the baking soda that had been sitting in the fridge since 1991. Just to be on the safe side, I also dumped in a can of tomato soup. It looked like a witches' brew.

"I'm not getting in that."

"You're gonna stink up the whole house."

"I'm not going to stink up a damn thing 'cause I don't damn stink."

I said, "Don't move. I'll be right back." I went to the kitchen and retrieved D.J.'s brownie from the fridge. When I got back to the bathroom, Pa was standing like a mannequin right where I left him.

"Eat this." I broke the brownie in two and handed him half.

He put it in his mouth and chewed brattily. Stuck out his tongue.

"Good, huh?"

"So-so."

I fed him the other half. He gobbled it up.

I said, "Let's watch some TV."

He followed me out of the bathroom. I laid a ratty blanket over his chair and sat him down on it. We watched an infomercial for twenty minutes before he started giggling. He didn't even know I

was there. He laughed and laughed. Holding his tummy. "Wheeeee!"
I snuck out of the room and ran some more warm water into the tub.

When I came back, he was staring at the TV, face stuck in a
blissful smile.

"Pa?"

"Yes, son?"

"I got an idea."

"Yes?" Giggle.

"I was thinking you might enjoy a bath right now."

"That so?"

"Wanna try?"

"Sure."

I helped him stand up. His hands floated around his head like
they were hanging on strings. I removed the blanket from the chair
and led him to the bathroom.

"That bathtub looks real good, don't it?"

"Sure does."

I put the blanket on the floor. "Take off your clothes and set 'em
right there."

He pointed to the blanket. "On that deal?"

"On that deal."

I exited, shutting the door behind me. After a few moments, I
said, "You got your clothes off?"

"Sure do!"

"Okay, now get in the tub."

Splashing sounds.

"You in there?"

"Yep."

I went back into the bathroom. He was sitting upright in the
tub. I handed him a washcloth. "Scrub yourself real good. I'll be
right back."

"Okay."

I looked at him sternly. "What are you going to do while I'm gone?"

"Scrub myself." He laughed. "Real good. Fried potatoes."

I bundled his clothes in the blanket and started them in the washing machine along with a handful of baking powder.

Then I sat outside the bathroom and listened to make sure he was making bathing sounds. There was splashing and scrubbing. He said, "Oh, wow," several times.

I must have fallen asleep. When I awoke, the sun was shining and Dad was gone.

CHAPTER 16

PA TAKES A RIDE

It was almost noon. The bathtub was empty. The TV was still on. The pickup wasn't in the garage.

Emmett Williams won the state 4-H tractor-driving competition in 1960. He used to be able to reverse a pickup into a crowded shed with two anhydrous tanks linked on back. You could set him blindfolded on the surface of Mars and he'd know which way was north. Now he couldn't tell left from right.

I wasn't scared of him killing anyone. Everybody knew what his truck looked like; if someone saw Pa driving in their direction, they would pull over and let him pass. I wasn't scared of him killing himself in an accident. He drove thirty miles an hour.

I was scared of him not coming back. He could drive and drive and get more and more lost. Eventually, he'd end up in Nebraska on a cattle trail, out of sight from the road. The pickup would run out of gas, he'd get out. Take a piss. Start walking. Get bit on the ankle by a rattlesnake. Scratch the bite every once in a while. Leg swells up to the point that he has to lie down next to a patch of soapweed. Wheeze. Confused. Sun burns his face. The snakebite turns his skin black. He doesn't know anything. He talks to Mom. Then he dies. At dark, the coyotes come.

It's best to approach these things pragmatically. Either he'd come home on his own, or someone would find him and lead him home, or he was dead in a Nebraska pasture. In any case, there was nothing I could do about it.

While I waited, I hoed the garden. The tomatoes were growing real good; they already had yellow flowers. Everything else was barely growing at all. Apparently, I hadn't been watering enough. The onions, carrots, and corn were all floppy, but they were alive, at least. The cabbages had leaned their little leaves over and dried up. I hoed the remains into the ground. Who likes cabbage, anyway? I turned on the soaker hose.

I ate lunch at three o'clock and went back outside. In the shed, I found a five-gallon bucket of red paint. I decided to paint the granary. I had to do something.

I popped the top off the paint bucket. The paint had separated. Thicker than mucus. I couldn't stir it with a stick so I bent a metal rod and stuck it in the end of the electric drill. A few minutes and it was mixed good.

Fill the brush, wipe the wood. The granary was old and dry. People pay good money for old wood. They chop it into foot-long chunks, paint the pieces with flower scenes, and sell them at flea markets.

No flea markets for this granary. I took lots of breaks. It was a hot one. Flies bit my neck. I drank water out of the hydrant. I couldn't find the ladder. I'm almost six feet tall. Standing on my tiptoes with arms stretched high, I was able to paint an eight-foot-tall band all around the bottom of the granary. I got a lot of paint on my shoes and my britches. My arms were wet with it. I could feel it in my hair. When the bucket was empty, I left it where it set. The paintbrush was solid with red.

I walked to the pasture east of the house and threw the brush as hard as I could. It spun thru the air, leaving a red spiral. We didn't have any damned paint—what did we need with a brush?

I went back to the garden and shut off the soaker hose. The plants looked happier, at least.

He came back at dusk. I was sitting on the front step, using a twig to scrape paint off my fingernails. He coasted the pickup into the driveway. The whole truck was covered in mud. Where do you find mud in this world? Driving up a sprinkler road, maybe. He got out of the truck. He was muddy. His shoes, his britches. He might as well have been a dog that had run away and come back home for all the answers he could give me. I didn't even ask.

We stood next to one another, me covered with red paint, him crusted with mud, and watched the sun sink. The edges of the clouds glowed orange. An owl hooted in the patch of trees north of the house.

I said, "That's a good sunset."

Pa said, "*Potential* sunset, son."

CHAPTER 17

CEMETERY

"I don't want you driving anymore."

Pa was quiet. We were eating breakfast. Canned peaches with syrup.

Pa said, "I'll drive where I want."

"I reckon you will."

"I'm going to go for a drive right now." He put down his fork and went to the garage.

I'd hidden the key. He wasn't gonna go for shit.

He came back. "Where's the?" He twisted his hand like he was turning a key.

"I ain't seen it."

"Bullshit." He was mad.

"Maybe you lost it."

His eyes went into slits. He wouldn't lose that key. He placed it on the dashboard every time he shut off the engine. Every single time. You could see him thinking, Do not lose the key. He had trained himself. He did not lose that key and he knew it.

"I don't need a babysitter."

"I suppose not."

"Get out."

"Get out?"

"Leave this place."

I said, "Who's gonna cook your dinners?"

"I know how to work the microwave."

"You gotta get food into your belly."

"I can make belly."

"You can't find your key."

"What key?"

"Touché."

"Get out."

He made a fist. I got out.

I took my car. First, I drove by Vaughn's place. His mom's car was in the driveway, so I went to Clarissa's. She wasn't home. I went inside anyway. I was hungry. Her fridge was empty. I sat down on her couch and started reading *Furious Desire*.

It was early afternoon when she came home. Before she came thru the front door, I closed the book and hid it behind my back.

When Clarissa saw me, she said, "Your dad kick you out of the house?"

"You hear that at the bank?"

"You just looked kicked out."

"He's in a bad mood."

"That's because you don't trust him."

"He's never trusted *me*."

"The hell he doesn't. He adores you. He follows you everywhere. Does anything you say. Thinks you're the bee's knees. He's like a puppy when he's around you."

"He ain't my dad anymore."

"No kidding. He's your son. You ain't figured that out?"

"I suppose not."

"Figure it out."

I said, "You been losing some weight."

She stood sideways. "I know."

"You're gonna need to get some new clothes."

"I'm hungry all the time."

"How is that?"

"It's something."

"I think I'm gonna go home."

Clarissa said, "You still wanna rob the bank?"

"Yeah."

"Any new ideas on how we should go about it?"

"Nope. I think our plan's good."

"Really?"

"Good enough."

"Me and Vaughn are ready when you are."

I said, "Don't tell Vaughn about Dad kicking me out."

"I'll try."

"Good enough."

Clarissa approached me, put her hand on my shoulder, and made me lean forward. She lifted up *Furious Desire* from where I had hidden it behind me. She said, "What do you think?"

"It's not as furious as I expected."

When I got home, Pa was poking a jack handle into the juniper bush.

"You sure like to do that."

Pa said, "What are you doing here?"

"You still mad?"

"I ain't mad."

I said, "You sound mad."

"Who gives a shit?" Pa poked the bush some more.

"Why do you keep doing that?"

"Cause God's in there."

"You wanna tell me what you're mad about, Pa?"

"I don't have to tell you things."

"You're just mad, then."

"That's right."

He cocked his ear. He put down the jack handle. Looked at the sky.

I said, "Something up there?"

He didn't reply. He kept looking up. His frown stretched into longing. I figured he was looking at his airplane and Mom and death and freedom. I listened. Faint, way away up there, was honking. Geese. Tiny specks spelling out a V. We watched them cross the sky. From all the years he spent hammering iron, he should have been deaf. But he heard those geese.

I said, "You want to go for a drive?"

"I reckon."

We looked for the pickup key all over the place. In the kitchen, in the junk drawer, in the truck, under the floor mat, next to the gas cap. All over the place. It was in my pocket. When Pa wasn't looking, I wedged it on the concrete floor under the left front wheel.

I said, "Let's look under the truck."

He tapped the dashboard. "It should be here. On this thing."

"Come on. Under."

I wanted him to find it.

He squatted and looked and he found it. "There she is!"

He held the key high.

Everything was okay. I said, "Let's go for a drive."

"Where should we go?" It was crazy how happy he was.

"How about a cemetery?"

Dad drove, of course. I figured we'd go to the old Mennonite church and poke around my great-grandparents' tombstones, maybe stir up some shred of nostalgia in Dad's head. Instead he drove north and west and north and west, following the right angles of the roads. The land grew hilly. Draws and gullies. Places where rustlers once hid. It was a bright, cloudless afternoon. Neither of us wore sunglasses. Dust devils swirled across the prairie. Instead of an intersection every mile, the road became a crooked, meandering thing. Houses, with their Quonset huts and patches of trees, became rare.

As Pa steered us farther and farther from civilization, we neither one spoke. A pheasant rooster scared up from the ditch and we both pointed at it. A jack rabbit raced alongside us. Dad turned the truck down a cattle trail. We called it a cattle trail, but it wasn't a cattle trail. It was a road that hardly ever got drove on. Two ruts with grass down the center. The ride got bumpy. The wildlife grew older. Tiny basking lizards scattered at our approach. Dad swerved to avoid a box turtle.

Finally, the road ended. We continued driving thru the grass. Sagebrush scratched underneath the truck. Dad had that half-smile he got when he was building something. I had that sense of dread I used to get when I rode copilot in his plane. He drove slowly, maybe twenty miles an hour. There were no fences, no power lines, no windmills. I looked behind us. I couldn't see any kind of road.

I said, "I never been out this far."

"Something, isn't it?"

"You know where you're going?"

"Where's that?"

"You know where you are?"

"In my pickup. In a pasture. Wearing clothes."

I saw a critter on the horizon ahead. On the crest of a short hill. Even though it was a long ways off, I could tell it was big, like a bull. There shouldn't be any cattle here. There weren't any fences. I blinked and it was gone.

"You see that?" I pointed to where the thing had been.

"Up there?"

"It looked like a cow or a bull or something."

"Maybe a heifer."

"Coulda been."

"Up there?"

I didn't speak. We continued to roll thru the grass. The truck bounced over a badger mound. On the horizon, the bull thing appeared again, this time with another next to it.

"Pa?"

"Son." He stomped on the throttle. "Let's get a look."

The animals skitted down the hill, away from us. The truck crested the hill. Dad stopped it there on the crest of that little gut valley. Staring up at us were a dozen buffalo, scared and dirty.

People sometimes raise buffalo in Strattford County. A man named McDonagh used to have a herd on Highway 59. But these buffalo didn't look like they were being raised. They looked like they hadn't ever seen a person. I asked Pa if he thought they were wild.

He said, "They're buffalo."

"But they're not the property of anyone."

"It's hard to say who belongs to what." He turned off the engine. The animals watched us with flared nostrils. A bull, some cows, a couple of calves. They were big. If you've seen them in Yellowstone or on the other side of a fence, that's one thing. But sitting in a truck in Strattford County with the window down, looking at a family of wild buffalo, it was like seeing Bigfoot. As far as I knew, outside of national parks, there simply weren't any wild buffalo, anywhere.

Satisfied that we weren't dangerous, a couple of the beasts resumed chewing on the grama grass. Dad opened the door, made like he was going to get out of the truck.

I said, "Hold on. Those things'll put a hole in your liver."

"Yep," he said, "and I hear they smell bad." He stepped out. The buffalo raised their heads again. Pa said, "Lean forward."

I obliged. He unlatched the seat back and tilted it forward. He pulled out a shotgun. "Open that deal there." He was pointing at the glove box. I opened the glove box. A couple of shotgun shells rolled out and landed at my feet.

Pa said, "Hand me them things."

I'm a good son, but I'm not a complete idiot. I didn't hand him the shells.

With an irritated grunt, he leaned into the cab and plucked them off the floor.

I said, "You mind enlightening me as to your ambitions?"

He ignored me as he loaded the shotgun.

"You are not going to shoot a wild buffalo."

The animals formed a nervous line. The big one scratched the dirt with its toe.

With a jerk, Pa pointed the gun toward the sky and pulled the trigger. The air around us popped with a twelve-gauge explosion. The buffalo scattered up the other side of the gut valley and over the hill. The calves sprinted to catch up. Dad laughed. My ears rang.

In the wake of their dust, we were looking at tombstones.

"Look," said Pa. "A cemetery."

The ground was dented with human-sized dimples, presumably from where the earth had sunk into caved-in coffins. There were maybe twenty of these dimples. At the north end of each one was a chunk of sandstone. Wore down, broke over. Only a couple of stones were still standing. No higher than my knees. We walked thru the graveyard in the footprints of the buffalo, looking for a legible word on one of the stones, a belt buckle, anything. Pa turned over a stone with the toe of his shoe.

"That one says something."

I squatted and cleaned the rock with my fingers. Carved indentations, stained the color of tobacco. There wasn't much to read: SHA–ES–EAR– –ILL–AMS. Looking at my own damned grave in a pasture haunted by wild buffalo. Time traveled in both directions at once.

Pa said, "Did you know you had a great-great? I don't know how much, but you had an uncle. We were going to name you after him. We decided not to because it'd be troublesome. But we called you it anyway, sort of. We named you one thing but called you something else. They said they called *him* that because he wanted an English name. The people at the place where his boat landed. Don't know when he died."

I said, "Thank you very much, Ellis Island."

CHAPTER 18

TEST RUN

He actually allowed me to drive back. I took Highway 36, which brought us past the school. Dorton Elementary/Middle/High School. K–12. In a good year, the enrollment for the entire school would reach one hundred and twenty kids. When the new school was built in 1954, it was state-of-the-art. Now it was in a state of disrepair. The windows were stained powdery white, the grass was trampled, leaky gutters left rusty streaks on the beige bricks.

Pa said, "There's a neat old building."

I slowed the truck. "Wanna go?"

"Why not?"

I pulled in. No cars in the parking lot. Thirteen years waiting for the bus, getting chased around the flag pole, trying not to watch car windows steam up while I got in my car to drive home alone after homecoming.

I parked right square in front of the building. We didn't have anything to be ashamed of. We were simply revisiting the old stomping ground.

I opened the glove box and found a Phillips screwdriver, which I put in my pocket. "Pa, let's go to school."

We circumnavigated the building. It remained as square as ever. The doors would be locked, of course, but the window into Mr. Schickle's room had a bad latch and, more important, it was on the back side of the building, hidden from the highway. I squatted, jimmied the screen out, and lifted the window. It slid up with an aluminum screech.

Pa said, "You know what you're doing?"

"I gotta pick up something I left here."

"Why don't you use the door like everyone else?"

I said, "It's locked."

"You know what you're doing?"

I was halfway thru the window. "Come on. It won't take a minute."

He followed me into Mr. Schickle's history room.

It still had the same shitty desks. Chalkboard. Lectern. Window-shade maps. All the lights were off. Ghosts lurked in the corners. Dorton was a small school. Elementary students were two grades to the room. In seventh grade, you moved to the west wing with the big kids. From then on, you had the same history teacher, English teacher, math teacher, and so on until you graduated. Everyone got to know each other real well. It's no good talking about it. But the air in that room was thick. No need to stick around and pry things out, we had a mission to complete. I had to steal something. I wasn't sure what that would be. I figured I'd know it when I saw it. I didn't see it in Mr. Schickle's room.

Pa followed me out the door and into the hall.

He said, "It's dark."

Sure was. It made things creepier. The lockers. The tile floor. Pa took a drink from the water fountain. He smacked his lips. "Good stuff."

Into the gym. Hopes and dreams and P.E. and dances and lunchtime lounging. We crossed the floor in our street shoes. Nothing worth stealing here. Not even a basketball.

On the other side of the gym was the entrance to the school shop. The door was locked. I gave Pa the screwdriver and said, "Can you pop out those hinge pins for me?"

He said, "We're not supposed to be here."

"Nope. But I don't give a damn."

He looked at me for a moment. "Me neither."

He whacked the handle of the screwdriver with the heel of his hand and worked the pins out. The noise echoed in the gym. We jittered the door out of the frame, leaned it against the wall. There, before us, was the shop. I wasn't so good in shop.

The Future Farmers of America creed was inscribed on a plaque nailed to the wall.

I believe in the future of agriculture, with a faith born not of words but of deeds—achievements won by the present and past generations of agriculturists; in the promise of better days through better ways, even as the better things we now enjoy have come to us from the struggles of former years . . .

I used to know that thing by heart. I suspect Dad did, too, when he was a kid.

The shop was clean. All the tools were put away, the welders in a row, the floor swept. It was nothing like the chaos of Pa's shed. I should have excelled here, but everything I made came out crooked and flimsy. I couldn't weld, saw, route, measure, hammer, or screw. I tried chewing tobacco and puked on my shoes. No regrets. Some people aren't built for chew.

There wasn't anything in the shop that I felt like bringing home with me.

The shop was adjacent to the music room. They were connected by a door whose purpose no one ever ascertained. It was kind of like one of those doors that links two hotel rooms. I crossed the floor, tried the knob. This door wasn't locked.

A word about our music teacher. Mr. Pridgon was his name. He didn't care for music or children. As far as I knew, he was still the Dorton music teacher. When I was in school, he yelled at us and pounded on the piano and generally made our lives crummy for forty-five minutes a day, three days a week, from kindergarten thru sixth grade. Even so, me, Vaughn, D.J., Clarissa, and the rest of the bums in my class would do our best to sit and sing "Old Black Joe" like good little boys and girls because if we acted real nice Mr. Pridgon would sometimes let us have Music Free Time.

Music Free Time meant we all got to go into the instrument closet, pick out anything we wanted, and play it as loud as we could for ten minutes. The first three minutes of MFT were typically spent arguing over who got to play the snare drum. Once we sorted ourselves out, the class became an avant-garde symphony. Snare drum, bass drum, piano, horns, out-of-tune guitars, and an assortment of percussive things. Mr. Pridgon never tried to teach us how to play anything. He just counted to four and away we went with our barbaric commotion. It was pure joy. It was like vandalizing the air itself. Something as simple as sliding a mallet up and down a glockenspiel could make you feel wild and free, as if you were throwing rocks thru windows.

Music class ended at seventh grade. The school didn't have enough money to pay Mr. Pridgon to teach the older kids.

For the first three decades of its existence, though, Dorton *was* able to afford a full-time music teacher and an actual high school pep band, which explained all the instruments in that closet.

Along with those instruments, there were two dozen band uniforms. They hung in the very back of that same closet, dusty and ignored.

I remember when I saw my first photograph of Jimi Hendrix looking stoned and cool. I was a sophomore, reading one of Vaughn

Atkins's *Rolling Stone* magazines, and there he was, the supreme badass of the universe, and he was wearing a band jacket.

The next day at school, I slid up to Mr. Pridgon in the cafeteria and asked if I could please have one of the band jackets.

"No."

"But nobody uses them anymore."

"They were bought with tax dollars."

"So?"

"So go finish your chimichanga."

No band jacket for me.

Pa was silent now, tiptoeing. I said, "Breathe with your mouth wide open. It's quieter that way." He complied. He was my accomplice. We were a team. This was excellent preparation for the bank robbery.

We crossed the threshold into the music room. High ceilings. No windows. The air was cool. Pa said, "I believe it's time to shed some light on the situation." He flipped the switch. The fluorescents flickered on. In the center of the room was Mr. Pridgon's blond, upright piano. "Old Joe Clark," "Blow the Man Down," "Biscuits and Gravy." I plunked a few keys. Dad sat on the bench next to me. We sang "Twinkle, Twinkle, Little Star."

When we finished "Twinkle, Twinkle," I closed the piano lid.

I said, "Let's get what we came for."

In the music room closet, past the shelves of horns and guitars that nobody ever tuned, past the forest of music stands that never got used, was the rack of uniforms, still untouched. It's possible that some of Pa's classmates wore those jackets years ago.

I took one off its wooden hanger. "DHS" was embroidered on the back. Epaulets. Black with gold trim. I slid into it. I was wearing the skin of Jimi Hendrix.

It fit tight. My arms stuck out the sleeves. It made me want to play an instrument. Music Free Time. With Pa's help, I pulled cases off the shelves until we found a trombone. I stuck the mouthpiece in the pipe and let Pa try. Nothing but wind.

I took the horn from him and said, "I'll show you." I gave a blat and slid the slide. It made a comical sound.

Pa laughed for ten solid seconds. "Your face turned ten shades of purple."

I showed him how to play it. "It's easy. Put your lips together and make fart noises."

He played the trombone. Fiddled with the slide. Random sounds, then more serious. His brow furrowed. He wanted to figure it out. He made a crude scale, which he repeated rhythmically. It sort of resembled the first few notes of a Johnny Cash song. I found some mallets and started playing along on the glockenspiel. Then I found a bigger mallet and whacked the bass drum. Dad banged on the piano. I played the snare drum, oh, beloved snare drum. THWAP THWAP THWAP. Dad marched and smashed the cymbals. KERRAANNNG! Pure racket, pure transgression.

When our song was played out, I conducted us to a triumphant conclusion. Dad applauded. I raised my arms in victory and then bowed. The band jacket split down the back.

Dad thought it was funny. I thought it was awful. Then I looked down at myself and realized I never would have worn the thing in public anyway.

We packed the instruments away. I left the jacket on the piano seat. I stole a tambourine instead. We exited the way we came in. It took a few minutes to put the pins back in the hinges of the shop door. I played the tambourine as we walked thru the gym, down the hall, thru the cafeteria and then we froze in place because we were not alone.

Someone had turned on the lights in the kitchen. I put my finger on my lips and pointed at the serving window. Dad understood the situation. He looked at the tambourine I'd been shaking. I stuck it under my shirt as quietly as I could. The jangles clacked together softly. Pa motioned that I should leave the tambourine on the floor. I shook my head no. That would be a waste of a trip.

In order to return to the history room and sneak back outside, we'd have to get past that serving window. From far back in the kitchen, I heard the sounds of cabinets being opened, then something heavy being moved. Whoever was in there, they didn't know about us. I crouched into a duck walk and scooted along below the view of the serving window. Dad followed in a crawl. Once we were past, we walked quickly to the history room. We twisted ourselves outside and stood, blinking and breathing.

Pa said, "What do we do now?" He sucked nervously on one of his cheeks. All his life, he hadn't broken the law or done stupid things. He'd never been in a situation like this before.

I said, "There's currently someone in the school. They're in the kitchen, which has a view thru the cafeteria right out onto the parking lot. If we get in the truck, they'll see us. Of course, whoever's in there will probably recognize your truck so they'll know it was us no matter what. But maybe they don't know we were actually inside. For all they know, we've been tossing a Frisbee on the football field. Of course, we were making a lot of noise, but the music room's a long way away from the kitchen. They might not have heard us. So, in conclusion, let's hide and wait until whoever is in there decides to leave."

He walked. I followed. There's a little hill next to one corner of the school. It comes up to about five feet below the roof.

Pa said, "That's where you want to go."

Standing on the hill, I boosted him up and then he lent me a hand and we were on top of the building. We sat still and waited.

The sun was bright. Pa lay on his back and instantly started snoring. I wandered around the building and looked out over the parking lot. There was our truck. Next to it was a '72 Chevy Nova. The one that belonged to our drug-peddling, skunk-smelling friend, D.J. Beckman.

I became more curious than nervous. I sat on the edge of the roof and resolved to wait for him to leave.

Ten minutes later, I watched as D.J. strode out the front door with a two-gallon can of tapioca pudding under each arm. I knew it was tapioca pudding because D.J. and I had hefted a million of those green-and-yellow things when the two of us were cook's assistants in sixth grade. He set the cans on the passenger seat, started the car, and drove away.

I woke up Pa. We crawled off the roof, got in the pickup, and went home. I hung the tambourine on a nail above Mom's piano.

Pa fell asleep in his chair before I made dinner. When I woke him up he didn't want to eat. I let him go to bed without brushing his teeth.

Later on, as I sat in bed reading the novelization of *Aliens*, I got to thinking about the last few days. A whole lot had happened. I lost Pa. I painted the granary. Pa came home. I went to Clarissa's. I came home. We saw buffalo in a cemetery. I learned how I got my stupid name. We broke into the school. I stole a tambourine. We didn't get caught.

I got to thinking that we really could rob that bank.

CHAPTER 19

MEMORIAL

The granary fell down. Maybe it was the paint I put on it. Maybe it was the wind. The building wobbled. Dad and I watched. Just before it happened, a white barn owl burst out from under one of the eaves and flew away with the wind. Then the granary slow-motioned to the earth like an old dog lying down. You could hear rusty nails creaking thru the wood as the building lost its shape. That was the that of that.

Dad said, "You can't win 'em all." I had to excuse myself to the bathroom so I could cry for a minute.

The farm was still falling apart.

Turns out Vaughn Atkins killed himself that same day. Clarissa called and told me. She was all tore up. Between sniffles, she said, "At least he's finally out of the basement."

I thanked her and hung up. Then I cried. I didn't make it to the bathroom this time. *Out of the basement.* It was corny of Clarissa to say it. But it got me. If I had just gotten him out of that hole and away from his mom. Just one more step. Dad asked me what was my damn problem. I rubbed my nose with my shirt.

"Vaughn Atkins's dead. Killed himself."

Dad got quiet. "Oh."

"You know Vaughn, right?"

"The kid with the . . ." He pantomimed rolling a wheelchair.

"Yep."

"What happened?"

"He killed himself."

"Oh. He wasn't real healthy."

I said, "Not for a long time. Not since he broke his back." I got profound in my misery. "The day he wrecked his car, that's the day he died." I sniffled.

Dad gave me his handkerchief. He said, "He's more dead now."

I turned on the TV. Clint Eastwood was eating poisonous mushrooms.

The funeral was three days later. We didn't go to the ceremony. Clarissa told me that she heard that Vaughn's mom didn't want us within a hundred miles of her boy. Vaughn's mom thought it was our fault. She thought we'd gotten him riled up. She wasn't altogether wrong.

We gathered in Clarissa's trailer instead. She was wearing a black dress. It looked new. Fitted good. More of a cocktail thing. She was definitely losing weight. Compared to her, Dad and I were a couple of sloppy dogs in our work shirts and dirty jeans. Clarissa offered us beers. I said no, thanks, and so did Dad.

"Still not drinking?" said Clarissa.

"When I drown my sorrows in booze, they always swim back up, wet and breathless." I'd been rehearsing that line.

Clarissa said, "That leaves more for me." She fetched a beer.

We sat on the couch. The TV was tuned to cartoons. Clarissa said, "You can change the channel if you want."

I found the remote and gave it to Dad.

I told Clarissa that I thought her dress looked nice. She didn't say anything. We watched Dad press buttons on the remote. He changed the channel, found snow, turned the volume up until white noise filled the room. He gave me the remote. "I don't know what to do with this damn thing."

I pushed the "Off" button. The screen shrunk into black. We stared at it for a while. I thought about Vaughn Atkins. Running in the playground, happy birthdays, not knowing what to say when he rolled into school after he got out of the hospital.

Dad said, "Why are you crying?"

I thought he was talking to Clarissa, but he was looking at me. I put a hand to my cheek. Sure enough, it was wet.

I said, "Well, Pa, Vaughn Atkins—"

Dad snapped his fingers. "That's right. He killed himself."

Clarissa shook her head like she had made up her mind about something. She spoke with her lips twisted. "It's a shame. It's a crying shame." She hugged herself and cried and moaned and shuddered. She tilted her beer up to her mouth but it was empty.

I fetched another one from the fridge and tried to hand it to her. Her eyes were squeezed shut. She waved me away, then beckoned me back. She grabbed my free hand and pulled me in close.

I wasn't raised as a hugger—there aren't many huggers in Strattford County—so it was awkward at first. She was sitting on the couch and I was holding an open beer. I kind of leaned over and put my arms around her shoulders. She stuck her face into my armpit and sniffled and heaved. I squeezed her arms. It's funny, the things you think about when you're hugging a woman. We hugged and I let a few tears fall out. Dad stood up and joined us. We were a sorry, hugging lot.

We moved to the front step just to get outside. Dad walked around the property, kicking weeds. The sun was about noon high.

"I'm inconsolable," said Clarissa. She was still crying but not so much.

I said, "Yeah."

She took a deep breath. "They're going after D.J. Beckman."

"Who? What for?"

"The sheriff. For giving Vaughn the drugs."

"Sleeping pills?"

"Something like that. They don't know for sure. But they think D.J. sold them to him."

"That ain't illegal, is it?" I realized that I had just said something stupid. "I mean, it's not murder. It's selling drugs."

"They can still arrest him." She played with one of her toenails.

I said, "I saw something funny the other day. Dad and I were sitting on top of the school building and D.J. Beckman came out the front door with two giant cans of tapioca pudding. What the hell would he want with tapioca pudding?"

Clarissa smiled a little bit. "What were you doing on top of the school?"

I smiled a little bit. "Stupid stuff. Working on our tans."

She slammed her fist against the step. "This town sucks. This place sucks. It makes you do stupid stuff. I hate this town."

"Everybody hates their hometown. Especially people from Dorsey."

"What do you know? You been gone. This place is falling to shit. You don't see how people are going broke. I work in a bank, you know. I see it all the time. It's sad. And poor Vaughn. He disappeared off the planet. He's just a cripple in a basement. He was. Nobody ever came to visit him. His mom was a mean old biddy. And you tried to be his friend but now you feel guilty about it because he's gone. You shouldn't, though. You were trying to be his friend. And D.J. Whatever you might think of D.J., he's just a big dumb person who says dumb things. He acts like a bully because he doesn't know what else to do. He tried to be Vaughn's friend, too. D.J. did Vaughn a favor when he got him those pills, but he's gonna go to jail. And everything Vaughn ever was, that's all gonna disappear." Her voice got loud now.

"And we aren't even allowed to go to his goddamned funeral!" She stood up and threw her beer bottle as hard as she could. It landed intact on a patch of buffalo grass.

I wanted to explain to Clarissa that I was pretty bent out of shape myself. My cat died. My dad was sick. Strattford County had pulled me back into its clutches. The bank stole our stuff. Vaughn was my pal, too.

This was Clarissa's time to be mad, though, so I buttoned my lip.

Dad wandered over and picked up the bottle. He brought it back to Clarissa.

She said, "I'm sorry, Emmett."

Pa said, "We should go for a drive."

Since Vaughn's mom wouldn't let us go to the funeral, we went to Vaughn's mom's house. We took Clarissa's car. She drove. Dad didn't object.

There was no one home, obviously. A bunch of casseroles were cooling on the kitchen table. We didn't linger. We went straight downstairs. Vaughn's bed looked weird without him in it.

I asked Clarissa what the room smelled like.

She shrugged. "A basement."

Dad said, "This is a dead man's room."

I said, "It sure is, Pa."

Clarissa said, "We should search for brownies or pills, anything like that. We need to dispose of any incriminating items. We have to protect D.J."

"I guarantee you the sheriff's already been thru the place."

She said, "Sometimes they miss stuff the first time around."

There was nothing under the pillows. Between the mattresses, we found a dirty magazine and an empty freezer bag. On the night-stand was a film canister full of fingernail clippings. No brownies.

Clarissa pulled out one of Vaughn's Paul McCartney records and held it to her chest. "He loved this album."

I said, "This feels weird. We should go."

"You're right," said Clarissa. But she had a look in her eye. "Emmett, would you mind opening that liquor cabinet over there?"

Dad put his hands on the padlock. He was hesitant. "Is it okay?"

Clarissa said, "It's what Vaughn would have wanted."

She and I excused ourselves to the bathroom and closed the door. She sat on the toilet.

I said to her, "You're after those coins."

"I am."

I said, "You thinking we could still rob that bank, even without Vaughn?"

She said, "I am. Maybe. I don't know."

"I think we could."

"Maybe."

I liked to hear that.

Her stomach growled. I said, "When was the last time you ate anything?"

"Not counting vitamins? June." She sniffed. "By the way, just for your information, this bathroom has a smell. It stinks like bleach and farts."

When we exited the bathroom, Pa was lying on Vaughn's bed with his eyes closed. The safe was not open. But sitting outside of it was a bottle of booze and a bag of coins.

We left the whiskey but we took the wampum.

We hustled out of the basement and into Clarissa's car. When she opened the door to get in, Dad slipped past her and sat in the driver's seat.

Clarissa said, "Emmett?"

Pa put his hands on the steering wheel and stared straight ahead.

I said, "I think he wants to drive."

"Let him," said Clarissa.

I tossed her the bag of coins, shouted, "Shotgun!" and jumped into the passenger seat.

Clarissa climbed in back. "The key's in the ignition, Emmett."

He started the car. Revved the engine. "Where to?"

"My place," said Clarissa.

He said, "What's our ambition?"

I said, "We're gonna decide what to do with those coins."

Dad said, "Those coins aren't yours. They belong to the old man."

I said, "They belonged to Vaughn, Pa. But he killed himself. Now they don't belong to anyone."

Pa was insistent. "They belong to the old man."

"What old man, Emmett?" asked Clarissa.

Dad looked out the windshield. Clarissa repeated her question. Dad didn't say anything. He drove. He turned left when he should have turned right.

"Where are we going, Pa?"

It was a mile before he spoke. "The old man had a place around here. We oughta go there."

Clarissa said, "Do you mean Ernie?"

Dad nodded. "Yes. That's him, Ernie Atkins. We should go see him."

Clarissa said, "Ernie's gone. The place has been empty for thirty years."

I asked, "Who's Ernie Atkins?"

Dad started to answer but Clarissa interrupted. "Vaughn's grandpa. Used to take care of the dump."

I said, "What dump?"

Clarissa said, "The town dump. Before we had the landfill, there was the dump."

"He had a Caterpillar," said Pa. "He pushed all the junk into a pile."

"That's right," said Clarissa. "Set fire to it every Sunday afternoon. You could set your direction by looking for that smoke. That's what they say, at least. He's been dead a long time."

Dad said, "He's dead?" He thought for a minute. "Seems I heard something about that."

All of a sudden, Clarissa got a look on her face. Kind of dreamy and excited at the same time. She said, "Let's put those coins in a hole in the ground."

That seemed like a weird thing to say. I didn't say anything back to her.

"Let's bury 'em," she continued. "They don't belong to you or me or Emmett. Vaughn's mom sure don't deserve 'em. Vaughn was the rightful owner but he's dead. So let's give them back to Ernie."

"You wanna bury that bag of coins in a hole in the ground."

"Or drop it in an old outhouse. Something like that."

I said, "What about the bank?"

"What *about* the bank?"

"We had plans. You were in favor of those plans a while ago."

"I said maybe. And I was being inconsolable at the time. But I'm feeling a lot better. I've got focus. Don't you see?"

I said, "I see that your head's all over the place. You're grieving. I had a focus, too. I *have* a focus. I want to rob that damned bank and scram ourselves out of Strattford County."

"That idea's pure crazy and you know it."

I turned around in my seat so I could look at her. "I don't think so. Not a bit. Up until half a minute ago, you didn't think so either."

She said, "I haven't eaten in weeks. I'm weak and tired and I'm getting annoyed with all your second-guessing. We're burying the coins. Shut up. Leave me alone. This is what Vaughn would have wanted." She crossed her arms and pouted. The way her arms pushed up her boobs, it was distracting.

I said, "The coins were important to him."

"You said yourself that they were just symbolic. We don't even need them."

"They represent Vaughn and everything he stood for."

She said, "What did Vaughn stand for again?"

I kept quiet. Vaughn didn't stand for anything.

"See?" said Clarissa. "He wouldn't give a damn what we did with the coins. As long as we did something." Her stomach growled.

"How do you know what Vaughn would give a damn about? Maybe he'd want us to rob the bank. And if you're so hungry, then eat something." I looked at her. "Jesus. You're just about sexy right now."

She hit me on the back of the head and half-screamed, "It's not about sexy, you cro-mag! It's about boredom and self-esteem and addiction. It's about everything *but* sexy. HAVEN'T YOU EVER READ *SEVENTEEN*?!?"

"Seventeen what?"

"It's a magazine. It's a stupid magazine that stupid people read and it has all sorts of stupid articles about stupid eating disorders and my point has nothing to do with that stupid magazine. I just want to bury those coins."

She wasn't going to get to me by being all dramatic. No pity here. She was breaking my dreams. "Why don't you jus—"

Pa slammed on the brakes so hard Clarissa bounced into the back of my seat and I bounced against the windshield. The car skidded to a stop in a cloud of dust.

I looked at Clarissa. She looked at me. We both looked at Pa.

He said, "Knock it off!" He said it like a father. "Yelling in my ear! I don't care about your anything. You both need to be quiet or I'll take you out of this car and put you in the ditch."

We told Pa we were sorry. He started driving again. We sat quiet and watched the prairie crawl past the windows. After a couple of minutes, Clarissa said, "Shakes, you're right. I was stupid. We don't need to bury the coins."

I'm worthless when people get apologetic. I tried to stay angry but I failed. I said, "No. I was an asshole. You were right. We should bury them. There's different ways to rob a bank."

Clarissa thought. "How about we bury just one coin? When we get to the old Atkins place, we'll bury one coin. It'll be our funeral for Vaughn. We'll take care of the bank with the rest. How's that sound?"

This was called compromise. I liked it. I said, "It sounds real good. And after the job, we'll still have those coins, right? We can bring them back to the Atkins place and bury them then."

She handed me the bag of coins. She said, "I'm sorry I got so mad."

I set the bag on my lap. "Me, too." I meant it. I don't know. When your friend kills himself it's hard to be normal.

She tapped my shoulder. "Did you mean what you said?"

"What part?"

"About being just about sexy."

"I wish you'd eat something."

Dad said, "Eat me."

"It's up here, I think," said Pa. He turned left. We were north of Highway 36. The highway divides the country into north and south. Being from the south side, I didn't know the north very well. Nothing much to distinguish one side from the other, just a bunch of wheat, grass, corn, and, every couple of miles, a house surrounded by a cluster of trees.

"You sure it's not on Road J?" said Clarissa. "I thought it was on Road J."

"We're okay," said Pa.

"We're going to the old Atkins place, right?" said Clarissa.

Pa said, "We're okay."

I could tell Clarissa wasn't so sure about that.

I said, "He'll get us where we're going."

We drove for half an hour. It seemed like he was zeroing in on a place, but we never got there. We'd come to an abandoned farmhouse, Clarissa would declare it the old so-and-so place but not the old Atkins place, and we'd move on. Clarissa kept nudging Pa to drive to Road J. He wouldn't do it. He started sweating. My pa was lost and he couldn't admit it. The bag of coins got heavy on my lap. It made my legs numb.

"What're we doing, Pa?"

"I'm driving."

"You know where you're going?"

"Well . . ." His voice was shaking. Not out of anger but uncertainty.

I tried a new angle. "Hey, Pa. We were thinking about going to the old Atkins place so we could drop off some coins that belonged to Ernie. How's that sound?"

"That sounds all right."

"You know which way that might be?"

"What might be?"

"The old Atkins place."

He said, "Just up here. I think."

It was hot. My forearm was getting sunburned hanging out the window.

In the mirror, Clarissa looked at me and shook her head. We pulled into the driveway of an abandoned farmhouse. A rotten barn, a chicken house, a windmill, and a stock tank. Everything rusted and shitted out. "This isn't the Atkins place," said Clarissa.

Dad ignored her. He shut off the car and put the key on the dashboard. He got out.

"I don't like this," said Clarissa.

"What about it?" I said.

"You hear things about this place."

I said, "Pa's never led us wrong." I thought about the buffalo and the cemetery. "It might not be where we want to go but it's something good, I bet."

She said, "I'll stay in the car."

I handed her the sack of coins. "Pick out a good one for burying." I followed Pa. The grass was tall. They say there's lots of rattlers north of the highway. I stepped carefully.

I caught up. "You think this is the old Atkins place?"

"Atkins place?" he said. "No. This ain't it. I think your grandma might have gone to school in that building." He walked toward the rotting house.

It didn't look like a schoolhouse to me. But Pa was never wrong when it came to this sort of thing. It was Grandma's old schoolhouse. Had to be. There was probably an old stove inside, where Grandma would have brought in wood for the fire on a snowy day. Pa didn't lead me wrong.

As we walked to the house, I noticed that the grass outside had been stomped down flat. I pointed this out to Pa.

He didn't seem to care. I figured it for cattle, maybe. Or deer or coyotes. There was a pile of beer cans. Fresh, not faded like cans get from sitting in the sun. Probably from high school kids using the place for parties and whatnot.

Pa walked up the front porch and opened the door. I followed. The ceiling was halfway caved in. I could see a blue tarp had been dragged over the hole. An empty can of tapioca pudding sat on the floor. Big old can.

I whispered, "We should not be here."

"It's all right," said Pa. He walked across the squeaky floor. There wasn't any glass in the windows. Just shards on the floor.

He was looking around like he knew the place. He probably did. It wasn't Ernie Atkins's house, though, and Grandma damn sure never went to school here. Pa knew the place. I saw him working over nostalgia that he couldn't place. It existed. He was here. But there was no putting it together.

I heard a noise. So did Pa. We stood quiet. On the far side of the room, there was a closed door. Something was creaking on the other side of that door.

He pointed to the door. "Let's go into that room there."

He walked across the room. I followed a few steps behind. He pushed the door open. It was the master bedroom. I could tell it was the master bedroom because there was a mattress on the floor.

It was stained with brown splotches and upon it was a woman on all fours, naked. Her hair was cut short and her elbows were locked. Her tits sagged like udders. A man was pumping her from behind. His fingernails, where they sunk into her ribs, were dirty like grease. The man and woman were totally silent. Creak, creak went the mattress. The man had his eyes closed, nose pointed at the woman's spine. The woman looked up at us. Her eyes were yellow. Dad and I stood like cattle. Dad's hand was still on the doorknob. The woman bared her teeth.

I pushed Dad's hand off the knob. He was staring at the woman with a look on his face. Startled. Shame. Amazement. He didn't have a lick of fear. He sort of cocked his head. It was curiosity is what that look was.

I pushed him backward, away from the door. The man with the dirty fingernails grunted. He still didn't see us. The woman saw us. She hissed. We ran thru the house, crunching on broken glass, and escaped to the outside.

There were children. Three of them. A toddler and a couple other kids, three, maybe four years old. They were all dressed in raggedy clothes and talking to Clarissa, who was leaning out the passenger window with her chin on her arms. When they saw us, the kids scattered. I pushed Dad into the driver's door, shoved him across the seat onto Clarissa's lap, and put the key into the ignition.

"What the hell?" said Clarissa.

I drove the car onto the road. I said, "Them kids you were talking to."

"Yeah," said Clarissa.

"We found their parents."

After we were down the road a ways, I pulled over and we got everyone rearranged with Dad in the back seat and Clarissa sitting shotgun. I drove back onto the road and explained about the mattress and what was going on in that room. Clarissa just said, "Squatters. Poor squatters. Leave them be."

"What about the tapioca pudding? There was an empty can of tapioca pudding on the floor of that place."

She said, "If you're curious about tapioca pudding, go see D.J. Beckman. I'm sure he ain't at Vaughn's funeral right now. And I bet he's freaking out about the cops and all the pills and stuff. He could use a visit."

It had been a long day. I said, "What do you think, Pa? You up for more running around?"

"Old Man Riles."

"Say again?"

"That place we were at. Old Man Riles lives there. He fixes watches. Smart fellow."

"Used to live there," said Clarissa. "He's in heaven now."

"There ain't much room up there," said Pa.

I drove us to D.J. Beckman's house. He was mowing his lawn in cutoffs and flip-flops. No shirt. One of those types that still think sunburns are fashionable.

We got out of the car. D.J. saw us and shut off the mower.

"Afternoon."

"Hotter than a witch's tit," said Dad.

D.J. said, "Why ain't you folks at the funeral?"

I said, "We were disinvited."

"What funeral?" said Dad. We ignored him.

Clarissa asked, "Everything going okay?"

A lit cigarette appeared in D.J.'s hands. He took a hard drag. "Dandy."

"What funeral?" said Dad.

"We were just at Vaughn's mom's place," said Clarissa. "We combed the basement for incriminating evidence."

"Find anything?" said D.J.

"Nope," said Clarissa.

D.J. cocked his head at Clarissa in her black dress. "You lost some weight, didn't you?"

Clarissa smiled. "Are you worried? About the sheriff?"

D.J. shrugged. "I got more on them than they got on me. You know who oughta be worried is your pals there." He pointed his chin at Pa and me. "Breaking into schools. That kind of thing will go on your permanent record."

"What are you talking about?" said Clarissa.

Good. She was making like she didn't know anything.

"Seems I heard somewhere that your two friends recently entered Dorton School in an unauthorized capacity."

I shook my head. "Hardly."

"I saw your truck in the parking lot."

"Because we left it there. We carpooled to Strattford with some friends. Gas ain't cheap."

"Is that why you were making all that noise in the music room? Banging on shit. Hollering like a pair of morons."

Dad said, "Who's having the funeral?"

D.J. said, "Musta been real fun, all that noise. Good old days. Music Free Time?"

No need to keep playing dumb. I said, "It sure was." My neck hairs stood up. "And maybe you could explain a thing or two about tapioca pudding."

"I don't know what you're talking about," said D.J. His lips were lines.

Clarissa said, "I don't know what either of you are talking about."

Dad said, "All I know is that someone died and there's a funeral but I don't know who it's for."

I said, "Tapioca pudding."

D.J. squinted at me, like he was trying to be Clint Eastwood. "You best leave it alone." He was scary in that way that angry, shirtless people get. Like he could try anything. I bet he carried a set of brass knuckles in his back pocket. I didn't care.

I opted not to leave it alone. "It's just weird, is all. How pudding travels from place to place."

Clarissa looked from D.J. to me and back. She chewed her lip, probably trying to decide if she should intervene.

D.J. made a little nod, like he'd made up his mind about something. "See, I'm helping out some friends. The economy being what it is and all. They're in the same boat you're in, Shakes. Or will be once the banker gets your pa's farm. Might want to stay on my good side in case I gotta go Robin Hood on your behalf, too. I'm an altruist, remember?" He pinched the cigarette dead and flicked it away.

I winked at him as maliciously as possible.

Pa yelled, "Whose fucking funeral?!?"

"Vaughn Atkins, Pa. Vaughn Atkins is dead."

Pa said, "Seems like I heard something about that. Killed himself."

"So they say," said D.J. "Believe half of what you see and none of what you hear, that's what *I* say. One thing I heard is that he had a real fancy coin collection. The kind of thing that people would"—he paused—"covet."

"So what?" said Clarissa, with just a tad too much defensiveness.

"I'm just repeating things I heard. Or read. Or saw."

"You're not making sense," said Clarissa.

"Death never makes sense," said Dad.

D.J. said, "Old Vaughn, he liked you guys a whole bunch."

I said, "That's comforting."

"Really, he actually said that. It's in his note." He reached into his pocket and handed Clarissa a piece of paper.

Clarissa looked at it for a few moments. "Where'd you get this?"

"Underneath his pillow. I snuck into the house last night after Vaughn's mom passed out drunk. I appreciate your efforts and all, but I like to clean up my own messes."

Clarissa handed me the paper. Her hand was shaking. "It's Vaughn's note."

I read it.

———————————

Dear God,
    I ate some pills. Tell Shakespeare and Clarissa
they can have my priceless coin collection. Mom,
you can eat shit.
    P.S. D.J., thanks for your help.

Sure enough, Vaughn liked us.

Nobody talked as Clarissa drove us back to her house.

Before we got out of the car, Clarissa said, "You think D.J. could help us with the bank?"

"How so?"

"I don't know. Something."

I pretended to think for a moment. "No."

"Why?"

"He's a jackass."

Clarissa said, "I suppose."

"Don't you go telling him about it."

"I wouldn't tell him."

I said, "Just don't."

"There isn't anything to tell him."

"That's right."

We got out of the car.

I said to Clarissa, "And put those coins somewhere safe."

"They're safe."

"Where are they?"

She smiled and twitched her head a little. "I gave them to those kids."

"All of them?"

"The whole bag."

I said, "That was awful nice of you."

I didn't know what else to say. It *was* nice of her. The kids were poor.

Vaughn was dead. The plan was gone. The bank job was a dream. Dumb. Over. Right then, I resolved to let it go.

She saw it in my eyes. She said, "The plan wasn't any good. It was just us talking to a dead guy in a basement."

I let Pa drive back from Clarissa's. He drove and drove, never getting anywhere close to home. He drove slower and slower and the pastures and cattle and wheat fields crawled by. There'd been so many moments when he was a compass that pointed us to where we needed to be. He didn't *know* he was a compass, but he *was*. It happened so many times that I assumed that he always, at the shriveled-up core of his brain, knew what he was doing.

After twenty minutes of random rambling, the fuel needle was touching red and we were nowhere near home. Pa had lost his true north.

He slowed the pickup to a stop. He rubbed the steering wheel with his thumb.

"I don't know where I am."

"Let me drive, Pa."

He agreed, but insisted on sitting in the back of the truck. He howled like a dog all the way home.

CHAPTER 20

PEACHES AND VENUS

Some mornings, while Pa was brushing his teeth or trying to climb into his britches, I'd sneak out of the house and go to the garden to watch the plants grow. I would lie on my stomach with my chin propped up on my fist and stare at one blade of a carrot leaf. At first, it would look as still as anything. Then there'd be a tiny movement, like a wake-up stretch. And as I lay on the ground breathing slow, I'd see that tiny blade uncurl and grow longer, cell by cell.

Mornings in the garden were the prettiest thing I ever saw. Apparently, I'd been watering properly. Everything was stout and green and climbing toward the sky. We had rows of sweet corn, onions, carrots, two kinds of peppers, and some fine, fine tomato plants. The tomatoes had grown out of their cages and started creeping up, out, and over. The plants were already heavy with fruit. It wouldn't be long before they turned red. The whole garden—every part of it—made me happy. Those mornings, I enjoyed every morsel of that happiness right up until Dad walked out of the house with his pants on backward and hollered for breakfast.

While we waited for the garden to get ripe, we continued our canned-food diet. The pantry, which had seemed bottomless a few months earlier, was now almost three-quarters empty. I allowed Dad to choose what we ate. I'd point him to the pantry and tell him to bring me two cans. Whatever he brought back, we ate. Chili and chowder. Ravioli and string beans. Peaches and peaches. I didn't much care for peaches. Sweet and syrupy and that furry, wet skin.

That pantry was going to run out someday. When that day came, I sure hoped the garden would come thru for us. If not, we were looking at a lean winter. I had counted our money and we had twelve dollars between us. Not counting the eighty thousand dollars of debt.

The thing is, we *could* have robbed that bank if Vaughn hadn't killed himself. This is assuming our plan would have worked, which it would have. This is assuming we could have gotten Vaughn out of that basement, which we would have, if he hadn't of killed himself. Now, though, with Clarissa being philanthropical with our coins and me spending my mornings staring at carrot leaves, it was ridiculous to even think about rallying for our last, victorious strike.

Poor Clarissa. In bed one night, dragging myself thru the piss-poor novelization of *Back to the Future*, I started thinking of her. I looked at the clock. It wasn't even ten thirty. She was probably reading a romance novel on her couch. Her TV was probably tuned to the news. I wondered what she was wearing. I wondered if she'd started back to eating yet.

Pa was downstairs, snoring in his bed.

I closed *Back to the Future*, pulled on a pair of britches, and found a T-shirt. It wasn't any trouble sneaking out.

I took the pickup. The moon was big so I decided to drive without the lights on. I eased along, admiring the silver-grey outlines of the ditches, watching out for deer.

A hundred yards from Clarissa's place, I shut off the engine and coasted into her yard. I parked a ways from her house. I didn't want to scare her. The shades were down but I could see the blue of the TV flickering thru the fabric. I sat in the truck for a while with the windows down. Crickets chirped.

I got out of the truck, careful not to make too much noise, and started toward the trailer. The crickets got quiet. I could hear the TV. A commercial for a used car lot in Lakewood. I walked up the steps and knocked on her door.

The TV went silent. The light was still flickering; she must have pressed "Mute" on the remote control. She didn't answer the door. I knocked again, softly. I didn't want to scare her.

Still nothing. Then a walking noise. I could tell she was still losing weight just from the sound of her footsteps. The porch light came on directly to the right of my face. I leaned back to avoid the mess of bugs that headed for the bulb. Then she opened the door and told me to stop lurking around and get the hell inside.

She was wearing a pair of sweatpants and a real loose T-shirt, probably something from her fat days. Her hair was blonder than I remembered it.

She pointed me to the chair across from her sofa and said, "What are you up to, Shakespeare Williams, visiting people at all hours?"

"I was just reading. Started wondering about you."

Her eyes got somewhat slitty. I wasn't sure if she was being suspicious or seductive.

I continued, "I bet myself a nickel that you were reading a dumb romance book and watching TV."

She leaned her head toward her end table. Facedown and open was a book called *Devil's Honeymoon*. "Dumb, yes. Romance, no." She picked it up. "It's this new genre called Jesus Fiction. My mom heard about it from Jerry Linkenbach's mom. Remember Jerry? He was a couple of years younger. I guess he lives in Denver and knows the guy who publishes these things."

She handed it to me. It featured a painting of Satan throwing fireballs at a heart-shaped bed whose occupants resembled Jennifer Aniston and a shirtless Christ.

"Looks pretty good."

"It's less blasphemous than you'd expect. You believe in God, Shakes?"

"Occasionally." I handed her the book.

She looked at the cover and then put it back on the end table. "Things okay at home?"

"Not bad. Dad's asleep."

She said, "What if he has another one of his sleepwalking spells?"

"It's unlikely." I smiled to show that I didn't take offense at the fact that she had just questioned my ability to watch over my own father.

She turned the TV volume back on, low. Curled her legs up underneath herself on the couch. "It's kind of funny, you coming here."

"How's that?"

"I was thinking I might start eating again. I wonder if I have the heart for anorexia anymore."

I said, "I hear it can be unhealthy."

"I saw a thing on the news the other day about pro-ana. You ever heard of it? It's a movement of women—girls mostly—who band together so they can starve themselves to within one foot from the grave. Pro-ana. Pro-anorexia. See? They're taking back the negative connotations of eating disorders. It's mostly on the Internet, with websites and stuff. They share tips on how to deal with hunger pains and they share pictures of each other and of supermodels. They call it 'thinspiration.' The news people were explaining about how awful it was that skinny people were celebrating themselves. It was annoying. Let them be, I say. I shut off the TV and I went online and found a pro-ana website where people were doing a forum to encourage each other."

"Like a blog?"

"No, a forum. You type in questions and other people give you answers. Anybody can do it. You ask for advice on how to avoid gaining weight for the holidays or what vitamins to eat so you don't die. The most popular question, though, was, 'Do you think I'm fat?' When you ask that question, you post a picture of yourself and then other people comment on it. All these people. All these girls were tiny, like they'd just been released from a concentration camp. Everyone would give positive comments. 'You go, girl!' Stuff like that. It was so positive.

"I wanted to be part of that positivity. So I put up a picture of myself. I don't have anything recent, though, so I posted something from last Christmas. My mom took it while I was eating a piece of pie. I was wearing a hideous sweater and I was as fat as I'd ever been in my entire life. It was disgusting. The perfect 'before' picture. I put it up with a note that explained that I'd lost seventy-four pounds since then and how neat it was to meet so many like-minded people."

I said, "You must have gotten a lot of good positiveness."

"The next day, I went back to the forum and there were one hundred and sixty-eight comments on my post. The first one said, 'Seventy four pounds is a good start. But you have a long way to go. Keep trying.' The next one said, 'Yeah. A couple more years and you'll look like a walrus instead of a whale.' The next one was, 'We want thinspiration, not something to make us puke. Next time you want to post a picture of yourself, do us all a favor and go to a bulimia site.' And on and on. I read every one."

I said, "Sounds like a bunch of assholes."

"They weren't all bad. I mean, the first seventy were aimed directly at me. But after that, they started going at each other. There was this one turd who called herself buli-pulpit75. She said,

'I'm bulimic and I think it's totally uncool of you people to say that we're losers.' It turned into a bulimia-versus-anorexia battle for a while. Vicious. Then a crew of badasses came on the scene. They called themselves the Athleticunts. I guess there's a thing called anorexia athletica where people are compulsive exercisers. They rolled in and told everyone to shut the fuck up and grow a pair."

I said, "Pair of what? Tits that look like busted balloons?"

Clarissa snickered. "Finally, someone called acuteangel came in and said, 'I have anorexia nervosa, bulimia nervosa, and anorexia athletica. I'm so weak I can barely type. You are all inside of my soul. It breaks my heart that we're fighting like this. I understand where you're coming from, but this destructive behavior has to stop. We must unite. Can't we all just agree that Orca is a fat cow and let it go?' Just like that, acuteangel saved the day for three types of eating disorders. They hugged and kissed and moved on to the subject of Fiona Apple's ankles. The end." Clarissa took a deep breath. "Sorry for boring you to death."

"You should post a picture of yourself like you are now. That'll shut them up."

Clarissa shook her head. "It won't do anything. Those gals are sick. Their priorities are screwed up, their brains are lying to them, and they can't see straight. I don't resent them. I feel sorry for them. I thought I could be their friend but I'm not one of them. They told me so. So why in the world should I keep trying to be like them? I'm hungry. I want to eat."

"You should eat."

She brought a tin of smoked oysters back from the kitchen and sat on the couch. She said, "Sit here, next to me." I did. Then she put her hand on the back of my neck and pushed my head down so my ear was against her belly. I never heard a stomach make so much racket in my whole life.

I said, "It sounds like a bowling alley in there." I tried to turn around to see if she thought I was funny, but she kept my ear clamped to her belly. My nose was basically in her crotch. I wondered what it smelled like.

I heard her open the oyster tin. Then she said, "Listen to this. Just one, for starters." I could hear her salivate as she put that first oyster into her mouth. *I* started salivating. My head was clamped right between her boobs and her Venus. She may have been skinny, but she was a good kind of skinny. Not that skeleton type, but something with a little cushion.

She swallowed the oyster. Inside her stomach it was like applause. A whole stadium full of people. I heard her slurp some more of the oysters. I could tell she was leaning her neck back and dumping the whole tin into her mouth, oil and all.

The applause grew louder. She thrust her tummy forward. She must have been arching her back in pure pleasure. Who wouldn't? It had been months since she had eaten anything but juice and vitamins.

Just to see what she'd do, I put my hand on her thigh. She ran her fingers thru my hair. It made me feel real happy.

Then she puked on my head.

There wasn't a whole bunch. A plop, really. Plenty enough to ruin the moment. I sat up and sort of waited for her to do something about it. I could feel it in my hair, working its way down to my ear.

Clarissa's mouth opened up and closed again. Her eyes jiggled back and forth. Then she screamed and ran into the bathroom.

She didn't come out for forever.

I went to the kitchen and wetted down a washcloth. I wiped my head clean. When I shook the cloth, a clump of half-chewed oysters landed in the sink. It wasn't terribly pukey. I ran some water, rinsed the mess down the drain. Then I took the cloth into the living room and wiped the couch clean. Wasn't much to it.

She was still in the bathroom. I put my ear on the door. She was brushing her teeth. I knocked on the door. The brushing stopped. I said, "You can come out."

I heard her spit into the sink. I pictured her with the toothbrush half hanging out of her mouth. She said, "I puked."

"It wasn't that bad."

"I have emetophobia, remember?"

"Emetophobia?"

"Fear of vomiting."

I said, "I'm pretty sure it won't happen again. I think you vomited out everything that you put in."

"It got all over you."

"Oysters clean up easy. Come out."

"You don't understand how awful this is for me."

"Sure, I do. You're freaked out. You can be freaked out in there, alone, or you can be freaked out here, with me."

A pause. Then, "Well."

"Good."

"Give me a minute."

The shower turned on. The minute turned into half an hour. I turned on the TV. *The Jeffery Towner Show* was on. All his guests were lousy.

When she finally came out, she was wearing a robe, a real thick, soft-looking number.

I said, "Feel better?"

She said, "Nobody takes emetophobia seriously."

"You're speaking to someone who doesn't have a sense of smell. Talk about not being taken seriously."

She sat down next to me on the couch and said, "Maybe I went too fast."

"You were in there for close to an hour."

"Not the bathroom. The food. The eating."

"That. Yeah, too fast." I took a chance, tried to be cute. "You're just out of practice. Judging by what landed on my head, it appears that you've forgotten how to chew."

Her cheeks bulged. She put her hand over her mouth. I jumped up from the couch.

She stuck out her tongue. "Gotcha."

I said, "Got me good."

She was still flirty. This might work out. I sat back on the couch and waited to see if she'd escalate things.

"You know, Shakespeare, I like the fact that you don't judge people."

I said, "I don't know about that. I got opinions."

"You take things as they come. You don't fight it when something bad happens. You know? With your mom and now your dad. It's tragic, but I've never seen you get overwhelmed. Even with Vaughn, you've been real calm. And when we canceled the bank robbery, you could have freaked out, but you didn't. You just accepted the reality of it. You're like that poem about changing things and not changing things and having the wisdom to walk on the beach alone."

When someone compliments you, you can either say thank you or give them some brouhaha about aw, you're just bein' nice. I kept my mouth shut altogether and instead tried to kiss her.

She turned her head and I ricocheted off. She sat up real straight, like she had an idea. "I was being stupid. Those oysters were too much too soon. I should try something easier." She went back into the kitchen. I heard her poking around in the cupboards. Cranking a can opener. Pouring something into a bowl. Clanking around the silverware drawer.

She came back into the living room with two spoons and a bowl full of peaches. With a fake English accent she said, "Fruit, any-one?"

"No, thanks. I've been eating too damn many peaches lately. Anyway, I'm not a big fan of sweets."

"This isn't sweets, it's fruit."

"When you don't have a sense of smell, peaches is sweets."

"But if you can't smell, then you can't taste. Right?"

"That's what everybody thinks. They're wrong. My nose doesn't work, but there's nothing wrong with my tongue. I get all the salt and sweet and bitter and sour I could hope for. Probably even bet-ter than you. It's the subtle stuff that I miss. Oregano tastes the same as pencil shavings. But canned peaches, they're sweeter than anything should ever be. Plus, I don't care for the fuzz."

Clarissa shrugged. She sat down on the couch and cut off a piece of fruit with the edge of her spoon. She put it on her tongue and savored it. Her eyes rolled up. She moved it from cheek to cheek, chewed twenty times, and swallowed. She waited a moment to make sure it stayed down and then took another, bigger bite.

I watched as she finished the whole bowl of peaches. It took a while because she ate so slow. It was fun how her lips would wrap around the spoon. When the bowl was empty, she brought it back to the kitchen and returned with it filled up with cold SpaghettiOs. She shoveled a spoonful into her mouth. "I can't believe how good this is." She held the bowl toward me. "You want some? It's not sweet."

I grabbed hold of her earlobe, real gently, and said, "You're pretty sweet."

She winked at me. "Sounds like somebody wants to fool around."

"That sounds about right."

She took another bite of SpaghettiOs. There was tomato sauce on the corners of her mouth. "Lemme finish this." She took another bite. A pasta *O* was stuck to one of her eyeteeth. "I've never been so happy in my life."

I stroked her eyebrow and said, "You could be happier, I bet."

"In a minute."

"Yeah, but—" I tried to sound jokey. I even used a fake English accent. "Shouldn't we have some fun now before you start gaining it all back?"

Her face changed. She frowned, her eyes got wet. She looked fat again. Fat and sad. She shook her head. She tried to say something, but nothing came out of her mouth. She pointed to the door.

I got up. "Fine. You slept with my dad."

"I did not."

"You said you did."

"I felt sorry for him. I didn't sleep with him, though. I just wanted him to think I did. What would be the point? He'd just forget about it anyway."

"Yeah, well, so would I."

Pa was still in bed when I got home. I went to sleep without reading any more *Back to the Future*. I thought about what I said to Clarissa. Sometimes you do stupid things.

CHAPTER 21

HERMITS

Me and Clarissa didn't work out. Not as drinking buddies, not as bank robbers, and not as whatever it was we didn't become that night in her trailer. If we'd been destined for some kind of big relationship, it would have started back in high school anyway. As for that night in her trailer, we just proved what should have been obvious already. We tried and it didn't work out. Just because you're the last two people in the world, that doesn't mean you're gonna restart civilization.

I suppose I could have apologized. Except I didn't want to. I just didn't want to. So long Clarissa. Other than Pa, she was the only other person in the world I cared to spend time with. Now she was out. Fine. Life would be easier without her or anybody else. Just me and Pa. For real, this time.

So we settled in. A pathetic, silent good-bye. Pa would grow more and more senile and I'd make sure he didn't do anything to hurt himself. At some point, the bank would take the farm away and then we'd move to a trailer park in Sterling. Once there, I'd get a job at the prison. That's a good job; I'd make enough money for us to enjoy three meals a day. Eventually, Dad would die and I'd be able to find a dream and follow it to its unsatisfactory conclusion.

But before any of that happened, I had a garden to tend.

It was morning, after breakfast, and I stepped out of the house. The biting flies had arrived. Biting flies look like houseflies but they behave like starving dogs. They latch onto your skin and chew. They're quicker than mosquitoes; try slapping them and you only end up giving yourself bruises. With biting flies, you spend a whole lot of time being sore and angry. That is, until you give up, which takes willpower. You have to pretend they aren't there. Sweat drips out of your eyebrows. But eventually you cross a threshold and you become used to them. As they eat their fill, blood trickles down your arms and neck and ankles and you go on with your life. That's how it works. Flies gotta feed their families, too.

Dad was still inside, in the bathroom. He was working on his morning shit, which could take up to half an hour. As I stood in front of the house appreciating the silence, a fly buried its snout into the back of my neck. I didn't move. I let that fly eat itself into happiness. It hurt and then it didn't. Then the fly flew away. I walked to the garden, ready to admire our great, bountiful potential.

At first, I thought the plants had disappeared, like some magical anti-miracle. They were gone, almost all of them. But then I saw the footprints. Deer tracks all over the garden. Big, medium, small. Papa, mama, and baby. Over the night, they'd eaten the carrots, onions, corn, and peppers, all of them right into the ground. You could even see how they'd pulled up the carrots and onions so they could get at the soft parts. Deer are smart.

They didn't touch the tomatoes. Every single tomato plant remained upright and glorious. I knew better than to think the deer had left those tomatoes out of decency. They left them because they knew that, in a few days, those tomatoes would ripen and taste better than anything they'd ever eaten in their whole entire lives.

I couldn't blame the deer for eating our garden. Deer have to feed their families, too. It was a beautiful garden. How could they resist? Except this was the first time I'd ever seen deer tracks this close to the house. Growing up, when I saw deer, they were either lounging in a wheat field, bounding across a pasture, or lying dead on the side of the road. Sometimes, after the grasses were covered by a big snow storm, you'd see signs that the deer had been gnawing on trees. But the deer never came all the way up to the house. It wasn't worth the risk; there was plenty of corn, wheat, and grass for them to eat elsewhere, especially in the summer.

From the front door of the house, Dad shouted, "Anybody out there?"

I hollered back, "Me. Just me."

He joined me in the garden. Even though it was at least eighty-five degrees, he was wearing a winter coat. He didn't seem to mind. He said, "Got something important?"

"Just some tomatoes."

"They're looking good. Did you grow those?"

"We did. Yep."

"That's a hell of a garden."

He was right. The tomatoes were looking good and I sure did grow them. Plump, brownish green, free of insects, well watered, and unmolested by hail or deer.

I figured the deer would get those tomatoes one day, but until that day, I'd enjoy watching them.

A few days passed. Each morning, I'd go out to the garden, expecting to see the tomatoes all eaten up. I suppose I could have sat out nights with a shotgun on my lap. But I probably would have fallen asleep. And if I did stay awake, I can't imagine that I'd actually have the guts to shoot a deer. But let's say I did shoot a deer. Then I'd have to either slaughter it so we could eat it or I'd have to drag it out to a pasture and let the coyotes go at it. Neither of those scenarios seemed worth the trouble. Instead, I relied on hope, but without feeling hopeful.

Every morning I went to the garden expecting to see the tomatoes destroyed. Every morning they were still there.

And then, one day, the tomatoes turned ripe. When I went to
bed they were green; when I woke up they were red. The plants
hung thick with fruit. There wasn't a deer in sight. Maybe those
fuckers just plain didn't like the taste of tomatoes.

I found a five-gallon bucket and brought Pa to the garden. It
was harvest time. Standing there in front of those plants with Pa,
I felt like a farmer. Well, not a real farmer. But someone who had
managed to not preside over the destruction of everything he
planted. Bullshit. I was a farmer. This was our farm. We made food
out of dirt, water, sun, and seeds. It was something, just to stand
there and breathe and let the biting flies chew our ears.

A dove made cooing sounds. Robins and blackbirds and sparrows flirted with one another around the big locust tree.

Pa took off his shoes, so I did, too. The dirt was hot and sandy
and fine. It was like walking in powdered cocoa.

Pa held the bucket perfectly still while I pulled tomatoes off
the vines and dropped them in. He became spacey. The handle
slipped out of his hand. The bucket landed on the ground. I wrapped
his fingers around the handle and helped him lift it up again.

"Hold the bucket."

"Kick the bucket."

"Funny man. Hold the bucket."

We filled the bucket with tomatoes and then brought them to
the house, where we piled them on the kitchen counter. There were
a lot of tomatoes. Bushels. We went for bucket after bucket. We
took lots of breaks for naps.

We brought the last of the tomatoes in just as the sun was starting to lean over. Probably around seven thirty. It was hot inside the
house so we sat on the back step and watched the tiny leaves on

the locust tree go from green to gold. As it got duskier, the millers came out.

A miller moth is about an inch long. They get into everything. They sleep all day. Open the door to the shed and they fly out at you like bats from a cave. Pick up a piece of wood and a hundred of them look at you like they just woke up. Leave the clothes on the line overnight and you'll find them in your underdrawers.

Millers are easy to kill, but they're gooey and their wings leave a shiny flour on your fingers. You'd best leave them alone. There's nothing evil about them. They're not like those biting flies. They're a nuisance, is all.

That twilight, after we'd brought in as many tomatoes as we could, the millers were something to behold. They gathered all around the big locust tree next to the garden. There were so many of them, the birds got scared. A dozen robins and blackbirds and sparrows flapped out of the branches. Millers kept gathering around the tree. Before long, the locust tree was surrounded. I'm not talking about a couple hundred moths. I'm talking about millions. They swirled around like electrified lint. There must have been something sweet in the bark that they wanted to lick with those curled tongues of theirs.

A robin decided to try to eat some of the millers. Birds eat bugs. It's only natural. A robin's gotta feed its family, too. The bird launched itself at the tree and then landed on a springy branch toward the top. The millers went crazy. They stirred up thick enough that you could hardly see thru them. They attacked that robin and he flew right out of there.

Pa said, "I never saw anything like that in my life."

When the sun got low, we walked to the road so we could get a fair view of the western horizon.

"There she goes," said Pa.

"Watch for the green flash."

"What's that?" said Pa.

"They say that when the sun goes down, right after the last bit of sun gets below the horizon, you see a green flash."

"I heard that, too. I think."

"You think it's real?"

He pondered for a moment. "I think it's just your eyes. You ever accidentally look at a welder without a helmet on? For a couple of minutes you have that, um, bright color in your eyes, even when you close them." He paused. "I'm not sure what we're talking about right now."

"That was pretty good, Pa."

The sun became a tiny arc and then it disappeared. I closed my eyes. The tiny arc was still there, in green. "You did good."

Early the next morning, Pa woke me up by poking me in the side. He said, "I want to ride the Rocket."

On the way to the shed, we passed by the ruins of the granary.

"What happened there?" asked Pa.

I said, "It fell down."

"Entropy," said Pa.

The Rocket had a flat tire. I patched it up, put fuel in the tank, and cranked up the engine. It sputtered, chattered, jittered, and settled into an idle. The exhaust was black smoke. I retrieved a screwdriver and twisted a screw on the carburetor until the smoke turned less black.

"Where'd you learn to do that?" said Pa.

"I have no idea." I really had no idea. I'm sure I'd seen Pa do it a thousand times but I had no idea what I'd actually done. Turn a screw and the engine works better.

Dad climbed on the seat, tested the clutch, and then rode the bike out of the shed and onto the farm. "Yippeeeeeeeeeee-eeeeeeeeeeee!"

While he played, I went into the house. The tomatoes were still stacked in pyramids on the counter. I looked thru Mom's recipe box until I found instructions on canning. Her handwriting was pretty. Cursive, with thin loops all leaning to the right at the exact same angle. Nobody writes like that anymore.

Boil water, insert tomatoes, remove tomatoes, put tomatoes in cold water, remove skin, add tomatoes to jars. Poke air out of jars with the handle of a wooden spoon, put lids on jars, boil jars for thirty minutes. Easy.

It was a big, wet mess. Tomato skins got stuck to my shoes. Boiling water spilled on the countertop. My fingers started to hurt from holding hot, wet tomatoes. Satisfaction. I made jar after jar, stacking them up in the pantry, which we had damn near cleaned out. With these preserves, we'd be able to make spaghetti sauce thru the winter. What else do you do with tomatoes? Soup. Other stuff. We had food.

I started to believe we could survive in this landscape, live off the land. If I could grow and can tomatoes, I could sure as hell raise chickens. You feed them, you steal their eggs. When you get hungry for meat, you twist their head off. Pluck the bird, boil it, gut it, cook it, eat it. No need to shoot a deer. Food is simple.

Dad was out there somewhere, riding the Rocket. I was doing domestic stuff. Not domestic stuff—*survivor* stuff. This is how life should be. This is how it should end. We could live like this forever. Fuck the future. Fuck the banker. Fuck Clarissa. Fuck the hospital.

Even after we got kicked off the farm, we'd settle on a spot in a pasture. Maybe in the cemetery where we saw the buffalo. We'd live just like my ancestors. Great-grandpa Williams didn't need a bank. Or a granary. He built his house out of dirt. When his wife died, he buried her in a hole. And he didn't get any hospital bills in the mail.

The mail. I looked at the clock. It was after one. Time for the postman. Time for Dad to bring in the bills so I could ignore them. I hadn't heard anything from Dad in a while. No putt-putts from the Rocket. I turned off the stove, wiped the counter clean, and went outside.

First, I listened. No putt-putts. Next step, I looked for him in the shed. That's right where he was. Sitting on the floor, surrounded by the Rocket. He was holding a combo wrench, sitting with his ass on the concrete.

"I believe I got her," he said, smiling proud.

Every piece of the Rocket was dismantled. The parts were spread around him. Engine out of frame. Piston out of engine. Rings removed from piston. Wheels out of frame, tires out of wheels, tubes out of tires. Reduced to a kit without instructions. Pa's hands were black with grease. His long-sleeved shirt was spotless.

He was proud. He was a little kid. He was my father. He ruined the Rocket.

I said, "Father."

He nodded at me. "Yes, son."

"Dammit, Pa."

"You got a problem?" Cocky.

"The Rocket." My face started curling up like it was about to cry.

He said, "What *about* the Rocket?" Perhaps he sensed that he'd done something wrong. Mostly, he sensed that I was mad at him. No shame. Just contempt at me for losing my cool.

He half-smiled, half-scowled at me. Completely clueless, but thinking he was in control. Up is down and down is down.

I didn't know what to say so I said, "Get out of my fucking face."

He blinked. It felt good to cuss. I did it again. "You stupid son of a bitch. You tore apart the Rocket. Do you know how goddamned hard we worked on that thing? And you tore the fucker apart. Why couldn't you have just driven it into the ditch and smashed yourself to pieces?"

For a split second, he looked hurt. Then he clapped his hands sarcastically. "Your panties are in a wedge."

I started walking. I walked out of the shed and around the building. I walked east across the overgrown runway and into the field where Dad used to plant wheat. It wasn't a field anymore. He'd stopped planting wheat when the government started paying him to let it revert into pasture. Now that the government wasn't paying him anymore, it was just dirt with grass on top.

I kept walking, thru the hip-high grass and over marmot holes. Dad didn't follow me.

A quarter mile from the house I came across a flattened patch of grass. The dirt was trampled with deer tracks. This was where they slept. I stood there, quiet, and turned around in a slow circle. I saw them. They poked their heads up out of the grass just on the other side of their flattened patch. There were three of them. Papa, mama, and baby. The buck had antlers on one side of his head but not on the other. Something must have knocked them off.

The deer stood staring at me, as deer do. I knew they were going to run. I wanted them to stay put. I wanted to pet their noses. I didn't want to hurt them. I smiled. They ran. Big floating bounds.

I walked again. Kept going until I came to the barbed-wire fence that divided our grassland from an irrigated circle that belonged to some farmer who still had a memory and a wife and a son who knew his ass from a hole in the ground.

I couldn't go any further unless I wanted to climb the fence and stomp half a mile thru a million dark-green, shoulder-high corn plants. After that, there would just be another corn field. Then a wheat field. Then maybe some soybeans. Some passenger in a 747 might look down with their binoculars and see me, a little black dot, crossing that endless series of circles and squares. They'd guess at what I already knew. I was nothing in the middle of nowhere.

I turned back toward the house.

This whole farm. My great-grandparents and my grandparents and my parents put it all together. One after the other, they made it better, cleaner, more perfect. But now Pa was tearing it apart. Not just letting it fall apart but actively unbolting the thing and spreading it out on the ground.

I had spent the whole summer trying to hold the farm in place, but there wasn't any good in that. I didn't know what I was doing. I had failed to learn from him when I had the chance. Pa had failed to teach me.

Tomatoes weren't good enough. Tomatoes couldn't stop the wind from blowing and the wood from rotting. They certainly wouldn't slow down a half-wit who could dismantle the place quicker than I could gather the pieces.

If Pa could comprehend what he was doing to his farm, he'd kill himself. He'd probably kill me, too. It made me envy Vaughn Atkins in his hole in the ground.

When I walked back to the house, Pa was sitting on the front step with the mail in his hands, looking lonesome.

He said, "You been gone a hundred years."

I said, "I'm sorry."

He said, "You're sorry, all right. A sorry excuse." Teasing. Not mad at me. He didn't recall anything. He just wanted to play.

When I was a little kid, I used to roughhouse with my dog Jumper. One time, he nipped me on the ankle. He didn't mean to do it. I knew he didn't mean to do it. But whether it's on purpose or not, a dog bite hurts. I swatted him on the head. I damned that dog to hell. He didn't hear me. Instead, he licked my ankle where he'd bit me.

That little act of ignorant fondness made me feel so bad, I swore I'd be kind to Jumper for the rest of his life. He was killed a week later when Ivan Pracht swerved his pickup into him on the dirt road in front of our house.

I said to Pa, "Let's get you burning that mail."

I gave him the matches and pointed him toward the trash barrel. While he fiddled with the fire, I went into the house to cook lunch. I made spaghetti with some of the not-yet-canned tomatoes that were still sitting on the counter. I didn't have a recipe. It didn't matter. You can fake your way thru spaghetti sauce.

As I was salting the pan of boiling tomatoes, the phone rang. I sort of hoped it would be Clarissa so I answered.

The voice in the phone said, "Stacey Williams?"

"More or less."

"It is I, Mike Crutchfield, your banker. The time has come to discuss your father's debt."

"I'm cooking dinner."

"*Pithecanthropus domesticus.*"

"That so?"

"May I speak with Emmett?"

"He's doing chores."

"Can you pass on a word to him, then?"

I didn't say anything.

"You've got a pen, I assume?"

I didn't. I nodded.

"Please inform Emmett Williams that, due to his inability to remit payment for a certain hospital bill and for various other whatnots that would require more time than you or I can reasonably expect to have, the unfortunate, yet inevitable, date of foreclosure is upon us. Necessary papers have been posted to you on several occasions but you have provided neither a response nor an acknowledgment. Not that this would have retarded the procedure. They were merely formalities. It is therefore my distasteful duty to inform you that as of the first of September, a mere seventeen days from now, the Williams estate will formally become the property of the Keaton State Bank. At that moment you will need to vacate the premises. This previous statement is of particular importance. I shall repeat it. As of September first, you will need to skedaddle yourself off of my farm. I can only wish you the best of luck. Good day."

He hung up.

Dad came back from burning the mail. We ate lunch. It was pretty good. Could have used more salt.

CHAPTER 22

RID OUT

On the sixteenth day before the foreclosure, we ate spaghetti with tomatoes for breakfast, lunch, and dinner. Over the course of the day, the phone rang on three separate occasions. I ignored it.

On the fifteenth day, Pa watched TV while I canned more tomatoes. Pa laughed at the commercials where people got kicked in the balls. The phone rang in the morning, in the afternoon, and twice in the evening. I ignored it.

One fortnight before the foreclosure, I tried to look at the finances. Maybe I had missed something. Maybe there was some sort of Medicare or Medicaid thing we could take advantage of. Maybe, shit. Probably. But I didn't know where to start and I didn't know who to call for help. I didn't want to call for help.

I went thru shoeboxes filled with receipts and bills and pieces of paper. I spread them out on the floor and looked at them until my back ached and my head hurt.

I picked up a ten-year-old tax return, tore a page off, folded it into a paper airplane, and gave it a toss. It flew toward the ceiling and crashed on the floor. I made another paper airplane. Then another and another. I made squadrons. Pa helped. He wasn't much for folding, but he could wad the paper into balls.

We threw them at each other. We chased each other thru the house, laughing. When we got tired, we stopped. Then Pa walked thru the house, gathering the airplanes. He placed them on the floor in front of the TV and began flattening them out. He smoothed them and stacked them on top of one another. I sat in a recliner and watched.

The phone rang.

Pa said, "Will you answer that damned thing?"

"Don't wanna."

Two rings.

He said, "It's bothering me."

"Then do something about it."

Three rings.

He stood up and walked to the kitchen, where the phone was hanging on the wall. Two feet from him. He looked around. Couldn't find it.

Four rings.

Pa said, "Where's that damned noise?"

Five rings.

He found the phone, lifted it off the receiver, and said, "Murphy's crematorium. You kill 'em, we grill 'em."

He listened for a moment and then said, "It's for you."

"Shakes?" It was Clarissa. I didn't say anything. It felt like we'd been caught. It felt like she'd poked her head into our private, crumbling world. It felt like I was in a coma and she was talking to me in a dream. It felt like I didn't have anything else to say to Clarissa after I'd messed things up the last time we'd seen each other.

"You there, Shakes?"

"Yeah."

"I've been trying to call. I was worried."

"We're having a good time here." Pa sat back down on the floor and resumed flattening his pieces of paper.

"I heard about it. About the house."

"Oh." Of course she had.

"I'm sorry."

"It's okay. Things happen."

"How's Emmett?"

"Lemme ask him." I said, "Pa, how are you doing?"

He looked up from his piles of paper. "I can't remember."

Into the phone I said, "You hear that?"

Clarissa laughed. "Yep." I heard her lick her lips. "What are your plans? With the house?"

I said, "I don't know. I guess we'll live here until we have to leave. Then we'll leave."

"I've seen this happen before. From where I sit in the bank. It's not that easy. You don't just leave. It's a difficult process. Mentally."

"We'll be okay. When it's time to worry, I'll worry. At the moment, I'm not worried."

She said, "It's time to worry."

"Not yet."

She said, "Don't you care?"

"About what?"

"The farm. Your dad. Everything."

"Whether I care or not, it doesn't make a tick's difference."

"What about Crutchfield?"

"Huh?"

"Don't you care about him?"

"I especially don't care about him. He's a plane-stealing, farm-nabbing prick. What's to care about that?"

"You're angry."

"Do I sound angry? I don't feel angry." I really didn't.

"I'd be angry if I were you."

"You wanna switch places for a couple of weeks?"

"Listen, Shakes. Just don't do anything crazy."

"Like try to rob a bank?"

She laughed again. "Exactly."

"I ain't gonna rob the bank. That idea's over."

"Good. That's not what you need right now. I mean, Crutchfield isn't evil. I know you imagine him as this big, mean, heartless demon."

I almost interrupted her. Plane-stealing, farm-nabbing prick, yes. But not a demon. I wasn't delusional. I let her continue.

She said, "He's just an asshole. He's an asshole doing what his asshole job allows him to do. But he has a family in Greeley. I hear him on the phone sometimes, talking to his kids. They talk about going to the swimming pool and pet chameleons."

I said, "You don't need to tell me all this."

"I do. I want to. Shakes, the problem isn't Crutchfield. The problem is— Wait. There isn't a problem. But the solution is in your head. You just have to pull yourself out of this mind-set. Stop letting things happen. Stop waiting for things to fix themselves. Start *worrying* and then start doing something about the things that worry you."

I said, "Are you reading this off a piece of paper?"

Clarissa said, "Maybe. I took notes. So?"

"So how much left is there to recite?"

"I'm almost done." She was frustrated. "I'm trying. Listen. I'm crumbling up the paper." Crinkle, crinkle. "It's just me, Shakes. I'm doing things so I can love myself and it's making me feel a lot better. I'm in control now. I don't need to starve. I don't need to feel like a failure. But that all has to come from within. Not from being angry at things and people. And not by giving up. Crutchfield's gonna get his. I know it. People get what they deserve."

"I hope so."

"See?" said Clarissa, "You've got some hope."

"I hope he dies in a plane crash."

"Maybe he will. Maybe he'll get cancer tomorrow. But whatever happens to him will have no bearing on whether or not you're happy unless you address the things within yourself that make you unhappy."

"You're still reading off that piece of paper aren't you?"

"Yes. It took a long time to come up with this. Listen. You need to make good things happen to yourself. Otherwise I'm going to worry about you. I *do* worry about you. That's why I called. All alone out there with Emmett. It must be hard."

"I try not to think about the situation." Dammit. She was getting to me. I don't *try* not to think. I just *don't.*

A pause. Then she said, "Listen, Shakes, I want you to know that I forgive you. I'm not mad about what you said to me that night. I'm eating food again. I feel good."

"I'm real happy to hear that." I looked at Pa, sitting on the floor. He was watching me with his mouth half open.

Clarissa said, "And I'd like to see you."

"Well." I thought about this. "You know where I am."

"So we could get together sometime? There's things we can share. Together, we might be able to pull you out of this. I'm so glad I called. I was nervous that you'd be angry and hang up on me. Or that I'd be angry and hang up on you. This is going pretty well."

"I agree."

"So," said Clarissa, "when's a good time to come by?"

"Let me check my schedule." I pretended to look at a calendar. "How about right now?"

She didn't say anything.

I said, "Tomorrow is also wide open."

She still didn't say anything. The phone was dead quiet. I blew into the receiver to check and see if it was even on. Nothing. I turned the phone off and on. No sound. No hum, no hiss. Just a dead line.

My heart raced. I closed my eyes. This was just another way for the world to kick us in the balls. Clarissa called and tried to cheer me up. And it was almost working. But I hadn't paid the bill so the phone went dead. That's what happens. Don't worry.

Pa and I had successfully subtracted ourselves from the world. A visit with Clarissa would only drag us back. I didn't want to go back. That phone call, it was a dream in a coma.

I opened my eyes. My heartbeats had slowed down again.

The thirteenth and twelfth days before the foreclosure, Pa and I went thru the house looking at stuff. There was a lot of stuff in the house.

On the morning of the eleventh day before the foreclosure, Pa said, "This house is messier than a coon's age. We need to rid out." Rid out. We started immediately.

There was way too much stuff to fit in the trash barrel. I decided to heap up the junk in the broke-down remains of the granary.

I walked to the granary and cleared out a path thru the busted-up wood. The way it had collapsed, the building looked like a bird's nest. Around the perimeter was a wall of busted-up wood. Once you climbed over that, the center was the flat of the galvanized roof sitting atop of where the floor used to be. Standing there, in the center, I felt like an egg ready to crack.

I went into the house, put all the financial papers in old shopping bags, and brought them outside with me. I stacked them in a pile right smack on the center of the granary's collapsed roof.

———————

Then we got busy. We used the wheelbarrow. We filled it with blankets, my old toys, Dad's trophies from the county fair. We worked without mercy. Photo albums. A wooden chair that had belonged to my grandmother. Quilts made by my great-grandmother. The pile grew and grew. We did not take breaks. I was strong now. Almost as strong as Pa. Sweat ran down our eyebrows. Boots, worn bare, went on the pile. Thirty years of *National Geographic*. Newspapers with headlines from the Big Thompson flood, Super Bowl victories, Nixon's resignation, the Moon landing, Monica Lewinsky. It all went on the pile. A surveyor's map of Strattford County, vintage 1932. Photos of the 1926 Dorsey High School basketball team. Deeper, we found a hatbox that had belonged to Pa's pa. The hat inside was too small for either of us. Pa winged it on top of the pile. 78 rpm records. So long, Paul Whiteman. Further back, a stack of rocks labeled with brittle masking tape, "From the first dugout built by H. Williams." A lantern whose bottom had rusted out. A box of broken pocket watches etched with German writing.

And then, the family Bible. Heavy old thing. As big as a dictionary. Massive, worn leather cover. We looked at the birth dates written inside. Helfrich's father, Johann Williams, born in 1851, the date inscribed with a quill. My sorry birth in 1971 was scrawled with a Bic. The text of the Bible was in a scary German typeface. *Am Anfang schuf Gott Himmel und Erde.* This Bible had sat on a shelf in a German house in Russia, crossed an ocean, ridden a train, and gathered dust in a basement in eastern Colorado.

We tossed it on top of the pile, like a cherry.

It was mid-afternoon on the eleventh day before the foreclosure and the house had been ridded out. We lay on the ground under the shade of the big locust tree. Gravel and sandburs stuck in our backs. Flies bit our arms. We didn't slap at them.

Heading into an outside nap, the sun feels good on your eyelids. Orange glow. Soon, Pa started snoring. I followed him into a slumber stirred occasionally by a quick breeze. Nonsensical dreams of daytime. Flat on our backs like two corpses.

Pa shook me awake, excited. "You gotta see this!"

I reassembled the world. We were still lying on our backs. The shadows were longer, the ground was cooler.

Pa pointed straight up. "The clouds! There's so many things in those clouds, I don't know where to start."

I looked up. It was nothing but clouds. Good ones, sure. Puffed up, lit orange and purple by the dropping sun and moving quick far above the top of the locust tree.

"Look there!" he said. "A cat. And a man on a bicycle." He jabbed at another part of the sky. "A tomato." He laughed to himself. "A tomato in the sky! Over there. A horse pulling a bus. I can't believe it."

I told him I didn't see anything.

We stood up. He pointed at a cloud. "Follow my finger. See it there? You see it?" I sighted from behind his shoulder, followed his finger. I didn't see anything.

He was patient. "Here. Look. Those are the eyes. Those big ones."
"Uh-huh."

"And that's the tail. Look quick, it's changing."

"I see it. Yep. I see one. It's a dragon." I still didn't see anything.

He looked at me sideways. Then followed my gaze. "That could be. Look over there, a fish with a woman's face. Everything, right up there. This is something else."

I squinted, let my eyes unfocus. I concentrated, relaxed. I did it all, but I didn't see anything but clouds. Dad was leaping, he was so happy. Watching Pa there, bouncing on the dirt, I had to agree that he was right. Being out there, with him right then, it was something else.

We didn't eat dinner that night. Neither of us was hungry. All those jars of tomatoes and not a drop of appetite.

We had pretty much cleaned out the whole house. All that remained was some furniture and few this-and-thats. The walls were bare. Whole rooms were empty. Our voices echoed.

I said, "What do you wanna do?"

Pa said, "It's dark. Might as well sleep."

I helped him brush his teeth and then I went with him into his bedroom to say good night. The closet door was open. Mom's clothes were hanging on the rod. Dresses and jackets and blouses. Things she wore to church and for gardening.

"We missed some stuff, Pa."

"Missed it how?"

"We threw away a whole bunch of things today. But we didn't throw out those clothes."

"Why would we throw out those clothes? They're your mother's. She needs those."

"I reckon she does."

On the tenth day, I decided we should set the pile on fire. But Pa wouldn't let me. "Not yet," he said. "You have to be safe."

We spent all day being safe.

First, we made a trench around the granary. The dirt was too hard for digging. We scratched a row with a hoe all the way around the granary and then ran water thru it, like a little moat. As the water trickled in, Dad dragged the hoe round and round the trench. Sometimes he ran, sometimes he got distracted by a bug. Eventually, the trench was deep and wide enough that we could get some good soaking going on.

With the water softening up the soil, we used spades to dig, dig, dig. It was another hot day. Even with the soaking, the dirt was still plenty hard and it made for sweat. Summer didn't want to let go.

Dad accidentally snapped the handle on his spade. It happens sometimes, especially if your shovel is seventy years old. After that, we took turns digging with the one good shovel.

It was a lot of work. I didn't want to dig a trench. I wanted to set a match to that pile. I kept hoping Pa would forget why we were digging so we could quit messing around. When I tried to distract him, he'd say, "We should get back to work." Give him credit for focus.

We dug and dug and dug. The trench was a foot deep and two feet wide by lunchtime.

Instead of eating, we napped outside for a couple of hours while the hose trickled water into the trench. When we woke up, we went right back to work. My back hurt. My hands were starting to blister. A few hours twisting a wooden shovel handle can do a number on your hands, even if you have calluses.

We didn't speak. Our britches became frosted with mud. That goddamned trench got deeper and deeper. It was like we were running a marathon. Not some bullshit Boston Marathon where people were cheering and handing us cups of water, but the real Marathon. The first one, where the guy died.

When it got dark, a rout of coyotes started yipping to the west. They were going good, making a racket like a bunch of junior high girls. We kept at it. The hole grew as wide as a coffin and half as deep as a grave. I was so tired I couldn't get more than a tablespoon of dirt with each heave of the shovel. Pa took over. Even he was moving slow.

I sat in a slump while the coyotes yipped and Dad dug. After several minutes, he tossed the shovel out of the trench and climbed up to solid ground. He was a dark shadow against the purple ink of the sun-gone sky.

He said, "What's the point of this deal, again?"

"Fire ditch."

He picked up a dirt clod and chucked it into the middle of the granary nest. "We're gonna set that afire?"

"That's the plan."

"Then we'll need some gasoline."

I fetched the shovel. I gave it a kiss and then pitched it on the pile.

Let me explain again how fuel works on a farm. You have two tanks: one for gasoline and one for diesel. Big tanks. Hundreds of gallons. As tall as a man and as long as a horse. The co-op sends out a truck to fill them up a couple of times a year. You never have to go to the gas station.

I brought an empty ice cream bucket to the gasoline tank and turned on the pump. It squirted out a handful of fuel and then started sucking air. Goddamned thing was empty. That tank was never empty. In my whole life, I'd never seen it empty. Fortunately, we still had the diesel tank. I tried it. It didn't even spit. Just dry pumping.

"Pa, we're out of gasoline."

"Diesel?"

"That, too."

"How about gas?"

"Negatory."

He said, "We'll get some from that car of yours."

I hadn't driven my car in weeks. It started up good. I pulled it up to the trench with the lights on, shining so we could see what we were doing. I went into the shed and, under the flickering glow of florescent tubes, went thru piles of junk until I found a length of surgical tubing. I brought it to Pa. Bugs were flickering in the headlights. Crickets chirped slowly. I noticed that it was cool.

I said, "You gonna do this or am I? Siphon the gas, I mean."

"You ever done it before?"

"Nope."

He said, "Now's a good time to learn."

"Asshole."

I siphoned every last drop of fuel out of my car, three buckets full. We poured it all on the pile.

Even without a sense of smell, you can tell when there's fuel in the air. It gets in your eyes and makes the inside of your cheeks tingle. The pile was waiting to be lit. It had to be lit. You could feel the fate of this thing. We were in the moment after the airplane hits but before the skyscraper collapses.

We couldn't find a match so we used a striker and a butane torch. I held a balled-up wad of my birth certificate over the blue flame until it caught fire. I tossed it like a baseball.

A thwoooop and the pile was alighted.

It burned for the rest of the night. Flames whirled up and disappeared into sparkling puffs of ash. The smoke blacked out the stars. Aerosol cans popped, glass cracked, plastic fizzed. Unseen things exploded, groaned. The remains of the granary caught fire. The old wood creaked into blackened oblivion. Bridges of boards collapsed, sending up bursts of blue. And throughout, the sound of wind created from nothing.

We stood with our arms crossed. Dad's ditch did its job; when glowing ashes floated into the sky, they burned themselves out before they could start a prairie fire.

I saw the eyes of animals on the other side of the fire. They were too tall to be coyotes. Too big to be deer. They were buffalo. Watching, waiting for us to be gone.

The wind shifted and the heat singed the hair on my fingers. When I looked at the fire again, the eyes were gone. The buffalo had left.

"Hey, Pa?"

"Son."

"What are your thoughts on religion?"

"Well." Long pause. "People have things they do."

"That sounds about right."

We stood silent as the granary, the oldest remaining structure on the farm, was reduced to carbon. Flames swallowed the final bit of wood just as the sun pushed over the horizon.

With faces and clothes and fingers stained with dirt and soot, we went to bed and slept until noon.

When we awoke, we were hungry. The pantry was almost bare. All we had were two packages of ramen and a whole bunch of tomatoes.

Apparently, the electricity had gotten shut off while we slept. The fridge sat there, empty. Water dripped out of the freezer.

You need electricity to pump water up from the well. Fortunately, Mom had always kept several gallon jugs of water in the closet under the stairs, in case of a blizzard. The water was at least half a dozen years old, but it was still wet. I poured some into a pot and let the ramen soak until it became mushy. I poured a jar of tomatoes on top, added a little salt, and we had edible food.

After we ate, we wandered around. Walked out to the smoking

embers of the pile. We walked around the shed but didn't go inside. We were tired. We didn't have anything to talk about. I wandered like a zombie. Pa wandered like himself.

Several hours later, night happened. Heat lightning to the south. The pile continued to smoke.

We slept again. In the middle of the night, we were awoken by thunder. It started raining. Soon, hail was clattering off the roof. We opened the front door and watched. Hail the size of teeth. Then eyeballs. Then fists. Punching the roof, the ground, everything. Splashing water, denting corrugated metal. Roaring, howling, mad winds. Lightning flashed. A hundred yards away, we saw a needle of black that pointed from the clouds straight to the earth. A tornado, just for us. It blew like a jet engine. Dad and I stood in the doorway, ready.

Another flash of lightning. The tornado was closer, just on the other side of the garden. Hearts thumping.

Lightning happened again, and now the needle was gone, replaced by wisps of black, like crows melted mid-flight. Our tornado had fled. And then suddenly, the storm, like all thunderstorms, passed and the rain and hail and wind stopped like a faucet shut off.

We went to bed. It was too dark to read.

CHAPTER 23

REBUILDING

I didn't know what day it was anymore. But whatever day it was, it was the day we rebuilt the Rocket.

We both slept good. The sun was halfway up the sky by the time we crawled out of our beds. We both had stubble on our chins.

For breakfast we each drank a glass of stale water. Dad didn't act hungry. I didn't mind a growling stomach.

We went outside to investigate the aftermath of the storm. The old locust tree was lying on its side. Like it had gotten tired and wanted to rest, with the garden as its bed. The dirt was stained where the tree's branches had squished the last of the green tomatoes.

Other than the tree, the storm hadn't messed things up too much. The hail had made dents here and there, shredded some leaves. But the house was still standing. No windows broke. The place where the granary had been was now a giant black spot encircled by a rusty moat.

We went to the shed and looked at the Rocket parts. When he dismantled the thing, Dad had laid everything out in a spiral in the order he'd removed it. The tools were all on the workbench. Ring expander, ring compressor, socket wrenches, gear puller. All of it. It was a kit. It had instructions. You just needed to know how to read them.

I said, "Let's put it together."

Dad insisted that we clean the parts before we assemble them. "Clean 'em with gas."

I said, "We don't have any gas."

"Siphon some out of your car."

"We did that already."

"Then get some out of my pickup."

"The only fuel we have is in the pickup. I ain't wasting it to clean an intake valve."

"Do it."

Asshole.

I stuck the surgical tubing into the tank and sucked. I felt like an idiot. Nothing came out. I climbed in the cab and checked the fuel gauge. Empty.

"How the hell did that happen?"

Pa said, "Someone must have driven it somewhere."

"Genius."

"Sounds like a personal problem."

There's always gas somewhere. I brought the surgical tubing to every engine in the shed, every tractor on the estate. Most of them were dust-dry, but I still gathered about a quarter gallon of gasoline, sloshing in that ice cream bucket.

By then, Dad had forgotten that he wanted to clean the parts.

He sat on a bucket and watched as I attached the Rocket back to itself. It was a real paint-by-numbers deal.

"I got this figured out, Pa. You ain't as smart as I thought you were. All this mechanical genius I thought you had is nothing but knowing what goes where."

He said, "Same as making babies."

"Putting the Rocket together is easier, I reckon. No wedding."

"You think you'll ever get married?"

I accidentally thought of Clarissa. "Doubtful."

Pa said, "I always thought I'd be a grandpa."

"You ain't."

He said, "You did other things good, though."

I said, "Thanks. Like what?"

"Oh." He paused. The pause expanded, stretched its legs, took a walk around the shed, and didn't come back.

I kept twisting the screwdriver.

Time lapse. Steady work. A string of small clouds brought strobes of shade, hours went by, everything went where it belonged, and then the Rocket was ready. I checked the bolts that held the wheels on the frame.

Dad steadied a funnel while I poured our last quarter gallon of fuel from the ice cream bucket into the tank.

Tweak the throttle. Pull the choke. Stomp the footfeet and putt-putt-putt. The Rocket was arisen for the third time. We didn't even bother to ride it. I shut it off. No need to waste fuel.

Pa patted the seat. "You know what I like about you?"

"What's that, Pa?"

"Nothin'."

"Me, too. Now let's get some tomatoes in our bellies."

Dad said, "I suppose I should get the mail."

While Pa went to the mailbox, I went inside. I cracked open a jar of tomatoes. They must of smelled grand. For a moment, I just looked at them, glistening. I plucked one from the jar and dropped it down my throat. Dear lord, that room-temperature tomato was heaven. The seeds sliding over my tongue. I poured two pint jars of tomatoes into a pot and stirred them on the dead stove. I flavored them with salt.

Pa was still getting the mail. I opened the door and hollered, hands cupped around my mouth. "Dinner, Pa!"

He yelled back, "Hold up. I got something."

His voice should have come from the direction of the mailbox, but it came from the shed. I hoped he wasn't taking the Rocket apart again. I hollered back, "Something good?"

"Yep," he said.

JUNIPER BUSH

I stepped out of the house and walked toward Dad. He was next to the shed, poking a jack handle into a juniper bush he'd planted twenty-five years ago. In a land where things refuse to grow, he always treated that juniper right. It was taller than he was.

I said, "It's lunchtime."

"There's a snake in there."

This had some potential. "Rattler or bull?"

"Bull, I think. Big one." He pointed from the juniper to where I was standing. "About that long." Twelve feet.

"Right."

He said, "I was thinking we should catch it."

"You say it's a bull snake."

"I believe it is."

I said, "Let's catch it."

"I was thinking I should get the grabber."

Dad had built the grabber several years prior. It wasn't anything special, just a piece of conduit with a handle and linkage and a pincher. A grabber. He'd built it from scratch in twenty minutes after he dropped a pair of pliers in a fertilizer tank. Sort of like you or I would bend a paper clip to fix a pair of broken sunglasses.

I said, "I think we burned it."

"We didn't." We did. Didn't matter. While Dad went to the house to look for the grabber, I crawled under the juniper and tried to see this snake. There wasn't a snake. Pa had been poking on that bush ever since I moved back to the farm. There was never a snake.

The ground under the bush was dry. Lying on my back, I could feel yesterday's warmth thru my shirt. I decided to rest there for a while until Pa either came back or forgot what he was up to. Then eat. Then what? Wait, I guess.

I closed my eyes. A fly landed on my forehead.

I heard a hiss.

I've seen dozens of snakes in my life. I watched my old dog Jumper torture a blue racer to death. I saw a king snake before they disappeared from the plains. Garter snakes, of course. Hognose snakes. You ever seen a hognose? They have a flipped-up snout for digging holes. If you surprise one, it'll play dead. If you keep poking it, it'll stop playing dead and flatten its head like a cobra. They're harmless. You can play with them all day long.

Even so, it doesn't matter what kind of snake it is, your first reaction on seeing one is always to yelp. It's born into us all, I suppose.

So when I opened my eyes and saw a tongue flick from the head of an actual, honest-to-shit snake, I yelped. I yelped right at that snake.

The snake's head swerved back and forth in front of my face. This wasn't a hognose or a bull or anything good. I was looking at a big-cheeked, slit-eyed goddamned pit viper of a prairie rattler.

I'd only seen a rattlesnake once in my whole life. It was during wheat harvest when I was a kid. I was driving the grain cart and had some time to kill before the combine filled back up with grain. I stopped the tractor and got out to take a leak. Right in the middle of my piss, a rattler crawled over my foot. I yelped. It didn't pay me any attention. It just went over my foot and then disappeared into the wheat stubble. I was so scared I zipped up my britches and climbed back into that tractor and didn't get out again until that field was harvested.

This was scary in a whole new way.

You think about the things you've heard. First, I concluded that there was no mistaking this thing. It was a rattlesnake. I couldn't see the tail. I couldn't hear any rattles. But its body was covered with diamonds and that head, it was an arrow, ready to fly.

I thought about the TV shows where Australians pick snakes up by their tails. About illustrations in pamphlets that tell you to back away slowly. I didn't recall anything about lying flat on your back under a bush while a snake stared at your nose.

Venom. If you get bit, pull out your pocket knife and make an X over the bites and suck the poison. Or don't. But whatever you do, stay relaxed. The less your blood pumps, the less the venom can spread. Baby rattlers were the worst. Why where babies the worst? Because they have more venom. Or because, because, because they had the same amount of venom but they couldn't regulate how much they spit out. When a baby rattler bites, it shoots its whole wad. An adult can control itself. Adults sometimes bite without releasing any venom at all. The snake in front of me was definitely not a baby. That was good.

What you gotta do, what you gotta do is make sure not to threaten the thing. I just had to relax and wait for it to go away. Then ease out from under the bush, walk to the house, and eat some room-temperature salty tomato soup.

Sweat was running down my temples. I couldn't breathe. I couldn't stop breathing. The goddamned snake crawled over a branch and dangled its head right up against my nose. The grassy tongue tickled my nostril.

It opened its mouth. The fangs were pressed flat against the top of its palate. The jaw stretched wide and the fangs unfolded. Then that goddamned biting fly landed on my forehead again. It dug its snout in and started chewing me up. I wanted to swat and shout and shrivel up. Still, that snake looked down on me, yawning, with its tongue flicking in and out.

The snake brought its mouth to my ear. I could hear it breathing in little raspy wisps. The tongue pushed against my hair.

It bit me on the neck, just below my right ear. There was a popping sound as the teeth punctured the skin, like pushing a straw thru the lid of a soda cup. Then the bottom jaw grabbed on and squeezed the fangs down. The snake just sat there, with its mouth clamped on my neck. It didn't feel like anything.

Dad's feet crunched toward me. The snake took its head off my neck and disappeared into the bush. I dunno. Maybe the whole thing took a split second. What's certain is that just as Pa's shoes came into view, that bite started to hurt. I scuttled out from under the juniper and jumped up, ran, staggered, and fell on my hands and knees. I put a hand to my neck and pulled it back. Two drops of blood on my palm.

Pa was carrying a five-gallon bucket. The tomato bucket. He said, "What's your major malfunction?"

I was dizzy and jazzed and upside-down. "I got snake-bit." My tongue felt like a shoe.

Pa put the bucket on the ground. He seemed concerned, almost fatherly. "What kind of snake-bit?"

"Rattler."

His voice caught. "You sure?"

I nodded. I pointed to my neck. "Right here."

Pa looked at the snakebite. "You got bit by something."

"Rattler."

"You sure?"

I nodded. This was a way of dying.

He touched my neck. "Does it hurt?"

I nodded. It was getting hard to move my neck.

"Those snakes don't always give you a full shot of their juice. It might not be too bad."

I was about to cry. I looked toward the sky so the tears wouldn't fall out. "It hurts, Pa."

Pa bit his lip. He was worried. He was my father and he didn't know what to do. He said, "Call the doctor?"

"Telephone doesn't work."

Dad's eyes darted to the juniper bush. He rushed over, stuck his arm in the branches, and pulled out the snake by its neck. It was as long as he was tall, wagging and flopping. He pushed the snake's face to the ground and stepped on it with the heel of his tennis shoe, twisting back and forth until red spilled onto the dirt. The snake's tail twisted here and there and then it lay still. Pa dropped the snake in the bucket and brought it to me.

"Recognize this?" He was smiling.

"We gotta get moving." We didn't have any gas. We couldn't get moving. My right ear was starting to ring.

I lay down. I heard Pa messing around. Touching things in the shed. "Pa, I'm snake-bit. We need to do something."

He said, "I know. I'm making it happen."

I rolled over so I could watch him. He was dragging a tarp along the floor. "That deal there." He pointed to the item that had previously been covered by the tarp. The jet-engine tractor. The last thing he worked on before he lost his mind.

"That thing." My throat was pinched. "It don't work."

"It might. In a coon's age." He climbed on the tractor seat. It had originally been a John Deere R. Made in the fifties. No cab. Squat and green.

He had reversed the seat and the steering wheel so the rear wheels pulled and the front wheels dragged behind. The engine was out and in its place was a jet turbine. He put his hand on the housing. Pa was gonna make that thing work. I wouldn't die on that slab of concrete.

I leaned my head back and closed my eyes. I heard Pa climb onto the seat. He clicked some switches. Then he said, "Vrooooooo-ooooooooooom!"

I looked at him. He was bouncing on the seat, moving the steering wheel back and forth. "Whoooooosh!"

I straightened out my crossed eyes.

"Pa."

"I'm driving."

"Pa. I need help."

"Sounds like a personal problem."

I pushed myself upright and crawled to the WBC Rocket where it was propped up on its kickstand. I draped myself over the frame and tried to climb on. I held onto the handlebars, stood up. The bike fell over on top of me.

Dad jumped off the tractor and lifted the bike off me. "Why's your neck so?"

"Snakebite," I hissed. "I got one."

"Black. Your neck is black."

I noticed the hair on his hands was singed short. Smoke floated around us. Pa looked around, worried. Then he smiled. "The trash is burning."

I nodded forward.

We are on the road. I'm balanced on the Rocket's seat. Pa is standing on the pedals. My hands are around his belly. They're tied together at the wrists. The world passes by slowly. I roll my face off of his back and see the five-gallon bucket hanging from the left handlebar. It's banging against the front fork. The engine goes putt-putt-putt. There's a quarter gallon of gas in the fuel tank. Where can we go?

I close my eyes again.

We are in a pasture. I'm curled on my side. Pa's on his hands and knees. He's digging the sand like a dog, scooping dirt out between his legs. I try to talk. My voice is a raspy squeal. I touch my face. The skin's taut.

Pa keeps digging. His eyes are closed, the lids dark with dust. The hole gets bigger. The sand is moist. I close my right eye and watch with my left.

"Look at this!" Dirt rains onto my face. Every piece of sand feels like a shot from a BB gun.

I work my left eye open. Pa is holding a half-decayed animal by its tail. I don't recognize it at first. Then it assembles itself in my head. The animal: cat. The cat: mine. We're in the pasture for dead dogs. Boy, does my head hurt.

Pa sets my dead cat on the ground. Then he grabs me by the wrists and drags me to the edge of the hole. I resist with all my strength, which is to say I barely resist at all. I'm on the edge of a grave.

"A real molly rauncher," says Pa. He picks up the bucket and tips it over the hole and out slides the dead rattlesnake. The scales hiss against the edge of the bucket and then it makes a thump and it's in the hole. Pa picks up the cat corpse, drops it on top, says,

"That'll give him someone to talk to," and then starts kicking the dirt back in.

My belly shakes. I can't breathe enough to laugh. I can't move my mouth to smile. I feel a tear drip out of my left eye and slide down my nose. Its coolness makes my skin feel better.

We're on the Rocket. My hands are tied around Pa's waist again. He sings, over and over, "Frère Jacques, Frère Jacques . . ."

The road is a smooth blacktop highway. I don't know where we're going. I don't know who I'm leaning against. It's my father. He's driving the Rocket. We pass the grain elevators of the Keaton Co-op. Why are we in Keaton? The hospital's not in Keaton. It's in Strattford, forty miles north and three miles west. We only have a quarter gallon of gas. The world's a smear. There is only now, which hurts, and not-now, which is a mystery.

CHAPTER 25

REAPING

It feels like someone's trying to yank my hands off of my arms. I'm awake again. My nose is bent crooked in Pa's back. I'm hanging on him like a cape. My hands are tied together around his neck.

He's walking me across the floor. My feet are dragging. I scan the room with my left eye. The floor is a crew-cut carpet, brown. People are sitting on the floor. There's a sticker on the wall. I can't read it, but I've seen it before. I know what it says: "Each depositor insured to at least $250,000. Backed by the full faith and credit of the United States government. FDIC."

We are in the Keaton State Bank. This is significant. My right lid opens up to a slit.

The people on the floor, they're looking at us. There's Mr. Pridgon, my old music teacher. He's lost most of his hair. His pants are too short. He's rubbing his ankles. There's Jimmy Young of the electric company. Red-faced, like he's been sunburned from the inside out. Too many electrons. There's Ezra Rogers, ninety-nine years old. Sitting with his legs straight out. He's staring at the knobby end of his cane. I can hear the breath pushing in and out of his lungs. I can see these people. They don't look at us.

Pa walks, drags me toward the teller window. Clarissa McPhail greets us. With my face behind Pa's shoulder, I can't see her, but I can hear her. "What'll it be today, boys? Deposit or withdrawal?"

Dad says, "If I told you I'd have to shoot you!"

Clarissa laughs. Dad laughs.

Clarissa says, "What's the matter with Shakes?"

Pa lifts my arms over his head and leans me against the teller window. My hands are still tied together. I'm able to stand, more or less. Clarissa is still pretty. She's wearing a purple V-neck T-shirt. There are two plastic barrettes in her hair.

Pa looks at me, staring hard at the right side of my face. He says, "You been rode hard and put away." He turns to Clarissa. "How's that go?"

"Rode hard and put away wet," she says. To me, she says, "You need some water?"

My head is a brick on a spring. I nod and it wobbles. My chin ends up on my sternum. I'm snake-bit. Can't she tell I'm snake-bit?

Clarissa says, "Why don't you fellas come this way?"

Dad grabs me by the left armpit and we follow.

She opens the wooden gate and leads us to the back, past the safe and the computers, to Neal Koenig's office. Clarissa opens the door without knocking. Neal, my father's classmate, master of the underhand free throw, bank manager, second in command under Mike Crutchfield, is sitting on the floor. His hands are duct-taped together and there's an apple taped over his mouth. He looks at us with hopeful eyes. When he looks at my head his hope turns to confusion.

I'm seeing better now. My right eye is mostly open. The skin on my neck and face still feels like it's ready to burst. A woman is sitting cross-legged on Neal's desk. There's a shotgun resting on her knees. It's a big one. Twelve gauge, I assume. This woman, her eyes are yellow.

Clarissa says to the woman, "They just showed up."

The woman with the shotgun points her elbow at me and says, "What's the matter with that one?"

Pa says, "Hell if I know. I found him in a ditch."

I gurgle.

Clarissa rolls a chair to me and helps me sit down. She fills a paper cup from the watercooler. I wonder why they need bottled water when they can get the same thing from a well, from the faucet. She pours some of it over my swollen lip and into my mouth. Most of it spills out. It doesn't matter. The water running over my chin and spreading down my shirt, it's a salve.

Clarissa says, "You want more?"

I lift up my hands, wave my fingers. My wrists are tied together with a bungee cord. With my eyes, I say, Please get this thing off me.

Clarissa shakes her head. She fills another cup of water and gives it to the woman.

Clarissa says, "Give him as much as he wants." Then she puts her hand on Pa's shoulder. "Emmett, I got a job for you."

She leads Pa out of the office and closes the door behind them.

The yellow-eyed woman sets the gun on the desk and climbs off. She says, "Lean your head back."

I do, and she pours water into my mouth. I swallow some. My tongue takes it in like a sponge. My throat opens enough so I can breathe. When I exhale, steam comes out. My body falls into focus. My hands are numb from the bungee cord. My ass hurts from the Rocket ride. The skin on my face and neck is fit to split wide open.

The woman looks at me, close. Yellow eyes. The blood vessels are little red rivers.

"You don't remember me."

I shake my head.

"I thought I made an impression." She falls to her hands and knees. "This help?"

I shake my head. She turns to Neal Koenig and says, "Don't look." Then she lifts her shirt over her head. She's not wearing anything underneath. She says, "How about this?" She bares her teeth, then bucks back and forth on the floor a few times so her tits hang and flop.

I'm not the smartest person in the world and I'm even dumber when I've got venom in my neck. But I recognize her. She's the woman on the mattress in the house that Vaughn Atkins's grandpa never lived in. The house with the tapioca pudding. I nod.

She laughs like a bully. "You can call me Miss Angie."

My right eye is completely open now. She pulls her shirt back on and stands over Neal Koenig. She says, "You looked at me just then, didn't you?"

Neal, with the apple stuck in his mouth, shakes his head. There's snot coming out of his nose.

Miss Angie kicks him hard in the knee and then does it again. He leans forward and weeps.

She climbs back onto the desk, puts the gun across her knees. "I don't mean to be rude, fella, but what the fuck is wrong with your face?"

I try to speak. "I been snake-bit." It doesn't come out clear.

Miss Angie leans toward me. I try again, forcing the muscles in my face against the swollen skin, "Rattlesnake."

She starts laughing. Neal Koenig stops weeping. With that apple taped to his mouth and the snot on his lip, he's a sorry-looking creature. And he's looking at me with pity.

"You get a rattlesnake bite and your old man brings you to the bank? What's he got, a snakebite kit in his safe-deposit box? Your old man is a dumb motherfucker."

If I was a superhero, I'd draw strength from the rage I feel right now. I'd flex my arms and bust the bungee cord and then punch this woman in the neck and steal her gun and rescue everyone. I am not a superhero. I slouch in the chair.

Miss Angie lights a cigarette. We're done talking. She smokes while Neal and I sit, helpless, dying probably.

Neal and I try not to look at each other. Miss Angie puts out her cigarette and plays with Neal's die-cast model of a 1962 Delta 88.

I fall asleep.

When I wake up, my hands are no longer tied. Clarissa is standing over me, nudging me in the thigh with her foot. She says, "Emmett isn't helping."

She didn't say "us." She said, "Emmett isn't helping."

I say, "So?" The word comes out. I can talk. I wonder if I'm getting better. I say "So?" again. I want to be tough but I'm about to cry.

"You gotta help him help us." Us. She's part of it. They're a gang. "Or bad things will happen."

"Who's us?"

"Who do you think?"

"D.J. Beckman?"

"Yep. And her." She nods to Miss Angie. "And her boyfriend."

My head wobbles.

Miss Angie says, "He's snake-bit."

Clarissa says, "No kidding." To me, she says, "You aren't gonna die. If you were going to die, you'd be dead."

I want to not believe her. You can't trust someone who robs a bank behind your back. Still, I think that she maybe is telling the truth. Maybe that snake didn't want to kill me.

Clarissa tells Miss Angie to help me up. The two of them lift me by the armpits. Miss Angie holds the gun in her free hand. They take me out of Neal's office, right up to the safe. It's one of those tall ones that you can walk into. The door is dark green with a yellow pinstripe painted around the edge. On the right side of the door is a heavy brass handle. In the center of the door is a dial. In front of the safe, there's a pile of tools all tangled in yellow extension cords. A drill, an angle grinder, a sledgehammer, a crowbar, and an oxyacetylene torch. The door is nicked, scuffed, dented, and blackened with smoke. And it is closed.

Clarissa sends Miss Angie back to keep track of Neal.

Miss Angie's ratty boyfriend is holding Pa facedown on the ground. The boyfriend's hands are wrapped around Pa's biceps. Pa's breathing hard but he isn't struggling. Clarissa says, in a sympathetic tone, "He got agitated. He started talking like your mom was here."

Miss Angie's boyfriend says, "I had to take him down."

I want to kill these rats. Robbing a bank, messing with an innocent old man. I glare at Clarissa. I'm sure, with my swollen face, she can't tell how angry I am. She says, "They aren't going to hurt anyone. Not if you can get Emmett to open that safe."

I say, "Where's D.J.?"

"Who?"

"Beckman? Where is he?"

"We sent him out front to keep an eye on the customers."

"I didn't see him when we came in."

"He was hiding behind the counter."

I say, "Seems like he'd rather be back here. In the middle of the action."

"He's not very popular right now."

"How's that?"

Clarissa points at the safe. "Neal told us he didn't have the combination, which I know is bullshit because I've seen him open that thing a million times. Angie and Kelly"—she nods toward Angie's boyfriend—"they figured they'd just make old Neal uncomfortable for a while and he'd fess up. They promised not to hurt him. But then, while we're taping Neal's hands together, D.J. sneaks out to his car and brings in all his tools and starts whaling away on the door. Before we can stop him, he's completely fucked up the safe so now the lock thingy won't even turn." She grabs the knob and tries to twist it. It certainly is stuck. "Like I said, he's not very popular."

I start to say something, but then I get dizzy. My legs bend and I'm on the floor.

Angie's boyfriend lets go of one of Pa's arms, reaches into his pocket, and pulls out a ball of aluminum foil, which he hands to Clarissa. "Give your buddy one of these."

Clarissa opens the foil. It's full of orange pills. She pushes one toward my mouth. "Kelly says to have one."

I allow Clarissa to put the pill on my tongue. I swallow. It pushes itself down my dried-up throat. I nod my head for another. She puts another pill on my tongue. It fizzes some. I spit it at her face. It sticks to her cheek.

Miss Angie's boyfriend, Kelly, jumps up from where he's holding Pa to the ground and slaps my face. A handprint of pain thrums thru my head. My breaths come faster and shallow. I can't take in any air. Clarissa holds me upright. She whispers into my ear, "I didn't want you to be here." I'm not sure if she's sorry or if she's irritated.

Out loud she says, "Get your dad to open the safe and this'll be done."

Kelly has returned to his spot, holding Pa on the ground. He says, "We're trying to be nice, buddy. Help him help us. Maybe you'll get something out of it."

I shake my head. No, I think. Eat shit, you dirt-fucking scum-hole.

Kelly pulls a revolver out of the back of his jeans. It's nickel-plated and shiny. He points it at me, right at my forehead. His hands aren't shaking like my hands would shake in that situation. What a prick. I can be a prick, too. I shake my head again. He points the gun at the back of Pa's neck.

I nod.

I've never seen Dad so confused in my whole life. They've allowed him to sit up. He looks so sad. He isn't wearing any socks inside his tennis shoes. His face isn't shaved right. He has long grey hairs under his nose and on his Adam's apple. I wish I'd shaved him this morning. I couldn't have shaved him if I had wanted to; we didn't have any electricity. I never learned to shave the old-fashioned way, with a razor and shaving cream. Electricity only. I try to recall if Pa ever shaved with a razor. I wonder if that makes us inferior to other men. I say, "Hey, Pa."

He says, "What's going?" He motions along his face, indicating the swelling on my cheek and neck.

I say, "Nothing much."

"Somebody hit you?"

"Naw. Just a snake."

He says, "You're a. Inflatable."

I say, "It's not the end of the world."

He nods. "I know. I been there plenty of times."

I say to Clarissa, "We have to leave him alone. That's the only way he'll do it. You know as well as I do." I'm feeling jittery. From the pill.

She says, "He's right, Kelly. I've seen it. Emmett won't do a damned thing if we're watching him. I saw him do it in Vaughn Atkins's basement. You just gotta forget about him. Next thing you know, he'll have the vault open. It's like getting rid of the hiccups. The more you try, the less it works."

Kelly points the gun at my chest. He says, "Your old man better not pull any shit."

I say, "He can't pull any shit."

Clarissa says, "Kelly, you go out front and wait with D.J. I'll take care of these guys."

Kelly scowls. "They better not pull any shit." Then he's thru the hallway and gone.

Clarissa says, "I'll give you one minute alone with him. Then you come directly back to Neal's office."

She walks away, into the office, and Pa and I are alone. I'd like to hug him and then climb on his shoulders, push aside one of the ceiling tiles, crawl thru the ductwork, and escape onto the roof. Instead I point him to the vault. He has tools. Dad can do this.

"Pa, we gotta get something out of that safe."

"What's in the safe?"

"A toilet. There's a toilet in the safe. And I gotta take a shit."

He looks at me like I'm crazy. I'm probably crazy. So far today, I've been snake-bit and I've taken an orange pill.

I say, "Do you want me to take a dump right here on this carpet?"

He says, "Hell no."

"Then you need to open that safe." I slap him on the back and shuffle toward Neal's office.

He follows, puts him arm around my waist. "You can't even walk right."

"Then help me."

He brings me to Neal's door. I knock. Clarissa opens it. I work my way out of Dad's arm and slither thru the door, which Clarissa shuts before Pa can enter. He knocks a few times. I hear him say, "Shakes?" Then there's no noise.

I lean against the wall and slide to the ground. I try to put my head in my hands but it hurts too much. Pa's out there, wandering. He doesn't know what's happening. I don't know what's happening. This is out of control. This is off the reservation. Whatever this is, it's conclusive. We burned everything.

I cry. It hurts to cry. The tears are stones birthing out of my eyes. I curl up on the floor and shiver. Sorry, Dad, this is your reward. You're the third generation of pioneers, people who built a farm, survived in a semi-arid landscape for a hundred and twenty years. And you end up wandering around a bank while your son's lying on the floor with a snakebite on his neck. Four generations. Lying on a floor. Wandering in the hall. I wish I would die.

Clarissa puts her hand on my back. Miss Angie is still in this room somewhere.

Clarissa winks at me. "I told you Crutchfield would get his." She seems proud.

I say, "It seems like you're doing all the getting."

"I'm sorry, Shakes, but D.J. had a better plan. A lot of people have asked me to help them rob this place. You wouldn't believe it. Kids, old-timers, everybody. If it makes a difference, you were the first person I said yes to."

"Out of pity." My head hurts.

"Partly. And also because it sounded fun. But it couldn't have worked. You need guns, Shakes. You can't rob a bank with collectible coins. D.J. was willing to use guns."

Miss Angie coughs a fake cough.

Clarissa says, "I mean, it wasn't entirely his idea. Miss Angie and Kelly, they started it. They're from Denver. They didn't bring me in on it until a couple weeks ago. After you and I had given up on the job."

I start to speak, but my throat's too scratchy.

Clarissa says to Miss Angie, "Can you get Shakes some water, please?"

"No."

Without replying, Clarissa fills up a paper cup and brings it to me. It helps.

She says, "You were saying something?"

I shake my head.

She continues, "I had started eating again and I was starting to feel good about myself. Like it didn't matter what people think. I felt like doing something bold. But I knew you weren't the person to do it with. You're not action-oriented. D.J. and Angie and Kelly, they've got it all figured out. And they promised no one would be hurt. And look, no one has been hurt. We'll get the money and then we'll go away."

"You have a getaway plan?"

"D.J. is in charge of that part."

She misinterprets my look of dismay.

"Don't worry, Shakes. You'll be right here. You'll be fine. You're not going to die." She sighs dramatically. "I never dreamed you'd show up in the middle of all this. I thought you'd be moping around the farm with Emmett. Of course it's good luck that you did. We'd be completely screwed without Emmett right now."

There are clanking noises coming from outside the door. Metal taps metal. Not aggressive. Exploratory. Pa is doing something out there. Clarissa's eyes brighten. Then she looks hard at me and the brightness goes away. "Remember the last time we talked on the phone? When I said I wanted to come visit? I was going to tell you about everything. I was going to tell you all about this and make you promise not to tell anyone. Then, afterward, I was going to give you some money so you could get back on your feet after the fore-closure."

I stare at her.

"But you hung up on me. So screw you."

I don't want to explain about the telephone being shut off. It doesn't seem important. I say, "D.J. is a jackass."

"Yep. And he's mean. But he has a heart, sometimes. He's been taking care of Angie and Kelly. He keeps them fed."

On the other side of the room, Angie slaps her belly. "He doesn't keep us fed enough."

I say, "What about Vaughn?"

Clarissa says, "What *about* Vaughn?"

"Is he even actually dead?"

"Of course he's actually dead."

"We didn't go to the funeral. I didn't see the body. All I know is that you *said* he's dead. Maybe you've kidnapped him and stuck him in that safe and this is all going to be a big joke on me."

Clarissa looks hurt. "Vaughn's dead."

I say, "You never intended to rob the bank with us. You gave him hope. You're always trying to give people hope."

"That's not true. *You* gave him hope when *you* suggested we rob this place. Not me."

"It's your fault he's dead. You lied to us. You lied to him."

Clarissa says, "Vaughn Atkins killed himself."

"He killed himself with D.J. Beckman's pills and now you're robbing the bank with D.J."

Neal Koenig groans. I had forgotten he was even there. Miss Angie kicks him in the knee. Clarissa clams up. She won't look at me. She's just as much of a weakling as I am, but being like me doesn't make me respect her.

We hear more clanking. This time, it's aggressive, purposeful clanking. Pounding. A grunt. Then the groan of iron being dragged across iron.

There's a commotion outside the door. People are hollering. Something heavy slams against the wall.

Clarissa runs out to see what's going on. She opens and closes the door too quick for me to see anything.

I hope Dad's killing them all.

Neal is wheezing. I know they aren't going to let us go. They never let you go. Assholes from Denver. I knew it, the second I saw them banging each other on that dirty mattress in that abandoned house. They were dirty, meth-eating assholes. They're the kind of people who would murder a cat for no good reason. I bet they killed my cat. They killed my cat and I drove my cat to the farm and I found dad living in squalor with a dead woman in the bathroom, and now we're all here except the cat and Unabelle.

I say to Miss Angie, "I expect you'll kill me."

She's playing with Neal's toy car again. She looks directly at Neal. "I don't know why a grown man has toys on his desk. It's immature." She pronounces the "t" in "immature."

Outside the door, there's an angry, whispered discussion. I hear voices but not words.

Neal's breath sputters around the apple in his mouth.

Miss Angie hops off the desk and squats in front of him. She rolls the toy car over Neal's face. She presses it against his nose so he can't breathe. The shotgun is lying on the desk.

The voices outside have grown calm.

I say, "Take the apple out of his mouth." I'm feeling hungry. It's been quite some time since I ate an apple.

Miss Angie removes the car from Neal's nose and says, "After I get out of here, I'm going to buy me a car just like this one." She giggles like a teenager. I suspect she's in her mid-thirties. Her meth face makes her look like she's a thousand years old. She continues, "Except when I buy my car, it'll be a real car. Not a Chinese toy.

Always buy American. That's what I say. It's practical. We need to bring back tariffs on foreign goods. They need to stop manipulating the currency."

More sounds of iron. Another burst of whispers. Someone says, "Fuck!" I can't tell if it's an exclamation joy or anger.

I want to know what they're doing to Pa out there. I don't want to know. I want Miss Angie to shoot me in the eye. The shotgun is sitting right there on the desk. Dirty cat-killing meth vampire.

Miss Angie says, "I'll drive my new car all the way to Cincinnati. I'm gonna go to Kings Island and ride every single ride 'til I puke ten times. I'm never gonna work again. I'll buy a Harley and take it to Mexico. I'll run with the bulls. I'll grow delicious apples in my own orchard."

She isn't watching me. My hands aren't tied. Why don't I just die? Pa's still out there. Something's happening. While Miss Angie rants her idiotic fantasies at Neal, I stand up slow. I make my hands into fists. I'm going to grab that gun and swing the butt into the back of her neck. It'll knock her out and then I'll untie Neal and then we'll take the gun and liberate everybody. And me and Dad will steal all the fucking money. It's our money. The banker owes us. Mike Crutchfield. Hadn't thought of him in a while. It makes me even angrier.

". . . I'm gonna buy one of those sea monkey aquariums. I'm going to buy X-ray specs and fake dog shit and everything. I'm going to become a magician. I'll be the magician and my assistants will be sexy faggots in Speedos . . ."

I reach my hand toward the gun.

". . . I'll start a restaurant that serves only my favorite foods. Peanut butter sandwiches, peppermint schnapps, um, rye bread. And tapioca pudding. I love tapioca pudding more than anything in the whole world . . ."

I close my hand over the barrel.

She spins around and shoots me in the stomach with a pistol.

I recall a conversation I had with Vaughn Atkins when we were kids, probably around seventh grade. We were talking about things we wanted to do before we died. At first it was stuff like screwing Christie Brinkley or doing a tomahawk slam dunk in the closing seconds of game seven of the NBA finals. But then we moved deeper. I clearly remember my top three things I wanted to do before I died:

1) Get bit by a shark.
2) Get shot.
3) Rob a bank.

When I lifted my hand off my stomach and saw the circle of blood on my palm, I thought, I gotta find me a shark, pronto.

This made me chuckle.

Miss Angie was still yapping. ". . . thirty-two kinds of ice cream, monkey brains, even though they're grody . . ." She was pointing the pistol at Neal's knee. Neal's eyes were squinted shut, waiting for her to pull the trigger.

I didn't feel that bad. Really, once you've been bit by a rattler, a gut shot is nothing. And this wasn't Dirty Harry. Judging by the look of that pistol and the fact that my ears weren't ringing, I'd been shot by a .22. Nothing. Barely a step up from a BB gun. I could take a few more of those before I dropped dead. Gimme some more orange pills and you could shoot me with a cannonball.

Still yapping, Miss Angie stepped over me, picked up the shotgun from the desk, and returned to her place next to Neal.

I slid to the floor. I said, "Would you mind removing that apple out of Neal's mouth?"

Miss Angie stopped talking. She pressed the barrel of the shotgun against the apple. If she pulled the trigger, the shot would send the apple thru the back of Neal's head. She said, "I would not mind."

There was a crash in the hallway. I heard Clarissa shout, "Leave him alone!"

Miss Angie's finger caressed the trigger of the shotgun.

Something happened. The room was filled with a terrible roar. It wasn't a gunshot. It was bigger. The gun was still in Miss Angie's hands and it wasn't smoking and Neal wasn't bleeding.

Miss Angie and Neal heard the roar, too. A mighty, apocalyptic sound. Neal didn't seem to care. Like he was used to thundering, rumbling, vicious noises. Miss Angie, though, she was startled. Her eyes opened up wide, her chest heaved like a frightened deer.

This was something bigger than snakebites and bank robberies and gunshot wounds and forgetful old men. The earth was peeling apart. Miss Angie and I looked at each other as if the world was going to end and we were both sorry it had to be this way.

Then we recognized the sound, both of us at the same time. It was an airplane. It was the sound of my dad's Cessna.

CHAPTER 26

FARTHER THAN A KITE

The roar became a thrum.

Kelly shouted, "Angie! Get out here."

The moment of unbashful fear that Miss Angie and I had shared was over. She made as if to hit me in the head with the butt of the shotgun and then ran out the door.

I said, "Neal. You all right?"

He nodded. I peeled the duct tape off his face and took the apple out of his mouth. His lips were stretched. His teeth were red with blood.

After a couple of deep breaths, Neal said, "Call him. Now."

I knew who he was talking about. I didn't want to call him.

"No. I gotta help my pa. I'm gonna get those cat-killers."

Neal gave me a worried, confused look. He said, "Call him."

"That man steals farms. And airplanes." I pointed to the hole in my stomach. "See that? It's his fault. I'm snake-bit and shot. So fuck Mike Crutchfield."

Neal nodded earnestly. He licked some blood off his lips. "I'll grant you, he can be difficult. But call him, please. He can save us. He keeps a gun in the plane. There's innocent people in that lobby."

From the sound, I could tell that the Cessna had landed. It was taxiing behind the bank.

Neal said, "There's not much time."

"Okay."

I walked to Neal's desk and picked up the phone. The line was dead. I shook my head. "They clipped the wire."

Neal said, "I've got a phone in my pocket. Untie me. Hurry."

I couldn't unfasten the cords around his wrists. The knots were tight and my fingers were slick from blood. My tummy was starting to ache.

Outside, the airplane engine sputtered to a stop. Neal pointed his head to one of his pants pockets. I reached in and pulled out his mobile phone.

I said, "I don't know how to use these things."

"Push 'Unlock' and then push star."

"Where's 'Unlock'?"

"Look at the screen. It's the button right under where it says 'Unlock.'"

I pushed the buttons, the phone lit up. I said, "Gimme the number."

He said, "I can't remember. It's in there. Scroll thru past calls."

"How do you do that?"

"Push 'Menu' and then hold the down arrow."

I pressed some buttons. A duck-shooting game came up on the screen. Fuck this. I put the phone on Neal's lap and ran out the door.

Clarissa and Pa were in the hallway. Clarissa had her arm around Pa. Pa was holding a handkerchief against his nose. Somebody had socked him hard. He had blood on the front of his shirt.

The safe was open. I felt a moment of pride. He did it. I felt regret. We could have done it.

Miss Angie and Kelly were inside the vault. Next to them, the shotgun was leaning against the wall. Miss Angie held a canvas bag, into which Kelly was dumping the contents of a safe-deposit box. He had a swollen eye and a split on his cheek.

Clarissa, Pa, Kelly, and Miss Angie, they all four stopped what they were doing and looked at me. Clarissa's eyes were wet. Pa's eyes were angry.

Miss Angie let loose of the canvas bag, reached into the back of her pants, and pulled out the pistol.

She said, "Mind if I shoot him some more, Kelly?"

Kelly shook his head. "I do not mind at all."

Miss Angie pointed the gun at my face. I was tired of having guns pointed at me.

Pa said, "Don't do that." His voice was shaking.

Miss Angie said, "How about I shoot them both, Kelly?"

Kelly said, "Go for it."

Clarissa just stood there.

I held Pa's hand. It was big and full of cracks and calluses. It was also warm. I tried to enjoy holding his warm hand. You don't get many tender moments in a lifetime.

D.J. Beckman rushed in, breathing hard and sweating out of every hole in his skin. "Hurry up, fuckers. Crutchfield is coming. He's got a machine gun." Beckman looked at me and Pa holding hands.

I said to D.J., "How's it hanging?"

He said, "Queer bait."

Kelly dropped the safe-deposit box on the floor. "How's he know? How's he know we're in here?"

Neal Koenig stepped out of his office, walking cocky, hands still tied behind his back. "Because," he said, spitting a pencil out of his mouth, "I warned him."

For a moment I thought, This is ridiculous. Then I saw that

everyone was thinking the same thing. We were trapped in a moment of collective idiocy. The things that were happening, they
simply couldn't be possible. Me, Angie, D.J., Kelly, even Clarissa,
none of us knew what to do. It was all too stupid.

Dad knew what to do. He grabbed me by the wrist and he started
running. I stumbled, ran, tried to keep up. Kelly and Miss Angie
just stood there. Pa put his shoulder into D.J. Beckman's chest and
dropped him to the ground. I saw Clarissa's face then, and I was
happy to see she was crying.

Pa saw her face, too, and he stopped. I bounced into him. He
reached into his pocket and pulled out a gold coin. He looked at it
curiously. It was the same three-dollar coin he'd picked up off the
floor at Vaughn's place.

Everybody watched him, ready for him to say something amazing. Waiting for him to wrap this all up with some profound one-
liner.

Pa tossed the coin to Clarissa. It spun slowly in its arc. Clarissa
opened her palm. The coin landed flat in her hand. She bent her
head down to look at it.

Pa said, "I swear I saw you in a movie once."

They can't all be profound.

Then he was dragging me thru the door to the front lobby, past
Jimmy Young and Mr. Pridgon and Ezra Rogers, all still sitting on
the floor. He pushed the front door open and we were out of the
bank and running on the blacktop under the sun.

I slid to my knees. Before Pa could help me, footsteps pounded
and Mike Crutchfield was sprinting right at us with a real-life M16
strapped over his shoulder.

He skidded to a stop and said, "You worthless old coot." He punched Pa square in the face.

Pa staggered back a step and then stood up straight. He didn't say anything. Punched in the nose twice in one day. Blood trickled out of his nostrils. He stretched his neck this way and that. Then he put on that smile he used to get when he was in the middle of building a contraption in his shop. He looked into the distance.

The vessels in Crutchfield's temples quivered. "I saw what you did to my farm."

Pa said, "Whose farm?"

Crutchfield said, "As of noon today—"

He didn't finish on account of there being a whole bunch of gunshots inside the bank. Pop! Pop! Poppoppoppop!

Crutchfield ran toward the bank. Before opening the front door, he pointed a finger at us. I know he was trying to be menacing but he looked silly. I nodded real easy, like a good country boy.

Crutchfield went into his bank.

Oh, was it a pretty day.

Pa lifted me onto his shoulder. I didn't feel hurt anymore. As he walked step after step, I watched the ground pass by. He ducked so I wouldn't bang my head on the wing of his plane. He sat me on the ground and leaned me against the wheel strut. He opened the door, put me in the copilot seat, and then walked around the plane and climbed into the pilot's seat. We were sitting in the airplane.

Pa slid the window open and shouted, "Clear!" That's what you say right before you hit the ignition.

He turned the key. The engine started right up. The prop spun so it became invisible. He pulled a red knob. Got it just right. Satisfied that the engine was running good, he taxied onto the road in front of the bank. No cars. He said, "It's a go."

He throttled up. We built speed, he pulled back on the yoke, we left the road, we cleared the power lines, and we were flying like two stones in a bird.

Clear over the country. The land fell away. We passed over the softball field, the school, and, further along, the little strip of town that was Dorsey.

The land became golden squares and green circles. Quarter-mile-long sprinklers sent thousands of rainbows arcing over the corn stalks.

A line of smoke points to a place that used to be a farm. Pa passes the plane low over our old house. It's burning. The roof has collapsed. Flames stretch tall over the crumbling walls. While the rattlesnake was biting my neck, Pa had been lighting that fire. Burning the trash.

Down below, the volunteer fire truck is on the way, followed by a cloud of dust, followed by endless dozens of pickups.

Floating, gentle.

"Hey Pa?"

"Yes."

"We're pretty high up."

"Higher than a kite."

"You think people get what they deserve?"

"They get lucky sometimes."

"There's always luck."

"Lucky slots."

"You win some."

"You lonesome."

"What do you think's on the other side of that horizon?"

"We're on the other side."

"Pot of gold."

"If you're lucky."

"You are."

Pa aims the airplane down toward the ground. We build up speed. Parts of the plane begin to rattle. The engine whines. Pa's got a half-smile on his face. Just before we slam into the earth, he pulls back on the yoke. The plane veers up. I'm squished into my seat. I blink my eyes. We're heading toward the sky now.

Pa says, "Let's see if this thing can do a loop-de-loop."

Acknowledgments

Maureen, I love you like crazy.

For reading early drafts and providing guidance: Rebecca Hill, Brett Duesing, Marrion Irons, Eric Allen, Kelly Kievit, Paul Handley, Chuck Cuthill, Jeff Thompson, Jennie Tower, Tim Sears, Paul Muller, Zack Littlefield, Brennan Peterson, Brittan Hlista, Kristin Aslan, Paul Epstein, and Lucas Richards. For educating me: Janice E. James, Renny James, Sue Terrell, Luis Urrea, Petger Schaberg, and John Vernon. For inspiring me: the good citizens of eastern Colorado, the Liberty High School Class of '91, the 1929 Joes High School Basketball team. For being my family: Aunt Jane, Uncle Larry, Aunt Marilyn, all the Hills, Hudiberghs, Williams, Walters, Heartys, and derivations of same. Special mention: Tony Parella, Phyllis Smith, and five thousand other extraordinary novelists. More special mentions: Louise Hughes, Theresa Alarid, and Merisa Bissinger. Still more special mentions: The folks at Penguin/Dutton who rendered this book ready for the public. Special, special mentions go to Jessica Horvath and Mary Beth Constant who edited with such a gentle touch. Continuing with the specialness: Judy and Elden Hill, for hiding their disappointment so well. And super special thanks to Thom Hill, whom we all miss very much.

I apologize to the people I've forgotten to mention here.

And now, in chronological order, I shall mention some rock-and-roll bands I've played in: The Screaming Cows, The Shivers, The Mudrakers, Armageddon Some, Mr. Tree and the Wingnuts, The Pork Boilin' Po' Boys, The Disklaimers, The Rugburns, The Orangutones, Six Months to Live, Manotaur, and The Babysitters. Thanks for putting up with me.